DRIVING BIG DAVIE

DRIVING BIG DAVIE

Colin Bateman

headline

First published in Great Britain in 2004 by
HEADLINE BOOK PUBLISHING

10 9 8 7 6 5 4 3 2 1

British Library Cataloguing in Publication Data

ISBN 0 7553 0919 7 (hardback)
ISBN 0 7553 0920 0 (trade paperback)

Typeset by Palimpsest Book Production Limited,
Polmont, Stirlingshire
Printed and bound in Great Britain by
Mackays of Chatham plc, Chatham, Kent
HEADLINE BOOK PUBLISHING
A division of Hodder Headline
338 Euston Road
London NW1 3BH

www.headline.co.uk
www.hodderheadline.com

For Andrea and Matthew, The Clash, Rudi and the portly punks of '77.

1

Everyone worth knowing knows exactly where they were when they heard Joe Strummer was dead. I know exactly where I was. I was sitting in a private room in a private hospital, trying to wank into a cup.

This probably needs some explaining.

Not everyone knows who Joe Strummer is. Or was. Joe was rock'n'roll.

He was The Clash.

For my generation, he was the man.

He sang 'White Riot' and 'Garageland' and 'London Calling' and 'Know Your Rights'. He ran the tightest, wildest, most exciting beat combo in history.

He made music important. He changed lives in a way that Spandau Ballet or The Hollies never could. He was my Elvis, my Beatles, and he never got fat, or bland, or shot.

The world is indeed cruel. I know that more than most people. And I take refuge from that cruelty in the music of my youth.

Joe was dead and he was only fifty years old, yet Elton John was still alive. Chris de Burgh was still breathing while Joe, the man who Fought the Law and stood for everything that was good and lush about rock'n'roll was pushing up daisies. Cliff Richard was still giving power to all his friends, for Christ's sake. But Joe was dead. It had already been a miserable few years for the punk generation. Johnny Thunders had succumbed in a seedy New Orleans hotel, Ian Dury had lost a battle with cancer. Two of The Ramones had snuffed it, and the other two were touring as The Remains. But Joe – it wasn't even a rock'n'roll death. He had taken his dog out for a walk in the countryside, then dropped dead from a heart attack. It was frightening.

Still, wanking into a cup.

The hospital was in Belfast West, that part of the city once known as West Belfast, until a £3m EC-funded tourism think-tank came up with a rebranding idea which was destined to fool all of the people none of the time. So we now had Belfast West, Belfast South, Belfast East and the Shankhill Road, because they knew better than to mess with those boys. I know a bit about tourism now, because it's kind of what I do. What I'm reduced to doing.

Sad.

I was about six months into my pipe and slippers years, with the exception of the pipe. I was happily reunited with my wife, I lived in a nice house in a nice suburb close enough to enjoy Belfast's many and varied shopping facilities but far enough away that we wouldn't be overly put out if things went all to hell, which they still did from time to time. I was for many years a journalist of some repute, mostly ill, reporting mainly on the troubles – usually my own – but for the past six months I had endured journalism of the last resort, commonly known as public relations. Now I was working in a small operation set up by the Government to promote tourism in Ireland. They didn't even call it Northern Ireland any more. The flag that hung lamely above Stormont was white. The project

I worked for was called *Why Don't You Come Home for a Pint?*. It was aimed at the tens of thousands of students who'd exiled themselves from their homeland during the course of thirty years of violence, and was supposed to entice them home with the promise of high-paying jobs, low cost of living, a grand social life and a guarantee that nail bombs were a thing of the past. Which they are. They're *so* 1970s. Whenever anyone phoned to enquire about grants or mortgages or business opportunities, I had to say, 'Hi, this is Dan Starkey, why don't you come home for a pint?'

Really. I had a script. I had to say it or I'd get a warning from the supervisor. You were allowed three warnings, then you got knee-capped. Old habits die hard.

But still, wanking into a cup.

You see, Patricia and I have had our ups and downs. And as the old nursery rhyme goes, when we were up we were up, but when we were down we were really fucking down. We had battled through separations, affairs, murder and mayhem, like any marriage really. Except there had also been Stevie, our boy, our boy with the red hair who'd starved to death in a bunker and been buried in a little white coffin. That had destroyed us and for a long time we'd gone our separate ways, knowing all the while that we still loved each other and that one day we'd get back together but neither of us prepared to make the first move.

And then it had happened, and needless to say drink was involved, and a party, and my old mate Mouse inviting us both without letting on and then deliberately seating us at different ends of the table during dinner so that we couldn't slap each other round the head. Then he played old songs by The Rezillos and The Mekons and Rudi which everyone else looked aghast at but had me up dancing like an eejit and Patricia up there with me doing a silent boogie and trying not to look at me but eventually not able to stop herself from smiling because Mouse put on 'You're a Disease, Babe' and we were pissed and pushing forty and dancing to The Outcasts, which we wouldn't even have done as teenagers because they were always the most unfashionable punk band in Belfast – but there, after midnight, pissed on red wine, with everyone else at the party begging for relief or Neil Diamond, we danced happily and punched the air every time Greg Cowan hit the chorus. We giggled and danced and eventually kissed and that was that. We went home together and we stayed together; we loved each other – with added ground rules. An end to the fecklessness, which translated as a proper job; I hadn't been in a bar in months; occasionally we had dinner-parties; I have been known to toss a salad. And they say punk's not dead.

We were happy.

And yet.

There was always the grey area, the invisible border we were not able to cross.

Little Stevie.

We would never forget him, but we had to. He would always be part of us. But he had to be removed. The memories of him took us high, but would invariably drag us low. It should have been easier for me. He wasn't even my son. He was the product of Patricia's affair with her work colleague Tony, an affair she'd largely undertaken as an act of revenge for my own philanderings. But then she'd half fallen in love with him. Of course he wanted nothing to do with the baby when it came along, because he was already married, and a ginger bap cunt at that.

Excuse me, the memory of it still riles.

And so it was that I said one night in bed, 'Let's have a baby.'

She cried and cried and cried, and I cleared my throat

a couple of times, and we decided that yes, now was the time.

So we tried. And tried. We went from this is fantastic, we're having sex three times a day to Christ do we have to? in about two weeks. We were having sex in the ad breaks in *Coronation Street*; we were having sex while Patricia bought pots from Argos – albeit on the phone rather than in the store. I even found out later that Patricia bought a tiny pair of white booties to present me with as soon as she was pregnant.

Except she never did get pregnant, and eventually we went to the doctor, and we found out that Patricia had all sorts of gynae problems you don't want to know about but mostly brought on by Little Stevie's traumatic birth. Even if by some miracle she did get pregnant the chances of her carrying a child full-term were fuck all squared in a box.

The doctor sat us down and told us in that bland patronising way doctors have. Had to have, really. They couldn't care about everyone or they'd blow their heads off. Patricia looked like she was going to cry. Her lip was quivering and her cheeks were flushed. I held her hand and said, 'Well, is that it?' to the doctor. And to Patricia I said: 'Sure, can't we always adopt?'

'Don't you think I've already thought about that?' she snapped. 'Do you think I wasn't aware the odds were stacked against us?'

I shrugged helplessly.

'Are you fucking brain dead?'

Patricia was always handy with the compliments when she was upset. The doctor, sensing three rounds of championship boxing coming up, told me adopting probably wasn't a good idea. 'Nobody gives their babies up for adoption any more. The only ones that are available are either badly disabled or they've been abused and taken away from their parents.'

I sat with my head in my hands. Partly depressed, partly to stop Patricia striking me.

'Did you ever think of IVF treatment and—?' the doctor began to ask.

'I can't carry a bloody child,' Patricia said angrily. 'What the hell use would—'

'*Let me finish*, Patricia.' The doctor gave her a hard look and Patricia took a deep breath. 'IVF treatment together with surrogacy. We could find a surrogate host for your child.'

I peered through my fingers. The doctor was nodding at Patricia.

Patricia wiped at an eye. 'Surrogacy? Isn't that, like, illegal or something?'

'No. Not at all. It's not illegal. It's strictly regulated. But certainly not illegal. It may be that your eggs are perfectly fine. It may be that they can be extracted and then fertilised in a laboratory with your semen, Dan. Then a donor can be found to carry the child. It could be the perfect solution.'

Patricia was smiling already.

'Dan?' the doctor asked. 'What do you think?'

'About what?'

Patricia tutted.

'About IVF treatment. Surrogacy.'

'Well,' I said, 'we were hoping for a Protestant – would there be any chance of UVF?'

And so, to wanking into a cup.

The New Haven Private Day Hospital was a redbrick building off the Falls, just opposite a heavily fortified – but beautifully landscaped – PSNI (Police Service of Northern Ireland) station. It had fifteen rooms where people were sliced apart and put back together. The hospital had a similar number. There was a water-cooler in reception and everyone was pleasant. There were none of those 'What the fuck do *you* want?' looks which you got when you walked through the doors of the Royal Victoria Hospital. This was a consultation, a first baby step on the road to surrogacy. Even so we'd each been advised of what to expect, and been provided with a set of instructions. The consultant was a white South African with a name that rhymed with pomegranate, but we called him Dr Love. He was nice and friendly and talked us through the infertility treatment even while he had a lubricant-soaked 12-inch plastic probe up inside Patricia's bits. The last time someone had been that personal with her I'd tried to knock him down with my car, and then become a father to his son. Dr Love looked at her ovaries on the monitor and tutted at the endometriosis then shook his head at the state she'd been left in after the birth of Stevie. He told us about the hormone injections Patricia would have to have, and that his clinic couldn't legally provide us with a surrogate to carry the child, but would put us in contact with an organisation that could.

As he peeled off his rubber gloves he turned to me and smiled and then said, 'So let's be having you then, Dan.'

I swallowed, and Patricia gave me the thumbs-up. 'Have a good one,' she said.

A pretty nurse – and she would have to be pretty, they couldn't have sprung some horse-faced hare-lipped hunchback on me who wouldn't have grinned knowingly like this one did – led me down a short corridor to a room with QUIET stencilled on the door.

'This is our Quiet Room,' she said.

No, it's not, I thought. It's your Wank-in-a-Cup room.

She was grinning as she led me into the room, she was grinning as she pointed out the bathroom within, the sofa, the table bearing three porn mags, and the cup for masturbating into. She was grinning even though she was well used to it. Of course I was well used to seeing Everton lose, but I still laughed every time it happened. So she grinned some more and said, 'And you've abstained from sexual relations for three days?'

'Days?'

'Yes. Days.'

'The bitch. She told me three weeks.'

Her grin widened. 'Perhaps she misread the instructions.'

'Perhaps she needs a thick ear.'

This was not very politically correct, but then who gives a fuck? Her grin narrowed somewhat. She told me to do my business into the plastic cup, and to then leave it on a small shelf outside the room where she would collect it and have it analysed to see how many swimmers I had. Then she left the room. I locked the door behind her, then checked that it really was locked – three times. Because there's something about masturbation: all men, and several women, do it, but it's a secret thing. You don't say to your wife that you're away upstairs for a wank; you wait until she's downstairs defrosting chicken cutlets or out getting her hair ruined. You don't wank into her favourite cup and then pop down and show it to her. 'Look what I done!' It's a private thing between you and an old sock. But there I was in a private room in a private hospital with official approval to look at porn and masturbate.

Clinical.

Loveless.

Of course if you think this put me off, then you've got another thing coming.

2

Any time, any place, anywhere. It's a man thing.

Women need soft light and candles.

Men need soft porn and five minutes.

I sat down on the sofa and undid my trousers. I lifted one of the porn mags. It was top-shelf stuff, but hardly hardcore. Basically, it was women with their legs spread. There are worse things in life. So I sprang into action.

You don't have to imagine this; it's probably better if you don't.

But I was sitting there looking at these heavily made-up women showing me their most private parts and thinking, What is a respectable time to spend masturbating before going back out cup in hand? If I spent three minutes they'd think I was a horn ball, or habitually premature. Thirty minutes, they'd also think I was a horn ball, or that I couldn't get it up. Was there a happy medium – say fifteen minutes? Ten? Twenty? Was there such a thing as a respectable wank-time? Should they have imposed a time-limit? I was turning the pages all this time. I came across, metaphorically speaking, a smutty crossword someone had taken the time to fill in. And then three pages later

– well, make that five, because the last two pages were stuck together. Freshly stuck together. In fact, they were still damp. I Frisbee-ed the porn mag across the room.

Bollocks.

I glanced at my watch. I was six minutes in. Soon they'd start checking the clock. Making wisecracks. Maybe they had secret cameras to make sure I wasn't doing anything I shouldn't. A pervy-cam. I was sweating now. Losing interest. Christ. Maybe I was appearing live on the giant TV screen above Donegall Square. Maybe I was live on the Internet. Maybe half the world was laughing. Maybe Noel Edmonds or some other beardless wonder would stroll in and announce I was on *Candid Camera*.

With my trousers around my ankles I shuffled across and checked that the door was locked again. Then I checked the light-fittings for hidden cameras. Nothing. But it didn't mean they weren't there.

Nine minutes, sitting there, half-mast.

Twelve minutes, even less.

Concentrate.

Concentrate? Since when did you have to concentrate on . . .

Jesus come on, it's all in a good cause.

I wonder how many games Liverpool need to win to be sure of European qualification?

Stanley Baxter did *not* star in *Zulu*.

Fifteen minutes.

Stanley Baker.

They're really getting worried now. Soon the nurse is going to knock on the door and say, 'Is everything all right?'

Just coming.

Okay. Okay. Relax. *Relax*.

Think about . . . think about sex, think about the best sex

you ever had. No, the first sex you ever had. The wonder of it. The absolutely fantastic wonder of it. Even the first kiss. Who was that with? It was lying in the snow with a girl. Not Patricia. She was my first proper girlfriend, but there were other fumblings in the dark. That's better, that's definitely better. Imagine the excitement of that, of the first time, of discovering an entirely new, long-dreamed-of but undiscovered world. Like the Vikings landing in America. Like Armstrong setting foot on the moon. Like kissing a girl for the first time, like feeling her tongue in your mouth, tasting warm cider and burgeoning lust – definitely, this is the business – like squeezing your fingers under bra wires, expecting a mouse trap but getting warm skin, getting pulled close safe in the knowledge that she was as young and naïve and absolutely up for it as you, lying in snow but it could be on a beach, you're as hard as a rock, you're going to do it, you're really going to . . .

Ejaculate.

And I did.

There and then in the snow.

And there and then in the room.

'Fuck,' I said then, as she said, 'What? What's wrong?'

'Someone's coming.'

There was, and I had. But she never knew.

And now I'd come again, thinking back twenty-four years and it was wonderful then and it was wonderful now.

And then I remembered the cup.

I remembered that I'd forgotten the cup.

That I'd made a fucking mess everywhere and I'd forgotten the god-damn cup. What the hell was I supposed to do now?

Jesus Christ.

What sort of a bloody idiot . . .

God . . . Christ . . . I hobbled in my half-mast trousers to the bathroom and soaked a towel. I rubbed at my trousers, I rubbed at the seat, I rubbed at the floor. Christ. I looked at my watch – twenty-five minutes. I was getting into 'we'd better check on him, he might have had a coronary' territory. I rubbed and I rubbed and I rubbed until no one but a crack police forensics team or a moron could tell the difference. Thirty-two minutes.

What the hell was I supposed to do now?

I was forty years old.

I couldn't just produce another cupful like that.

It would take at least thirty-seven minutes, and probably a doze, then a bit of a walk and a ham sandwich.

I wasn't fucking Superman.

And even if I did produce another dribble, they'd be weak and tired, barely interested, forced out under sufferance, not the Gold Medal swimmers we needed to progress with the surrogacy. I'd be humiliated. My sperm count would hardly register. They'd fail their O-levels. They'd get a *must try harder* stamp from the nurse. The pretty nurse would be grinning so hard she'd split the top of her head off.

Bloody hell.

What was I going to tell Trish? Here for possibly the most important, relationship-defining day of our lives, when all I had to do was concentrate for five minutes, and look what I'd done, and look where I'd done it.

Christ.

Thirty-seven minutes.

Soon the SAS would come swinging through the windows to rescue me.

I would have to think of something.

Something *now*.

A migraine.

A stroke.

The nurse grinning.

Christ.

I pulled up my trousers and hurried to the door. I unlocked it and peered into the corridor. It was empty. Directly across from me there was a shelf with a small door behind it where I was supposed to leave my sample. I heard footsteps and ducked back into the room, leaving the door open just enough to see a nurse – a different nurse – hurry past.

Patricia – I have good news, and I have bad news.

The good news is, ejaculation was no problem.

The bad news is, if you want to count it, you'll have to get down on your hands and knees.

What was I like?

I had always brought shame on my family – through no fault of my own, of course, except in cases of extreme stupidity – but this brought it to an entirely new level.

I had sworn on our most recent reconciliation to be honest with Patricia at all times.

That if I strayed, or put our house on a horse, or gave her tacky ornaments to Oxfam with instructions to smash them, then I could and would be brutally honest. But this? How could I tell her this without utterly humiliating myself? I wouldn't be able to hold my head up even in my last refuge, my own house. And even if she stuck with me, even if she swore never to tell a soul, it would get out there. These things always came out. She'd get drunk and tell my friends. And they'd all snigger into their cocktails and they'd tell their friends and it would soon evolve into an urban myth.

I peered out into the corridor again.

This time a male nurse was coming past. I had to do something. I had to do something quick. He was a big fella, six foot at least, squarely built. I hissed across at him, 'Hey, mate, c'mere a minute.'

He turned towards me. Close-cropped hair and small, inquisitive eyes. He came over.

'Listen,' I began, not really sure where I was going. 'I'm in a bit of a hole. I'm . . . look, my son died . . . we're desperate to have another kid. We came here to get help . . . You know what this room is? The QUIET ROOM. You know what the QUIET ROOM is – of course you do. I've . . . Christ, look, mate I've had a bit of an accident, and I can't go back there and say . . . like, what do you say? I just can't go back and look like a total eejit. I was like wondering . . . do you know where I'm going? Do you understand what I'm saying?'

'No,' he said.

'Look, it's quite simple. I need you . . . I'd like you . . . Look, mate, no strings attached, I know it's kind of odd, I'm not a weirdo, I'm just really stuck. I'm too old for this, I can't just produce it like . . . I really need some help.'

'What sort of help?'

'I need you to come in here and wank into a cup.'

His eyes widened slightly, then narrowed again. I could almost hear the clogs turning in his brain. Or perhaps cogs. He glanced up and down the corridor, then moved slightly closer.

'What sort of a cup?'

'What?'

'What sort of a cup do you want me to wank into?'

'What do you mean? What the fuck does it matter?'

'You mean like a big cup, like a pint glass, or a wee one, like an egg cup?'

'What the fuck does it matter?!'

'I'd just like to know.'

'I'm inviting you in here to masturbate and you're worried about what sort of a cup you'll have to wank into? What sort of a fucking mental are you?'

14

'Please yourself, mate,' he said, and started to turn away.

'No! I'm sorry. I'm sorry.' He stopped. 'Look – okay. Okay – it's a small plastic cup. Please. This is so important.'

He turned back. 'How much?'

'How much? How the fuck do I know. A cupful? Half a cup?'

'No – I mean how much are you paying?'

'Paying?'

'I'm not going in there to wank into a cup for nothing.'

'Well – fuck, how much do you want?'

'A hundred.'

'Quid?'

'Yes.'

'Okay. All right. That seems fair.' I took out my wallet. Luckily, and rarely, I had enough. 'Fifty now, and fifty when you deliver.'

'A hundred now.'

'What if you don't deliver?'

'I'll work at it until I do.'

I looked at my watch. Forty-four minutes.

'All right – deal. Come on.'

I ushered him into the room. I showed him the bathroom and I picked up the porn mags. 'Here,' I said, 'this might help.'

He held up a hand to refuse them. 'That's not what I'm into.'

I nodded. He closed the door. He locked it. I gave him two minutes.

'Everything okay?' I said.

'Yes.'

'Are you going to be long?'

'Not if you shut up.'

'Okay. Fine. I'll . . . just sit over here.'

It would be okay, everything would be okay. I could

15

explain it away to Trish. I was nervous. The antiseptic surroundings of the hospital. She would somehow perceive it to be a compliment to her that I was unable to do it without her being with me. It was only a sample they were looking for. It wasn't as if they were going to match it up with Patricia's eggs. It was just to check the sperm count. He would have a fine and healthy sperm count. It wasn't like he was some albino dwarf. He was a strapping big guy with normal sperm.

What was I even *thinking* of?

Christ.

I should crack the door open and toss him out of there for being such a pervert.

What sort of a guy goes into a room and wanks for money?

And what sort of a guy asks him to?

I buried my head in my hands.

From inside the bathroom, he said, 'Oh baby.'

I blushed. I really blushed.

He said, 'Oh, *baby* . . .'

I cleared my throat.

He said, 'Give it to me.'

Then he cranked up the volume. 'GIVE IT TO ME!' he bellowed.

Christ.

And then my mobile phone rang.

I pulled it out, fearing it was Trish. But I didn't recognise the number. I pressed the button. Before he, she or it could speak there came a:

'HARDER. HARDER.'

I swallowed and said, 'Hello?'

'Dan?'

'OOOOH YES!'

I cleared my throat. 'Yes.'

'Dan, it's Davie.'

'OOH YES. YES. YES!'

I cleared my throat again. 'Davie?'

'Yes, Davie.'

'Davie?'

'*Davie*, Davie.'

'GIVE IT TO ME, GIVE IT TO ME HARD.'

'Davie Kincaid?'

'Yes, Davie Kincaid.'

'Davie Kincaid? *The* Davie Kincaid?'

'OOOOH YES!'

'Yes, Dan. How're you doin'?'

'I'm . . . fine. Davie Kincaid? But I haven't—'

'I know, Dan, it's donkey's years. But I had to call. As soon as I heard, I had to call.'

'*OOH yes, yes, yes, yes, yes!*'

'Dan, is this a bad time? There seems to be—'

'No, it's fine. We just . . . we have the painters in.'

'Are they having sex?'

'No. They're just . . . admiring their work. They're doing a mural, you see. But what do you mean "as soon as you heard"?'

'You haven't heard?'

'I don't know what I haven't heard, Davie. Davie Kincaid. My God.'

'He's dead.'

'Who's dead?'

'Strummer.'

'Strummer?'

'Joe's dead, Dan. I had to call. He's gone. It was just on the news. Of all the people in all the world, I had to call you.'

'Joe?'

'Joe.'

'But he's only . . .'

'I know, Dan.' His voice was shaky.

'Davie.' Christ Almighty, so was mine. Joe Strummer. Rock'n'roll. Bottles of cider on the beach, pogo-ing madly, parties, gigs, fanzines, singles, spiked hair, anarchy, gobbing, missing the last bus home, forming bands, posing with sunglasses, writing lyrics, wailing into a mike, trying to learn a chord, abusing people wearing cords, flares, big permed hair, being attacked for wearing drainpipes, being chased by Rockers, throwing up, sniffing Poppers, having just the best time of our lives. And all traced directly back to Joe. It was just miserable to know that he was dead. And then the tears came. It was just the most shocking, horrible news I could think of.

'Dan, are you okay?'

'Yes . . . yes. It's just – devastating.'

'I know . . . I know. I knew you'd understand. Everyone round here's looking at me like I'm a head the ball. But Strummer. *Jesus.*'

I tried to wipe at my tears but they kept coming.

Then there was a knock on the door.

'Mr Starkey? Is everything all right?'

'*Yes!*' It wasn't a shout, it was a wail.

Strummer was dead.

'Are you sure?'

The nurse didn't wait for an answer; I heard a key in the door, and it opened inwards. She was standing there looking concerned, her mouth open, her eyes wide. Patricia was standing behind her, looking perplexed, but not, I later thought, unduly surprised. And I was standing there, with my zip down, my trousers slightly damp, tears tripping me.

From the bathroom, my new friend bellowed: **'GIVE ME YOUR BIG COCK! YESSSSS!'**

I swallowed. I raised the phone again. 'I'm going to have to call you back, Davie,' I said.

3

Davie. Big Davie Kincaid.

Davie was six foot two before he was fifteen years old, a lanky big fella who could get served in off-licences years before anyone else in our crowd but always went bright red when a girl talked to him. For two years from the summer of 1977, he was my best mate. My parents, in one of their rare moments of adventure, had moved the fifteen miles down from Belfast into a seaside village called Groomsport in search of a quiet life. I was fifteen years old and full of testosterone, hormones, spunk and punk and it was like moving to another world. I was a product of the rough tough streets of Belfast; Groomsport on the other hand had some rather nice cul-de-sacs. The nearest it had to a paramilitary organisation was the Boys' Brigade. It was my particular claim to fame that I introduced punk rock to Groomsport. Before my arrival it had been a tasteless wasteland of showbands and Genesis; within a week it was dancing to Richard Hell and The Voidoids. The local youth club grooved to Patrick Hernandez and 'Born to be Alive'. Within a week I'd kids pogo-ing to The Stranglers' 'No More Heroes'. It was a mini-me version of 'Anarchy in the UK' and I loved it; it was a great time to be alive, and the perfect time to get beaten up.

Because of course there was the slightly older generation, into Queen and Zeppelin, who felt threatened by punk – dinosaurs staring into the pit of their own destruction. Actually they were just pissed off by spotty-faced drunks causing a racket. Either way, they'd chase us and nail us from time to time, but it didn't put us off or slow us down. Me and Davie would sail into The Stables, the biggest local bar, every Saturday night without fail, looking like twin clones of Sid Vicious, and order our pints. We'd be refused, because I looked about twelve. Then we'd fire off the verbal abuse and we'd be thrown out.

'Two pints of Harp, mate.'

'How old are you?' Vernon the barman would ask.

'Nineteen.'

'Date of birth?'

'Thirteenth of the sixth 1960.'

They wouldn't even bother to work it out.

'ID?'

'I'm nineteen, right?'

'Sorry, son, try again when you've got some bum-fluff on your cheeks.'

And the whole bar would laugh.

'Fuck you, you fat cunt!' Davie would shout, dipping into his *Penguin Book of Oscar Wilde Epigrams*.

'Out!'

'Yeah, you and whose army?'

Well, actually, him and most of the bar would throw us out.

It was a ritual.

We always had an ace up our sleeve – the off-licence round the corner where Davie would get served those big flagons of Olde English cider. We'd take them down to the park and sit with our little shoe-box cassette player and get completely pissed listening to The Clash and The Buzzcocks and Belfast bands Protex, Ruefrex and Rudi. Then we'd call for Karen.

Ah now, to be fifteen again.

Karen Malloy was fifteen, going on twenty-one, the most beautiful girl either of us had ever seen. We were both totally in love, smitten, in lust; and because we were both too shy to ask her out, or to face the absolute certainty of a humiliating rejection, we did what teenage boys have always done: we hung around, annoying her. Where she went, we went; where she played, we played; when she went to school, we were there at the bus stop, when she came off her bus, we were idling nearby; when she took her spaniel for a walk we went too, trailing behind like we were in heat – and we were; it was the only exercise either of us got. We shadowed her to church, we followed her home; her parents called the cops on us half a dozen times for loitering outside her house, but it didn't stop us. And looking back, I don't think we ever even spoke to her. The occasional, 'Hi,' maybe. She had short blonde hair, thin lips, a big smile; we followed her into Unicorn Records once and saw her buy an Electric Light Orchestra album, but we dismissed that as pure innocence we would soon correct. The interesting thing was that we both pursued her with never any talk about what we'd do if she *did* happen to take an interest, as if somehow she would want to go out with both of us at the same time rather than split us up. Or she would make her choice, and Davie would go off and commit suicide, and I wouldn't mind in the slightest because I was going out with Karen Malloy. But she was never going to go out with us. I think we knew that, deep down. We just couldn't give her up. We thought that by hanging around her we would grow on her. That she would see us for the wonderful, dynamic, funny boys we thought we were.

I remember one night, we went round to her house after midnight and threw stones at her bedroom window. Of course we were pissed at the time. We missed completely and cracked the next door's glass. We took off, cackling. We were still laughing about it in the park when the neighbour caught up with us. We debated briefly whether to make a fight of it, but decided to be meek and apologetic instead; the fact that she was seventy years old and on a walking stick meant that we probably would have won the fight, but then be lynched by her family. She'd been down the pub for a drink and was hobbling home when she happened upon us smashing her window.

So we said sorry.

'Sorry, missus.' She didn't seem too put out, actually.

'You boys are always hanging around.'

We shrugged.

'It's Karen, isn't it?'

We shrugged.

'You're like sticking plasters.'

We shrugged.

Davie, emboldened by drink, said: 'She's the most beautiful girl I've ever met.'

'You've never met her,' I pointed out.

'She is beautiful,' the old woman said. 'Up to a point.'

'What're you talking about, up to a point?'

She smiled benevolently at Davie. She took a seat on one of the swings in the children's playground she'd cornered us in. She put her hand out and Davie was confused for a moment, then the penny dropped and he gave her the flagon. She took a long drink of the sweet alcohol. She wiped her hand across her mouth. 'Ah,' she said, 'that takes me back.'

Davie winked at me. 'Don't fancy yours much,' he whispered.

'Any port in a storm,' I replied, and probably meant it.

'Anyway,' Davie said, 'what shite are you talking about – "she's beautiful, up to a point"?'

The old woman explained: 'She's a nice kid, and yes all right, she's pretty enough. But lads – I see you hanging around her all the time and she's not the slightest bit interested. She's fifteen. Fifteen-year-old girls don't want fifteen-year-old boys. They want older boys. Believe me, I know.'

We looked at our feet. She was speaking the truth, we knew it.

'Besides, she's only beautiful in Groomsport.'

'What the fuck are you talking about now?' Davie snapped.

'Listen to me. Look at this place. Groomsport. About a thousand people. And in a place this size, yes, she's considered beautiful. But go a mile down the road to Bangor, put her in with the girls there, she'd merely be good-looking. Go ten miles up the road to Belfast, and what's considered good-looking in Bangor would be merely okay, maybe even plain. And send her to London, they'd think she'd been beaten with the ugly stick.'

'What the fuck are you talking about?' Davie snapped again.

She took another swig of his cider. 'If you want to pursue beauty, go to the big city. That's how it works. Beautiful people get better jobs and gravitate to the city. There they meet other beautiful people and have beautiful children. It's the way things are. That's the thing about little country villages. The slow and the plain and the unambitious get left behind, and they marry and they have slower and plainer and less ambitious children. Don't let it happen to you, boys.

23

You're bright, I can see that. You're individuals. Get out of here while you can.'

I started to think about this. It seemed to make sense, but then I was pissed on cider.

Davie was nodding sagely as well.

Then he pushed her off her swing and stole her handbag.

He took off into the night, cackling wildly.

And I ran after him.

I drove down to Groomsport two nights after the incident in the Quiet Room. This was a calculated risk as I hadn't possessed a driving licence for some considerable time. There had been a small 'incident' which forced some dozy judge to remove it until, and I quote, 'hell freezeth over'. But now that terrorism was largely a dying art there weren't so many security checkpoints on the roads, so the chances of me being caught out were much reduced. I just had to drive carefully. It wasn't a problem. I'm a careful kind of a guy. I drove down the coast at a steady thirty-five miles per hour. Other motorists screamed abuse at me, but it was water off a duck's back.

Somehow it didn't surprise me that Davie had never moved away from the village. We'd enjoyed two golden years of punk, but then my parents had grown tired of the constant sniffles of Irish seaside life and gone back to the city. For a while Davie came up to see me at weekends; funnily enough I can't remember ever going back down to Groomsport to see him. I met new friends, different girls, then Trish, my first proper relationship, my only proper relationship. She met Davie a couple of times and seemed to like him, but was quite wary of him as well. Maybe she was jealous of how close we had been, but she needn't have worried because we really weren't close at all any more. After a while he stopped coming up; there was the occasional phone call, then Christmas cards. Then nothing. I heard on the grapevine that he had joined the police, and then a couple of times while out reporting I ran into him. He was big and imposing with his uniform and gun; I was usually bedraggled and hungover. Our conversations were stilted and embarrassing. He was a cop, and being a cop changes you. It goes with the territory. God knows what he made of me. We exchanged numbers and promised to give each other a bell, but we never did.

Sad, really.

And then Joe Strummer pops his clogs and I'm motoring down to The Stables in Groomsport to meet him and really not knowing what to expect. It had to be at least eight years since I'd last bumped into him; then hurried words on a mobile and an agreement to meet up soon while a gay nurse jacked off in the background and my wife screamed at me.

I pulled into The Stables car park. Patricia had given her tacit approval to me driving down to meet him but warned me against drinking and driving. Davie said he'd put me up for the night. Fair enough. The bar had changed quite a bit over the years; it had once boasted the kind of musty smell you get in pubs that don't bother to clean their carpets from one decade to the next, but now everything was new and polished and family-friendly. Same staff, though. Big Vernon, who'd once terrorised us, thumping us around the ears and hurling us out into the car park, Vernon whom we'd terrorised in return, running a hose pipe into his car and filling it with water, ordering tonnes of coal for his apartment – he was behind the bar, paunchier, balder, but still recognisably Vernon.

He saw me, looked puzzled, then surprised, then pointed to the doors. 'Out,' he said. 'You're barred.'

I stood my ground. 'Yeah? You and whose army?'

'Me and this army,' he scowled, and nodded at the bar before him and the three guys sitting with their backs to me. One by one they turned around, growling.

'All right, lads,' I said.

I was forty years old. I was too old to run away, and too old to stand and fight. I was caught in no-man's land cursing the mistakes of my youth and the eternal memories of smalltown hard men.

And then they smiled.

They came off their stools laughing and said: ''Bout ya, Dan – how're you doin'?'

I was staggered.

I looked closer. Jesus. Bald – fat – bearded . . . these were *old friends*. Mark, Tommy, Sean – punks of my generation gone to seed. They had their hands out and were clapping me on the back and saying how great it was to see me and what the hell had I been up to.

'Jesus, guys, bolt from the blue or what. Let me get you a drink.'

'No,' Vernon snapped. Then quickly followed with: 'The drinks are on me. Eh, Dan? Local celeb returns home.'

'Celeb?'

'Dan, you're never out of the papers. Your column, we used to love that. And then your books and all the trouble you get into. You're the closest thing Groomsport will ever have to a celebrity.'

I shrugged helplessly and happily. I was a celebrity in Groomsport in the same way that Karen Malloy had been a great beauty; it meant bugger all just a mile up the road. But still, Vernon was buying me a drink.

'So what are you havin'?'

I ordered a pint. 'I'm supposed to be meeting Big Davie. Have you—?'

And with perfect timing, the opening chords of 'Should I Stay Or Should I Go?' pealed out of the jukebox, and the boys parted to reveal Davie leaning against it with his arms folded across a leather jacket and his hair slightly quiffed up. Very rock'n'roll. I wasn't sure if this was still his normal style, or whether he'd made a special effort. I, on the other hand, was dressed head to foot courtesy of Kays Catalogue. Polyester Man. I was getting old. I felt it now, and Trish did nothing to help me, ordering all this crap out of a catalogue. 'How're you doin', mate?' Davie grinned. 'Thought I'd get the boys back together to mark the occasion. Little Danny Starkey's back in town.'

'Davie.'

'Whaddya think – The Clash on The Stables' jukebox! It only took Vernon twenty-five fuckin' years.'

Vernon grinned across, but it seemed to me that a flicker of anger crossed his face. The boys themselves looked a bit awkward.

'C'mon and get a pint, Davie,' Mark said. 'Vernon's buying.'

Davie stood by the jukebox for a moment longer, then came across with his hand extended. 'Dan,' he said.

We shook.

'Shakin' hands like we're all grown-up,' he said.

'I know. Happens to us all.'

I nodded around my old friends. It did happen to us all. We managed to get a couple of rounds in, chatting about the old days, without me talking to Davie directly at all; there was something between us, an awkwardness, a holding back. But then one by one the others began to make their excuses and leave. One was driving and didn't want to risk his licence. One had to relieve a babysitter. One couldn't take another drink or he'd be up all night burping. They shook my hand again and said how great it was to see me, but I could tell they were kind of relieved to be going home. The pub was no longer their natural environment. They were family men. Davie and I never were, never had been.

'Great to see them, all the same,' I said.

'Ah, part-time punks,' he replied dismissively. 'You see them more than I do.'

'But you're still in Groomsport.'

'Oh aye. Fucking fixture in here.' He nodded around the bar. Vernon glanced over, but stayed talking to another punter.

'What about Joe, then?' Davie said.

'Aye. Dreadful.'

We looked at our drinks. I'd come all this way to reminisce about The Clash, but we seemed to have exhausted it with one exchange.

Davie nodded back up to the bar. 'Ah, fuck it,' he said. 'Vernon, give us four pints of snakebite.' He winked across at me. 'It's like we're on a first date, mate, isn't it? Awkward as fuck. Let's sink these and then the barriers will come down.'

I nodded.

I was in a quiet village getting quietly drunk with an old mate. It wasn't the sort of place where you could possibly get into trouble.

4

Vernon, my new best buddy, threw us out just after mid-night. He barred Davie for ramming bottle-tops into the coin slot on the jukebox and screaming, 'Daniel O'Donnell's a cunt! Daniel O'Donnell's a cunt!' at the top of his voice.

The sentiment wasn't wrong, just the means of expression.

I was drunk, but Davie was pissed. He was funny though, which makes up for a lot of things. We'd talked for hours. He was right. We needed to get pissed together to break down the barriers that had been erected over the past twenty years. Now we were rolling along the main street like kids, the wind off the sea battering us, the rain soaking us, but neither of us caring. We were just having a laugh. Big Davie. My mate. He'd even managed to persuade Vernon to sell him half a dozen cans before throwing him out. It was like the United States selling weapons to Iraq. Sooner or later he knew Davie was going to come back and slap him in the face with them.

'That fucker bars me every week,' Davie growled as he drank his first can in one.

It was a comment I should have taken on board at the time.

Davie crumpled the can, threw it up in the air, then kicked it hard. 'He shoots! He scores!'

Except that he had scored through the front window of a terraced house. The glass shattered, and for a moment we just stood there in shock.

Then we took off, racing up the street laughing madly.

Davie led me along several back streets at a gallop, then down a lane where we stopped for a piss against a brick wall, still laughing our socks off.

'Jesus,' I kept saying, gulping for air. 'I'm gonna have to get fitter.'

'Ah bollocks,' said Davie. 'Come on.'

He turned and walked further along the lane. I was drunk. I followed without asking. He opened a small wooden gate and led me down a garden path. He patted his pockets, clearly searching for a key. 'Ah bollocks,' he said. He looked up at the kitchen window. The small top window was partially open. 'Ah bollocks,' he said again, and climbed up onto the sill. He opened the small window fully, then reached down towards the larger one below. 'Ah, bollocks,' he said, straining to reach the handle. But he got it and opened it and then manoeuvred himself through the window and into the kitchen. A moment later a light came on and he opened the back door.

'Enter,' he said, bowing, 'my humble abode. But . . .' and he put a finger to his lips '. . . Mother is sleeping.'

I nodded. I'd heard that his dad had died, but he hadn't mentioned it, so I hadn't either. This was a smaller house than he'd lived in when we'd been mates. Just a little terrace. He led me through the kitchen into the front room, flipping the light on as he went. It was small, but packed with dark wooden furniture and shelves full of china figurines.

'Now,' Davie whispered, 'let's organise a little drink, eh?'

He moved to a teak sideboard and began opening drawers. I stood somewhat ill-at-ease. I was out of practice with the drink. I felt like lying on the sofa for a doze, but knew that Davie wouldn't let me get away with it. He tutted as he crossed to a glass-fronted display cabinet in the opposite corner. I glanced at the photos on top of the sideboard. There were none of Davie. None that I could see of his mum. Probably relatives, but I didn't recognise or remember any of them, although I'd probably met a few of them at some point.

'Ah bollocks,' Davie hissed. He wasn't having any luck with the drink. 'I'll try the kitchen.'

He walked past me and started opening cupboards there. I bent to a plastic box containing several dozen albums, and began to flick through them. Most of them were of Scottish pipe bands, my personal idea of hell, but each unto their own. Although I didn't remember his family being much into the whole Orange culture thing, it could easily have slipped my mind.

Then I heard footsteps coming from the stairs.

There's nothing as loud as two drunks trying to be quiet.

I steadied myself against a chair and prepared to make polite conversation with Davie's mum. I wondered how much she'd aged. She'd be in her seventies now, for sure, bent and grey, perhaps on a walking stick.

Except the woman who came through the hall door was in her forties at most; she had on a pink dressing-gown, curlers in her hair, and she was carrying a shotgun.

She said, 'I don't know who the fuck you fuckers are, but you better get outta my house or I'll blow your fucking arseholes off.'

I stared at her aghast for several moments, desperately waiting for her to break into a smile, to crack up at the great fright she'd given us. Or indeed *me*, as I heard the back door open and Davie take off screaming down the garden path.

'Okay,' I said. I started to back away.

'You're the worst fucking burglars I ever met,' the woman hissed.

'We're not burglars,' I said, reversing through the lounge doorway into the kitchen.

'Well, what the fuck are you then?' She jabbed the gun at me, as if it had a bayonet on the end.

'Pissed,' I said.

'Well fucking piss off then!'

I reached out blindly to find the kitchen door, then turned. She poked me in the back with the barrel.

'I know that fucker from around town, but I'll remember *you*, you fucken no-brain dickhead.'

I cleared my throat and stepped out into her back garden.

'I'll just er . . . dander on here.'

'You do that, arse face. And close the fucking gate!'

Davie was at the end of the lane, laughing his legs off. I said, 'Thanks a bunch. Thanks a fucking bunch.'

'Don't mention it.'

'She nearly shot my fucking balls off!'

'Ah bollocks, she wouldn't have done nothing.' He cackled. 'You should see your face, mate, you're as white as a—'

And then he stopped. He sank to his knees, then turned abruptly and threw up into a hedge. Then again. Then again.

From somewhere in the distance, a man shouted, 'Why don't you go and boke on your own house, you fucker!'

When Davie had got up as much as he was going to get up,

I helped him to his feet, and guided him out of the lane and back along the main street. I glanced warily back towards the house where we'd broken the window, but there was no sign of activity. Davie staggered sideways. I kept on his right, trying to stop him from falling off the path onto the road. There weren't many cars about in Groomsport at this time of night, but it only took one.

I'd known Davie was pissed, but thought he'd still be pretty much in control of himself. Now I remembered that he had always been like this: the life and soul one minute, completely comatose the next. I'd presumed he'd grown out of it, rather than into it.

'She's a fuckin' bitch,' Davie slurred.

'She was just worried about her house.'

'Not her, not fuckin' her.'

We staggered on a bit.

'Who then?' I said. 'And where are we going?'

'My house. My house. Really. My house. Just up here.'

We turned a corner. Davie had forgotten what we were talking about. I'd confused him with two questions in one. 'Who's a bitch?' I asked again.

'She is. My fuckin' girlfriend. My fuckin' fiancée.'

'Your fiancée?'

'Fiancée? Yeah, that's a laugh.'

'Davie, what are you talking about?'

I should have left it. I should have just let him slabber on, got him home, had a good night's sleep, woken up with a hangover, collected my car and gotten the hell out of there. I was past all this. I wasn't exactly grown-up myself, but I was more grown-up than Davie. I should have just shut my mouth there and then. Possibly none of the shit that happened later would have happened.

But I was – I am – a glutton for punishment.

'Davie – what friggin' fiancée?'

He stopped then and grabbed my shoulders, and for a moment I feared he was going to be sick over me. But he merely used me as leverage to push himself into a more erect position. He sucked in a lungful of the fresh sea air. The eyes seemed to rotate in his head for a moment, as if deciding whether to okay a complete collapse or grant a moment of clarity.

Clarity came through.

Davie squeezed my shoulders. For a few moments his eyes were as focused as mine. That is, partially.

'Joe Strummer is dead, Dan.'

'I know.'

'It's a tragedy.'

'I know, Davie.'

'Joe Strummer is dead and I was supposed to get married next week. But the cow's run off.'

Davie and a girl and marriage. It was the first mention of it all night. 'Seriously?' I asked.

'Would I joke about something like that?'

'Yes, frankly.'

'Well, I'm not fuckin' jokin'. I'm not fuckin' jokin', Dan. She ran off.'

He shook his head, then slowly folded to the ground. He was sick again, then lay still on the pavement, his face inches from a puddle of boke. I tried to pick him up, but he was a dead weight.

'Davie,' I said, 'you gotta get up. You gotta get home.'

'Uuuuuugh . . .'

I sat down on the kerb. It was the sort of night a sailor would call fresh, and the rest of us fucking freezing. I pulled up my jacket collar and looked at Davie. My mate. I couldn't imagine him being married. Neither, apparently, could his fiancée.

I took out my mobile and phoned Trish.

'Is the car all right?' were her first words.

'Yes, the car's fine, and thanks for your concern.'

'It's the voice of experience, Dan. Where are you? What's wrong?'

'Nothing's wrong. I'm sitting on a kerb freezing my bollocks off.'

'Where's . . . Davie?'

'He's lying on the footpath, sleeping.'

'Right. I see. So why are you calling exactly?'

'For moral support, mainly. Am I within my rights to just leave him here? I can get a taxi home.'

'Don't even think about it,' Trish said firmly. 'You're responsible for him.'

'But he's irresponsible.'

'Kettle, pot and black are three words that spring immediately to mind. Now if you don't mind, I'm trying to sleep. Get your act together, Dan, do the right thing. You know you can't be a dad if you can't decide what the right thing is without phoning someone in the middle of the bloody night for advice.'

She cut the line.

She was probably trying to make some kind of point, but it was lost on me. It was too cold to think. I was getting a sore head. I wanted a nice warm bed. And a cup of hot chocolate. I wanted a hug from my wife and some late movie to snuggle down to. I was getting old and I really didn't mind.

Fuck it.

I made another attempt, really put my heart and soul into it, and finally managed to hoist Davie onto his feet. 'Come on, mate, come on, have to get you home.'

His legs went all floppy. But I held him up. I slapped at his face. 'Come on, Davie, come on.'

Eventually, eventually, he started to come round. He

mumbled incoherently for a bit as I led him further up the street.

'I need to know where you live. I need to know the house, Davie.'

'Isssabiginjusuphere.'

I led him on.

'I'm sorry,' he said, 'I'm really sorry.'

'That's okay. Let's just get you home.'

'I'm sorry,' he said again. 'Really, I'm sorry.'

'Let's just get home.'

'But I'm sorry.'

'Will you shut the fuck up and keep walking?'

We did the old three steps forward, two steps back for another five minutes before Davie stopped me outside a large house with a sweeping drive. 'Thisit,' he said.

I looked up. There were lights on. 'No one's going to try and shoot me up there, are they?'

Davie sniggered. 'Don't be daft,' he said.

He lurched forward.

I followed quickly, just in time to stop him falling over, then guided him to the front door. He leaned his head against it and I rang the bell. There was a short delay, then the bolts went back and a woman I gratefully recognised as his mum opened the door. Then she stepped back as her son fell through it.

She blinked down at him for a moment, then fixed her gaze on me.

'Well,' she said, shaking her head, 'I see nothing's changed with you pair.'

She was a nice woman, but sad since her husband died, and clearly not entirely over the moon at how her son had turned out. I was sobering up quite quickly. Davie was upstairs in bed, and I was sipping tea. It was nearly two in the morning. I wanted to sleep, she wanted to talk.

'He took it very hard,' she said.

'His dad?'

'No – Joe Strummer.'

'Yes. I know.'

'He should have retired and taken up gardening.'

'Yes. I know. Joe Strimmer.'

'What?'

'Joe . . .'

'I mean his dad. He worked too hard. Worked himself into the grave. It's very lonely. Don't work too hard, Dan, it's not worth it.'

'Don't worry about that. It's extremely unlikely.'

She smiled and sipped her tea. 'Did he ask you?'

'Did he ask me what?'

'About the trip.'

'What trip?'

Mrs Kincaid rolled her eyes. 'Heavens to God, that boy.' She shook her head. 'Big strapping fella could shoot a Fenian at two hundred metres, but he can't ask his best friend a favour.'

I wasn't entirely sure about the Fenian, but in this land you have to make allowances for all creeds and bigotries. And as for being his best friend . . . he had to get out more. The idea of Davie looking for a favour from me was somewhat worrying as well. Again, I should have left it.

But I never do.

Just shut up, Dan. But no, slabber your way into more trouble.

'What sort of a favour, Mrs Kincaid?'

'He's just a big shy lump, so he is.'

I nodded. She would get there eventually.

'He's shy, yet he's loud, he's got no confidence, yet

sometimes he's the bravest person in the world. He was shot, you know. Several times. He should have been retired on the sick years ago, but he stuck in there because he loved it. But he hated it as well. Do you know what I mean?'

'Yes, Mrs Kincaid.'

'I really thought he was going to settle down with this girl, but Davie's such a handful, I think he scared her away. So he's kind of stuck.'

'In what way, Mrs Kincaid?'

'With the honeymoon.'

I nodded. She nodded. She showed no immediate inclination to continue, so I said, 'In what way, stuck?'

'Well, it's all booked and paid for. One of those fly-by-night holidays in Florida.'

'Fly-drive . . .' I began to correct and then stopped as an idea of what she was about to ask sprang fully formed into my drunken head. 'Right . . . right. I see what you're getting at. He's stuck with the honeymoon.'

She nodded sadly. 'He'll lose it all, you know, at this late stage. Different if he was ill or she got her head sliced off in a tragic elevator accident – he could claim the money back. But he'll get nothing for getting dumped within sight of the altar. So he was kind of embarrassed about approaching you.'

'Well, he shouldn't have been. I'm . . . flattered he even thought of me. As long as we can – you know, come to some agreement – I'd be delighted.'

Mrs Kincaid smiled now. 'Ouch, that's great, Dan.'

I smiled too. Patricia would be over the moon. I'd arrive home with a hangover and a cut-price holiday to Florida. We hadn't been away in years. It was exactly what we needed. Romance. Rest. Set her up for her egg harvestation and my second attempt to wank into a cup.

'He'll be delighted.'

'No trouble, Mrs Kincaid.'

'He said you always talked about going to America together. When youse were kids.'

'We . . .'

'He said to me, "Dan and I were going to do a real rock'n'roll tour when we got the money together, but we never did. This is the perfect opportunity. Forget my troubles and have a cracking time with my old mate, Dan Starkey".'

Gulp is the correct word, I believe.

'So you're up for it, Dan, are you?' Mrs Kincaid asked.

'Absolutely,' I said. 'But would you mind phoning my wife and letting her know?'

5

She's an old trouper, my wife. Swears like one, too. Consideration for her reputation prevents me from relating in detail the torrent of abuse which was hurled at me when I told her I was going to Florida with Davie – although the words *fucker* and *wanker* figured strongly. This was of course understandable; she was in quite a delicate state because of the whole infertility/surrogacy situation. It might even be considered as indelicate in some quarters that I was contemplating disappearing off for a holiday in the sun when she was feeling so vulnerable, but I mean, it was free. All I needed was spending money, and I could borrow that off Patricia. She wasn't going anywhere.

'You are the most callous, insensitive little fucker I ever met.'

This was after the first torrent had abated and I had politely enquired about her fiscal liquidity because the PR job with *Why Don't You Come Home for a Pint?* paid bugger all, but I was so pissed off with her attitude that I am now forced to reconsider my concern for her reputation. Sometimes you have to present a woman with all of her inglorious flaws for others to understand how difficult she can be to live with. Perhaps, as an artist, I am just overly sensitive, but some of her language was uncalled for.

'You have to look at the bigger picture sometimes, Trish,' I said.

'Fuck your biggest picture, you're sloping off to America without me.'

'I'm doing it to help Davie.'

'Aye fuck you are. You're going off on a two-week bender.'

'I'm not, I'm just trying to help him through a difficult time.'

'Aye fuck you are.'

'I am, he's—'

'I don't give a fuck, Dan. What about me – what about *my* difficult time?'

'What difficult time?'

'Christ!'

'I mean – I know it's been hard. But we got good news, didn't we? We can do the IVF treatment, my swimmers are world-class . . .'

'If they *are* yours.'

'That's not fair, Trish. I made a mistake – they're mine now.'

'Yeah, right.'

'They're going to help us find a surrogate, aren't they? It'll be fine.'

'You've really no idea, have you? You've no idea of what's involved. The injections I'll need, the pain, the waiting, the counselling. We have to go before a fucking ethics committee, we have to meet a surrogate, we have to trust her to look after our baby for nine months, and you know at the end of it, at the fucking end of it she can hold onto it if she wants. Legally she can just keep it and we can do fuck all about it – and you'll have to fucking pay for its upkeep. You do know that, don't you?'

'Yes, of course.' I did indeed have some vague memory of a counsellor at the hospital telling us about that, although I have to confess most of my thoughts at the time continued to be about Joe Strummer. 'But it'll be fine.'

'That's just you all over, isn't it? *It'll be fine.* Everything will be fine. Everything's always fine with you, Dan.'

I had no idea what she was talking about, but I made all the appropriate noises. She appeared to calm down. I said I was going away to America and I'd really miss her. She said she'd miss me too. I said perhaps we should make love now. I went to give her a hug and she punched me in the stomach. I pulled her hair and she bent my fingers back until I screamed. It was another uneventful day down at the Ponderosa.

I had to see my psychiatrist.

I know, me and a psychiatrist, where's the sense in that? Me and some chrome dome with a file and a couch saying I have *unresolved issues*, like he'd know anything about it. I think I am a well-adjusted individual, although clearly not perfect; I am willing to concede that I may occasionally have an attitude problem, and that perhaps from time to time I don't act my age, but I'm no head the ball. So why a psychiatrist?

Well, not out of choice.

There are actually many and varied reasons, but the one best worthy of your consideration contains the words 'court' and 'appointed'.

Dr Raymond Boyle, psychiatrist to the stars in their own heads, was foisted on me by a senile judge who seemed to think my clearly accidental reversing of a car into Patricia's former lover Tony had enough elements of what he laughingly referred to as 'the sinister' to warrant some form of punishment. My solicitor was canny enough to indulge in a bit of plea bargaining in which I, against my better judgment, and mostly because Patricia ordered me to, admitted causing Tony grievous bodily harm but got off with a conditional discharge, the condition being that I voluntarily undergo psychiatric evaluation and treatment if required. Either that or jail time.

The road to hell is paved with gypsy flagstones.

I have tried to live a good life, it's just that I always end up wearing clown shoes. I have a hoop in my trousers.

'I wasn't trying to kill him,' I told Dr Boyle at my first appointment.

'You ran over him in your car.'

The mitigating circumstances were that I was drunk and really angry, neither of which were likely to carry much weight with the judge. So the only person who really knew the truth was my solicitor, and only because I trusted her, and the fact that she had a nice smile and a spiky fringe. 'I just wanted to flatten him. You know like, in a cartoon, when you flatten someone in a car and he gets up again and he's all kind of . . . flat. That's what I wanted to do.'

'Life isn't a cartoon, Dan.'

'You should look at my CV.'

Wisely, she warned me to shut the fuck up.

Patricia, though she told me she believed it had been an accident, didn't really. I could tell. It was in her eyes. Besides, she should have been grateful for my rather admirable restraint. I hadn't actually *killed* him. And if he'd had any sort of reactions at all, even those of a particularly lethargic sloth, he would have been able to leap effortlessly out of the way. I'd even sounded my horn. Really, I just wanted to give him a bit of a shock. But no, he stood staring at my reverse lights, like a rabbit frozen by the sight of Art Garfunkel. There was no particular *intent*. It was more, well, opportunistic. If his having to spend three months in traction in the Royal Victoria Hospital allowed Patricia and me the space and time to get back together, well that was just an unforeseen happy consequence of a tragic accident. Besides, lying with his feet up – admittedly in plaster – for most of the winter wasn't a punishment: that was a career break.

Alcohol, no matter how practised you are at it, is a real mind-fucker. It conspires to turn coincidence into conspiracy. I could see it in Dr Boyle's eyes, and in the way he had the temerity to suggest that the fact that I'd removed the number-plates from my car shortly before the incident was somehow indicative of my desire to also remove Tony from this mortal coil. Clearly, nothing could have been further from the truth. Besides, as I pointed out to him, only a complete idiot would remove his number-plates in an attempt to hide his identity, but neglect to remove the letters emblazoned across the front windscreen: *Dan & Patricia*. They had been there all the way through our marriage and subsequent separation; somehow as long as they remained in place I felt there was hope for us, and wasn't I proved right? Actually, the windscreen wasn't big enough to get on what I really wanted: *No, I Don't Want To Buy A Fucking* Big Issue *You Romanian Bastard*.

Reluctantly I must concede that there were also several snippets of evidence available to the police which, if presented in a certain light, might possibly have strengthened their case against me and led to a substantial amount of prison time – if they'd had the opportunity to present them. They did have fifteen positive witness identifications plus a video tape from a security camera in which I was plainly visible behind the wheel of the car. If I had been content with merely knocking him down I might have gotten away with it, because my face on that part of the tape was mostly in shadow, but my decision to reverse back over him meant that I was caught clearly from a different angle.

Don't misunderstand me. I am not a violent man. I was merely in love. I did not deliberately reverse over Tony *twice*. I reversed over him once by accident. I then drove forward, allowing him plenty of time to crawl out of the way. Aware that I had struck something, I then reversed back again to see what it was, totally unaware that Tony had shown the rank stupidity of the ginger-haired by agonisingly dragging himself *forward*, only to be inadvertently struck again. The other hugely positive thing to come out of this unfortunate accident, besides allowing Patricia and me to get back together, was the fact that it revealed a blind spot in the car's mirrors, which I was able to quickly communicate to its manufacturers. I probably saved thousands of lives that day, instead of merely endangering one.

'Dan?'

'Mmmm?'

'You're wandering again.'

I cleared my throat and looked Dr Boyle in the eye. 'Sorry.'

'Last time we spoke you'd been offered the largest advance of your publishing career.'

'The *only* advance of my publishing career. The only one worthy of being called an advance.'

'But you rejected it.'

'You know why.'

'You don't think it might have been a cathartic process, Dan? The fact is that you still find it impossible to unburden yourself to me – whereas a book about your son might enable you to do that in a medium to which you're obviously much better suited. The written word.'

'They want me to cash in on my son's death by writing

about it. They want pornography for necrophiliac paedo-philes. It's not for me.'

'Well, how is it going to get out then?'

'How is *what* going to get out?'

'Your hatred and guilt.'

'I don't have any hatred or guilt.'

He fixed me with a look. 'Dan. A blind man in a coal bunker can see the hatred and guilt.'

I glanced at my watch.

He said, blankly, 'Thirty-three minutes, Dan.'

'And three more sessions. Then I'll be done.'

'Unless you volunteer for more.'

I smiled.

He smiled.

'And I'm going to have to miss our next appointment.'

His smile faded. 'The court made it a condition—'

'I'm going to be on holiday. I didn't think it would be a problem.'

He lifted a pen and tapped it against his teeth. I had already told him about the IVF and the surrogacy. He didn't think either was a good idea. He seemed to think we could do without the stress.

'Well,' he said after a while, 'a vacation could be ben-eficial. Somewhere nice and sunny, I hope.'

'Florida.'

'Lovely. You'll be able to talk this whole surrogacy thing through away from the distractions of daily life.'

'That's what I thought.'

'It's really a very positive step, Dan. I'm pleased.'

'I thought you might be.'

'Though of course you're not doing it to please me.'

I smiled. 'I try not to do anything to please you.'

'Do you ever think about him, Dan?'

'Who? My son?'

'No. The Colonel.'

'I try not to.'

'Out of sight, out of mind?'

'Something like that.'

'What about Patricia?'

'You'd have to ask her psychiatrist that.'

'You still don't discuss it.'

'There's a joke I know, Doctor.'

'Excuse me?'

'A joke I know which kind of explains my attitude to this, to just about every bloody thing you want me to talk about.'

He sat back in his chair and folded his arms. His hair was thinning and he'd crow's-feet around his eyes, which was the best place for them. He wore a brown suit and a yellow tie and beige brogues. He was as bland as a New York cheesecake. He had a hangdog look about him which was more Clement than Sigmund.

'Hit me with it,' he said, and then added, 'metaphorically, of course.'

'How many country and western singers does it take to change a light bulb?'

Most of us would just say, 'I don't know, how many?' but he was a psychiatrist. He tried to figure it out, which says it all really. I gave him ten seconds and then answered my own question. 'Six. One to change the bulb, five to write a song about it.'

Dr Boyle didn't smile, but he nodded appreciatively. 'You don't want to write songs,' he said.

'Nope,' I said, and walked out.

When I let myself into the house, I heard voices from the kitchen – Patricia's and a man's – and my blood immediately ran cold. I still got stressed about the possibility of Patricia rekindling her relationship with Tony, or anyone else for that matter. She'd told me a million times since that she'd never be unfaithful again, but once bitten and all that. So I stood in the hall for several moments trying to hear what was being said, but it was too muffled to really make it out. Had Tony's car been parked out on the street, and I hadn't noticed it? He drove a blue Siat, recently augmented with a Disabled sticker. I peered back outside, but the street was empty. No sign of wheelchair grooves or crutch imprints on the carpet.

The only male friend we had who was likely to call unannounced was Mouse, but since he had a voice that could lift lead off a church roof it seemed unlikely that it was him.

I walked down the hall, paused by the kitchen door for a moment, took a deep breath to prepare myself for unarmed combat or tears, then opened it.

'Davie,' I said.

He was sitting at the kitchen table with Patricia. There was an open bottle of whiskey between them, half-empty, and she was rubbing tears from her face.

'Dan,' he said, 'I've been talking to Trish.'

'So I see. What have you said to annoy her?'

He held up his hands in denial, but before he could say anything Patricia pushed her chair back and came towards me.

'I've got more understanding out of Davie in twenty minutes than out of you in twenty months.'

I glanced at him. 'Well, big fucking—'

But before I could finish she put a finger to my lips, and wrapped her arms around me. 'I love you so much, Dan Starkey, and I want you to have a fantastic holiday. When you come home we're going to have a baby and live happily ever after.'

'Okay,' I said.

'Good. Now pull up a chair and pour yourself a drink.'

'Okay,' I said.

Patricia wiped at her eyes again, then turned to Davie and smiled. 'See? As long as he does exactly as I say, we hardly ever fight.'

6

Shankhill Airways Flight 101 was to take us direct from Belfast to Sanford, twenty odd miles north of Orlando, Florida, home of theme parks, expensive shops, cheap villas and the hundreds of thousands of British tourists too middle-class to do Spain, but not middle-class enough to afford Hawaii. My flying companion was Davie Kincaid, once my best friend, and as it turned out, now an ex-cop.

'I never really got you as a cop anyway,' I said.

'What's that supposed to mean?'

'Well, y'know, we were punks. Remember that Rudi song about the cops? We used to scream that chorus at them: *SS RUC! SS RUC!*'

Davie smiled at the memory of it. He shook his head wistfully. 'It was long ago and far away. And then I became a killing machine.'

I laughed.

We had little screens on our seat-backs on which you could choose to watch either a movie, a little map illustrating our progress through the skies, or pictures from cameras mounted to the front and underside of our aircraft showing how things looked outside. Bearing in mind that I hated flying at the best of times, that I classed all flying as a near-death experience, the last thing I needed to see was a map showing destination oblivion or cameras showing how ludicrously high we were flying. I never have understood why planes have to fly so high. Why can't they just skim the top of the waves?

'It's to do with the curvature of the earth,' Davie said, by now onto his third Bushmills whiskey. 'Flying over the top of the waves would prolong the flight by days.'

I was prepared to put up with it. We could always stop somewhere for a picnic.

'Besides,' Davie said, 'I thought you couldn't swim.'

'I can't.'

'I thought you had a morbid fear of the water.'

'I do.'

'Then what the fuck are you talking about?'

I pointed down. 'We're on a plane, and they stick life-jackets under the seat. Big fucking point. That's like handing out parachutes on a ship. At least if we skimmed the waves they'd have some bloody use.'

There were lots of kids on the flight. They were running about screaming. I didn't mind so much. I'd dreamed about taking Little Stevie to Disney. But that wasn't going to happen. Davie wasn't quite so relaxed. There was a baby crying constantly across the aisle from him and a kid of about six kept nudging his seat from behind.

'If he kicks my seat again,' he hissed, 'I'm going to fucking deck him.'

I didn't know him well enough any more to know if he was joking. I didn't know if the fact that he was now ordering his fourth whiskey meant that he had a drink problem or that he was even more of a nervous flier than I was. But what I did know was that even at this early stage it was hopeless to try and keep up with him. I was badly out of practice. I had to be in a state where I could at least walk off the plane. I smiled to myself. Showing some sense of responsibility at last. Patricia would be proud of me. Of course, with my luck, I'd be as good as gold for the eight-and-a-half-hour flight and then drop dead of a clot on the brain.

'I really appreciate the fact that you're coming with me,' Davie said. His voice wasn't slurred at all, which was slightly worrying.

'Don't mention it,' I replied. 'It'll be great.'

'I know. But a blast from the past, then a couple of days later we're on the road. You don't really know who I am any more or how I've changed.'

'Ditto.'

He smiled. 'You haven't changed at all, Dan.'

'I know,' I said. 'That's the problem.'

He unscrewed the miniature's top and drank without pouring it into the plastic cup. He sighed contentedly. 'You know, you have changed a little bit. You're more diplomatic.'

'What's that supposed to mean?'

'Well, you used to open your mouth and talk without always putting your brain into gear. Now you seem a little bit more circumspect.'

I shrugged. Clearly, he hardly knew me either.

'For instance, I said I had to leave the police, and you never asked why. I mean, you could be travelling with a maniac.'

'And so could you.'

'Fair point. But you were a journalist – what's the worst you could do? Give the pilot a bad review?' It didn't feel like a put-down, although it probably was. 'I used to be Special Branch. I am highly trained. You see all that bullshit security we had to go through before we got to Departures?'

I nodded. 'The metal detectors and the body search and the X-rays and the dogs sniffing our shoes for Semtex? It's all just for show because of September eleven. They know it, I know it. Anyone with even the most rudimentary training in bomb-making could have walked into Duty Free and bought all the materials you need to construct a bomb. Alcohol, batteries . . . I swear to God, I could blow this plane to pieces if I had a mind to.'

I nodded pleasantly at the air hostess as she passed, while smiling at Davie at the same time and saying, 'Very funny, good one.'

'I'm serious,' he said.

'I know. Just keep your voice down. Jesus.' This time I took a drink.

'Theoretically speaking,' he said. 'I don't really have a bomb, Dan.'

'Good.'

'Go on then.'

'Go on then what?'

'Ask me why I got drummed out of the police.'

'You got drummed out?'

Davie raised his eyebrows. 'Look at me, I'm forty years old, fit as a fiddle, prime of life, I got paid to carry a gun about and shoot bad guys. You think I'd just walk out of that?'

'I really don't know.'

'I was pushed.'

'Why?'

'Why do you think?'

'I really don't know.'

Davie laughed. He lifted two of the miniatures and clinked them together. 'Any closer?' he asked. 'Take a wild guess.'

'Drinking,' I said. He nodded. 'Sorry,' I said.

'Don't be sorry, Dan. It's not like I'm a raving alcoholic.'

'Well then, why?'

'Three convictions for driving while under the influence. Cop's bugger-all use to anyone if he can't drive. So they drummed me out. Full pension and all, but it's a fucking hard lesson.'

'Sorry,' I said again.

'That's why it's so fantastic that you're doing this, Dan. Driving me all round Florida for three weeks. It's like having my own personal chauffeur.'

He winked, then drained his miniature. He pressed the call button for another.

I sat there, kind of stunned. He could tell by the look on my face that something was up. 'What?' he said. He signalled at the barmaid – sorry, hostess – for a repeat prescription, then smiled across at me. 'You look a little . . . ?'

'I'm fine. I'm just . . . a couple of minor points, Davie.'

'Shoot,' he said, making a gun with his fingers as the hostess handed over the miniature.

She scowled. 'That's the last of your complimentaries,' she said.

Davie nodded as he broke the seal. She turned away.

'Will you stop doing that with your fucking fingers?'

'What?'

'*This.*' I made the gun shape. The hostess, passing back in the opposite direction, scowled at me this time. I sighed. I put the gun back in its holster. 'Davie, listen to me. Three weeks. I was under the distinct impression that it was two.'

'No. Three. It was always three. Can't do America in two.'

'But I told Patricia two.'

'Nobody ever said two.'

'But I'm supposed to—'

Oh God. Patricia would be furious. She was supposed to go into hospital to have her eggs removed. I was supposed to go back and wank into a cup. The sperm would be analysed to be sure there were no infections and the eggs examined to make sure there were no imperfections and then the whole lot would be frozen for six months while we went through the mandatory legal channels and counselling procedures. All our appointments were already set up. Patricia liked to know what she was doing. She liked organisation. She did not like last-minute changes of plan. She would scream that our entire future together rested on us fulfilling this first appointment. It didn't, of course. But it would seem like it. Davie had definitely told me two weeks, although that was neither here nor there. She would still blame me. She would say, 'Why didn't you check the tickets?' Because I never had them, Davie had them. Then she would tear her hair out and scream, 'What do you think would have happened if they'd had to postpone the fucking invasion of Normandy because someone was too fucking brain dead to check the tickets?' The fact was that they did have to postpone the invasion, but it would be lost on her. She would say this was the final straw and run back into the broken arms of her lover. I sighed again.

'Come on,' Davie said, 'it's not such a big deal. She'll be fine about it.'

It was, and she wouldn't be. But I would have to jump that hurdle when I came to it. The fact that he seemed to think I was going to be his chauffeur was much more pressing.

'If you think I'm driving you from pub to pub for three weeks, then you've another think coming.'

'Ah Dan – for godsake, it won't be that bad. There won't be that much driving.'

'There won't be *any* driving, Davie.'

'What're you talking about? It's a fly-drive holiday.'

'I haven't got a licence either, Davie. They took mine away as well.'

And that flummoxed him. He sat back into his seat. 'You're serious?' I nodded. He started laughing. He slapped his leg. He probably would have slapped mine too if I hadn't moved it. 'What are we like? We're a pair of fucking numskulls.'

He had a point.

'What the fuck did you lose yours for?'

'Same sort of nonsense.'

As it seemed like we wouldn't be driving anywhere when we landed, we decided to get pissed. Or he decided to get more pissed and I made a valiant effort to catch up. It didn't take long. There's something about flying that gets you drunker quicker. Perhaps it's the altitude, or the stale air circulating through the system, or fear that at any moment you could be blown into a million bloody smithereens.

About an hour out of Sanford the hostesses announced that the bar was shut, then came through with landing cards which had to be filled in to get us through immigration and customs. It was a struggle; we had to remember our names and our flight numbers and our destination and we had to squeeze all this information into little boxes and write it in capital letters. It was like sitting our eleven-plus while underwater. Or trying to do something sensible when pissed.

Davie was busy giggling to himself.

'Just fucking concentrate,' I hissed, 'or they won't let us in.'

Davie sniggered and pointed at the back of his form. 'They're not going to let us in anyway. Look at this shit.'

I turned my form over and studied it.

Davie jabbed a finger at the top question in a list of half a dozen. 'They want to know if we're Nazis.'

He cackled. I read the question. They did.

'Like you're going to answer, "Yes, I'm a Nazi".'

The next question asked if we'd ever been involved in acts of genocide.

'Yes, when I was a Nazi. I mean, what sort of stupid fucker is going to answer *yes*?'

The third question asked if we'd ever been involved in international terrorism.

The fourth was about our involvement in smuggling narcotics.

It was ludicrous and surreal, although not as ludicrous and surreal as Davie seemed to think it was. He went on and on about it. Eventually I closed my eyes and pretended to be asleep. And before very long I *was* asleep. I dreamed about Little Stevie, but he wasn't so little, he was all grown-up and pushing me around in a wheelchair. He was pushing me down a footpath, but the paving stones were all cracked and there was no suspension and every time we hit a bump the whole contraption shuddered. He kept saying, 'Watch out, old man, watch out,' and I tried to say something but dribbled out of the side of my mouth instead.

When I woke my mouth was as dry as a bone. Davie was half-turned, glaring malevolently at the kid behind. 'You kick the back of me again and I'll break your fucking neck,' he hissed between the seats.

The kid looked petrified. Luckily, from our point of view, the woman he was travelling with had her earphones in and her eyes closed.

Davie turned back, satisfied, and winked at me. 'Hiya, Sleepyhead. Another twenty minutes and our walking tour begins.'

According to the map on the screen in front of me we were just slipping from Alabama into Florida. I peered out of the window. We were noticeably lower in the air, although not so low that we would be okay if our engines failed and we plummeted to the ground and exploded in a fireball.

Davie was gazing down at the land below as well. Perhaps he was just as panicked about flying as I was, and sought to cover it up with the drink and the bravado. As I looked at him gazing at America below, unaware that he was being watched, I thought perhaps that he was a little bit lost, that he was thinking of something else, something darker. I know dark things, I recognise them. I hadn't really known Davie for the best part of twenty-five years; although we were older, we were not necessarily wiser. He had been a policeman, he had been in Special Branch all through the bad times. There was no telling what he had seen or what he had done. We were about to spend three weeks in each other's company, and it could be heaven, or it could be hell, but the reality would probably lie somewhere in between.

I put a hand on his arm and said: 'We'll have a ball.'

He glanced back and gave me a half-smile.

'I'm sorry it didn't work out with the fiancée.'

He nodded.

'I'm sure she was nice. I'd love to have met her.'

His head turned more fully towards me, away from the window. 'You did meet her.'

'What do you mean?'

He laughed. 'What I say. Dan – it was Karen. Karen Malloy. We used to hang around outside her house: she was the most beautiful creature we'd ever seen. Remember?'

I nodded.

'You took off to Belfast and I stayed behind, because I knew if I hung around long enough she'd eventually fall for me. And she did. I came within a hair's breadth of marrying Karen Malloy. How close to perfection can you get, eh, Dan?'

He smiled at the memory of it, then closed his eyes for

the final run into Sanford airport. I thought about different things: Patricia, life and love and the prospect of a fiery death on the runway, but mostly I thought about the fact that five years previously, I'd attended Karen Malloy's funeral in Belfast.

7

Way back in punk, we had both been jokers. The anarchy of The Pistols had always been counterbalanced by the comic lunacy of The Damned. But now we were twenty-five years further on, punk really was dead, and I had to decide whether Davie was winding me up, a complete and utter bullshit artist or whether he really did think he'd been about to marry Karen Malloy – in which case he would need medication, and lots of it.

The simple solution would have been to confront him with it: point out that Karen was dead and tell him to stop talking crap. But we were about to spend three weeks in each other's company: what kind of atmosphere would that make for, him exposed as a liar and fantasist? Especially as I like to think of that as my own personal territory.

As we queued up to go through passport control Davie kept joking that he was going to claim political asylum. He threatened to declare his genius like Oscar Wilde. He was on fine form and I was staring black-eyed into the distance wondering not for the first time in my life what I'd gotten myself into and realising that the expression, 'There's no such thing as a free lunch', now had a wider and more international perspective.

The question was, how much was I going to pay? And how painful was it going to be?

Davie's hair was all over the place from several unsuccessful attempts to sleep in the plane, his shirt was hanging out of his trousers, he was cracking funnies and taking the piss out of the uniforms. I was trying to walk steadily, look focused, be polite and helpful. Inevitably, he sailed through and I was given the third degree, mostly because I'd misspelled my own name on the entry form. I had to stand there and fill the form out again while Davie, at the next booth along, offered them his form, then withdrew it, then offered it cackling, 'What do I win then? What do I win?'

By the time I finally passed the written exam, Davie had already collected our bags and was standing outside smoking and sweating. I could see him through the glass as I approached the exit, but it wasn't until I got a blast of the hot air that I realised why he was dripping.

Heat. HEAT. We Irish aren't built for it. An analysis of one hundred years of Irish weather shows conclusively that we get one decent day a year and drizzle for the rest of the time. Warm days in Ireland are often described as 'close', but in reality they're about as close to being muggy as a cripple is to skateboarding down Everest. I walked out of the terminal and got slapped round the face by hundreds of Fahrenheit, not to mention the centigrade; they then drenched me in sweat for daring to hang around looking gormless. We were, of course, dressed for a summer's day in Belfast, black T-shirts, black jeans, black zip-up jackets and filthy attitudes. We looked more like we were waiting for a Stranglers reunion gig than a cab to the holiday capital of the world.

Davie took a final drag of his cigarette and said: 'Sorry.'

'What for?'

'Getting pissed. It's the smoking. I can't handle nine hours without a cigarette. I've got so many nicotine patches on I look like Pongo.'

'Pongo?'

'*Hundred and One Dalmations.* I'll be fine after a sleep.'

'Never worry,' I said. 'C'mon. Let's find a taxi.'

Davie dozed off, his head bumping gently against the window, as we were driven towards Orlando. I watched him in the fading light. We were the same age, but there was something still quite boyish about him. We had prized him in our youth for his ability to get served in off-licences while under age, but it was the only time he had actually looked older than any of us; in fact it wasn't older, it was taller. The rest of us had gotten tall as well, but we'd also aged, some of us quite dramatically. But Davie remained just Big Davie. Big Davie with the cavalier attitude to life and, as I was beginning to fear, a cavalier attitude towards the truth.

What he had said on the plane had kick-started a process of sobriety in me, sucked the benefits of drink from my soul and left the nag of a hangover in my head, which wasn't helped by the rap from the radio the cab driver insisted on blasting out. Davie started to snore.

Maybe I was just being supersensitive. Maybe I was jealous that he'd had his way with Karen Malloy. Maybe he was just pissed and mixed up. Perhaps it was as innocent as that. He was supposed to be on honeymoon with the love of his life, but she'd left him within sight of the altar – that was bound to fuck up your head. Add huge amounts of alcohol, deprive of nicotine, ascend to thirty-six thousand feet, then wait for hallucination to kick in. He had confused fantasy and reality, and come out with Karen Malloy.

Perhaps he didn't know she was dead.

Perhaps when he sobered up I'd tell him that she'd been virtually cut in two by an articulated lorry outside the newspaper office where I was then working. That she'd been on her way to a job interview, that where we might have ended up working together, I had instead ended up going to her funeral. I might have flirted innocently with her, become her confidant. We might have exploded the Harry and Sally myth that men couldn't be friends with women without sex rearing its ugly head. Or we might have gone at it like rabbits, Patricia be damned. Even in the fleeting glimpse I had of her as she crossed the road to our office that day I had registered that she was more beautiful as an adult than she had been as a girl. The old woman in the park had been wrong. There was nothing small village about this girl. She looked magnificent. She had gone blonde; she was wearing a fine business suit which also managed to show off her figure; she had breasts that could poke your eyes out; and then she passed out of my field of vision, and half a minute later she was dead. The next time I saw her she was in her coffin, her cheeks puffed up with cotton wool and somewhere beneath her funeral shroud her legs were stitched back onto her torso. I watched the wooden box shudder along a moving track and then come to a halt while we sang 'The Lord is My Shepherd'; I stood outside and shook hands with relatives while smoke billowed from the crematorium.

I thought the chances of her recovering from a slight case of death and getting engaged to Davie Kincaid were small to remote. Stranger things had happened, although mostly in *Dr Who*.

I shook myself. For Christ-sake. I was on holiday. I was taking it all much too seriously. Davie was winding me up, or talking the piss-talk. I needed to lighten up. I'd been in the air for nine hours. Back home it was two in the morning. I needed to sleep. Wind down. Enjoy America. Maybe take anything he said with a pinch of salt. Or wind him right back up.

We arrived at the Ramada Inn on International Drive in Orlando forty-five minutes later. It wasn't that far from Sanford, but the traffic was heavy. Big, in fact. Big traffic. Big hotels. Big weather. Big cars. It always takes a while to acclimatise to the bigness of America. Davie rolled out of his side of the taxi after some prodding and paid the driver, who looked at the colour of our money and said, 'What about a tip?'

Davie and I glanced at each other, then sang together: 'Don't sleep in the subway.' We cackled our way into the hotel and the desk clerk, a fruit in a suit, looked us up and down and said, 'Ah, Mr and Mrs Kincaid, welcome to the Ramada.' He then gave us the keys to the honeymoon suite.

Davie immediately suggested that he stick them up his arse. Luckily, his accent was thick enough to confuse, and before the penny dropped I quickly suggested that single beds might be more appropriate.

He looked us up and down again, then leant forward and whispered conspiratorially: 'You don't have to be embarrassed. I understand what it may be like in Ireland, but we're quite open-minded here. We host many gay weddings and honeymoons.'

I looked at Davie. 'It's only for one night.'

Davie shrugged. 'Any port in a storm,' he said, then added needlessly, 'you big ride.'

The desk clerk smirked. Davie tried to hold my hand as we walked across to the elevator. We went up eight floors and let ourselves into the honeymoon suite. It had a lounge, Queen-sized bedroom, ensuite bathroom, TV,

DVD, Internet and minibar. We held a long discussion about which facility to use first, and chose the minibar. We pulled back the curtains and enjoyed glorious night-time views of the traffic. It was Davie's honeymoon, so after a couple of drinks he wandered off into the bedroom and I lay down on the couch. I sort of drifted for a while without ever quite getting to sleep. The door to Davie's room was open and I could see the flicker of his TV screen. There were groans and squeals coming from inside.

'Davie?' I called. 'You awake?'

'Yipee!' he shouted back. 'Hot and cold running porn! Come on and take a look!'

'You're okay,' I said.

'It gets really boring after about an hour!' Davie yelled. 'They've all got inflatable tits!'

'You're paying for them. You do know that?'

He didn't answer, but the TV suddenly went off. A few moments later he appeared in the doorway pulling his T-shirt back on. 'We should go and get breakfast,' he said.

'It's the middle of the night.'

'So? This is America! Come on!'

Davie was an enthusiast.

I would hate enthusiasts with a passion if only I could summon one. As International Vice-Chairman of Sloth and Slow plc, I fixed him with two weary eyes and said, 'Catch yourself on, I'm knackered.'

He laughed. 'Come on, Dan, we're on holiday!' He pushed his T-shirt into his trousers and headed for the door. 'Come *on*!'

I moved into a more comfortable position on the couch.

'C'mon, Dan, you're only young once.'

'You're right,' I said. 'And I was. Good night.'

I closed my eyes. He tutted. 'Sure?'

'Sure.'

He opened the door. 'Well, see you later, alligator.'

'In a while . . .'

But I was asleep before I got to 'crocodile'. Or at least I pretended to be.

And I did get to sleep, eventually. I woke just after ten in the morning. The sun was blinding. I showered. I phoned Patricia at home and exchanged words of love. At the end she said, 'See you in two weeks,' and I didn't have the heart to correct her. And maybe it would be two weeks. Maybe it would only be one week. Davie was already showing the energy levels of a teenager, or speed freak. Or both. I put on my summer gear – black T-shirt, black jeans and sunglasses – and went to find breakfast.

Davie was already in there, eating an omelette. He was hollow-eyed and stubbled, but he smiled with real warmth and said, 'What aboutcha, big lad?'

'Great,' I said. 'What about you?'

'Fantastic.'

I sat down opposite him and folded my arms over the placemat. There were words printed all over it, but they were too difficult to read with my sunglasses on, and my sunglasses were too difficult to take off with my hangover head on. Davie reached into his pocket and produced a set of car keys. He set them down on the table. 'Have wheels, will travel,' he said.

'Brilliant,' I said, as the waitress approached and poured coffee for me without asking.

'How do you like your eggs?' she asked.

'Fertilised,' I said, but it was an in-joke.

She said, 'Excuse me?'

I wasn't entirely sure of the terminology. Americans like variations in their food and drink; they have a thousand different ways of serving coffee, whereas we have black or white. It's the same with their eggs. All that over easy and sunny side up shit. I looked her in the eye and said, 'I'd like them oops outside your head, I said oops outside your head.'

She said, 'Excuse me?'

I said, 'I'll have Frosties.'

She said, 'Excuse me? Do you mean Frosted Flakes?'

'That's what I mean.'

'And how would you like your eggs?'

I sighed.

She looked pained. I ran up the flag of surrender and said I'd pass on the eggs. I could tell by her eyes that even if she got satisfaction on the eggs front she'd immediately move onto the even more complicated ham or bacon argument; then we'd get to discuss whether I wanted pancakes or biscuits or sausage and biscuits or pancakes and syrup and sausage or French toast or white or rye and then I would ask for Veda and she would look like I'd slapped her in the face and Davie would have to intervene and explain it was a Northern Irish baker's delicacy and not a sexually transmitted disease, although not before I'd committed suicide. America. Big traffic. Big noise. Big breakfast.

She eventually went away. There would have been smoke coming out of her ears, but smoke had been banned in Floridian restaurants.

'Guess who got out of the wrong side of bed,' Davie said.

I shook my head and smiled. I had a hangover, sure, but I wasn't upset. I was frustrated by choice. 'She should have given me a fucking menu,' I said.

'She did.' He nodded down. The placemat was the menu, I could see that now. I thought briefly about apologising to the waitress, then didn't. It's the thought that counts. Besides, I'd other, more important things to deal with.

I said, 'Seeing as how neither of us have a driving licence, where'd you find someone buck eejit enough to hire us a car?'

'I didn't,' Davie said. 'I bought it.'

'You bought it?'

'Nineteen eighty-five Dodge. Seventy-five thousand miles, five hundred dollars. You owe me two-fifty and I'll throw in the gas.'

I lifted the keys. They were rusty. 'You never thought of consulting me before buying? You never thought of asking me if I wanted to invest two hundred and fifty dollars in a car?'

'It's not an investment, Dan. You hope to profit from an investment. Look on this more as a donation to charity, plus we get to ride around in it until it gives up the ghost. One saying and one motto come to mind. "Beggars can't be choosers", and "never look a gift horse in the mouth".'

I sighed. I shook my head across the table at Davie's big grinning face. He looked so pleased with himself.

'Okay,' I said. I would let it ride. I didn't ask about insurance. There didn't seem much point. It felt somehow unAmerican to have insurance anyway. I couldn't remember a movie where Vin Diesel refused to partake in a high-speed chase until he'd checked his insurance documents. I couldn't recall Indiana Jones arguing over the finer points of his third party fire and theft policy.

'Good man,' he said. 'This'll be class, Dan. This'll be class.'

'If you're happy, Davie, then I'm happy too. You're right, you know. We're on vacation. We should enjoy ourselves.'

'That's the spirit, mate.'

'And to that end . . .' I produced a clutch of pamphlets I'd picked up in the lobby on the way into breakfast. They covered pretty much all of the local theme parks – Sea World, Disney, Epcot, Universal Studios. I spread them out at random before Davie, or at least as close to random as I could make it look. Actually I put the Universal Islands of Adventure leaflet in the most prominent position, because I was completely determined to have a go on the 3-D Spiderman thrill ride. It was the kind of subtle attempt at mind-control I was famous for.

Davie nodded down at the leaflets for several moments, then pushed them together into a neat pile and tore them in half.

'We're not doing the theme parks, Dan. It's not that kind of a holiday.'

He reached into his own back pocket and produced a different leaflet. It showed the other Ramada Inns dotted around Florida, but he'd clearly only picked it up because on the reverse of it there was a fairly detailed road map of the state. He jabbed a finger at it. 'Here,' he said. 'This is where we're going.'

He was pointing at the Gulf Coast, at the beaches south and west of Tampa.

'But why? What's down there? What's so great about . . .' I trailed off. He looked kind of hurt. And a little bit angry.

'Because it's my honeymoon, and that's where we planned to go, all right? Is that too much to ask?'

I sat back. 'No,' I said.

'Okay. I'm gonna pack my stuff. See you back down here in ten minutes, and we'll get on the road, yeah?'

'Yeah,' I said.

He got up and started to walk across the restaurant. Then he stopped and came back. He put a hand on my shoulder and said, 'Sorry. I didn't mean to . . . you know.'

'Don't worry about it.'

'It just gets to me, you know?'

I nodded. I could understand. It was getting to me as well, as was the realisation that I had agreed to spend twenty-one days driving around Florida with a complete looper.

8

We took the 14 from Orlando to Tampa, then cut off onto the 275 for St Petersburg. I drove, Davie read the map. There wasn't a lot to it. Big road. Big traffic. Big easy. We didn't say much. Davie cracked a few funnies and I grunted. We listened to the radio. We heard 'London Calling' on an adult-orientated rock station, and looked at each other grimly. We liked that The Clash were recognised now, but lamented it as well. The sun was cutting our eyes out through our shades and the air conditioning on our Dodge rust-bucket was about as strong as a dead man's last gasp. We were sweating through our shoes. All around luxury cars were laughing at us as they cruised past. I'm not a car-boy, never have been, but even I felt embarrassed.

About halfway there, an hour and a half on the road, I insisted on stopping for doughnuts and Diet Pepsi. I insisted by pulling off the road and driving to a 7–Eleven while Davie flapped about in the passenger seat like he'd been hijacked. But he didn't reject the custard doughnut I bought him. He glanced at his watch as he ate it and I said, 'What's the big fucking hurry, Davie?'

'No particular hurry.'

'Then stop looking at your watch.'

'We have to check in. It's on the itinerary.'

I nodded and swallowed some doughnut. 'Anything else on that itinerary I should know about?'

Davie shrugged. 'Not really, no.'

'You know, you've been whining on about me relaxing and enjoying the holiday, you should take a leaf out of your own fucking book.'

I finished the doughnut and threw the napkin out of the window. I started the engine. As we pulled back out onto the interstate Davie said, 'You're pissed off, aren't you?'

'No.'

'Yes, you are. And it's my fault. I'm sorry.'

'And you don't need to keep apologising. Just stop *doing* it.'

'Doing what?'

'Winding me up.'

'I'm not doing it on purpose, Dan.' I gave him a look. 'Really. Maybe we're just different. Maybe we've grown apart.'

'Maybe we are. Maybe we have.'

Frankly, I didn't think there was much doubt about it.

'So what's the solution?' Davie asked.

I should have left it. But I never do. 'How about you get over the fact that you're not on fucking honeymoon. How about you get your story straight.'

There. I'd said it. I'd meant to keep it under my hat. But it was out there, slapping him round the face.

'What story?' he said quietly.

'What story?' I was getting angry now. 'C'mon Davie, how much of a fucking doughbag do you think I am?'

He raised his hands off the map and held them about twelve inches apart. 'This much?' he asked.

I couldn't help but laugh. We drove on. About another three miles down the road he said: 'What story?' again.

The road was straight and the traffic had thinned out after Tampa so I could afford to give him a long, hard look without writing off the car. He kept eye-contact for just a couple of seconds, then returned his attention to the road. I kept looking, daring him to look back, but he wouldn't.

'What story?' I said.

'What fucking story?' Davie snapped.

I snorted. 'What story. You know what story.'

'I wouldn't be fucking asking, you Clampett.'

'You and Karen.'

'Me and Karen who?'

'You tell me, you slabber.'

'No, you tell me, you wanker.'

'What the fuck are you calling me a wanker for? You're the one doing the slabbering.'

'Christ! Dan, what the fuck are you talking about!'

'About you and Karen Malloy!'

'Karen Malloy from Groomsport?'

'Yes – Karen Malloy from Groomsport!'

'Karen Malloy's dead!'

'I know that! So how the fuck can you be engaged to her?'

'I'm not! Christ Almighty, Dan, what're you on?'

'I'm not on anything!'

'Patricia told me you were seeing a psychiatrist, but I didn't think you were a fucking mental!'

'I'm not a – Jesus . . .'

I slapped the wheel in frustration. I took a deep breath. I tried to concentrate on the road. Someone was singing on the radio about taking their love to town. 'On the plane,' I said as calmly as possible, 'you said your fiancée was Karen Malloy.'

'I did not.'

'You did.'

'Why would I say that?'

'I don't know why you would say that. But you did. I swear to God.'

'Karen Malloy?'

'Karen Malloy.'

'But Karen Malloy's dead.'

'Yes, I think we've established that.'

'Then why would I say she was my fiancée?'

'I really don't know. Because you're *barking*.'

'Because *you're* barking.'

We both stared angrily at the road. I wanted to stop the car, pull him out and hit him with a spanner. I wanted to . . .

. . . and then I heard it. A low chuckle. He kept his eyes on the road, and his face straight, but the chuckle was coming from way down in his stomach, like he'd swallowed a frog and it was reading a joke-book. The dull angry stare began to morph into a moist shine, the chuckle grew louder and a crease began to creep across his brow. Slowly his head turned towards me.

'Gotcha,' he said.

I glared at him.

'Got-*cha*,' he half-sang.

'You bastard.'

He laughed and slapped the dashboard. 'I fucking got you! I burned you up!'

'You fucker.'

'The thought that I got to her, that I had sex with her, that she chose me over you.'

'You wanker.'

'And even though you knew she was dead, the remotest possibility that she might not be, that she had somehow survived having her legs cut off and then being cremated, for Christ's sake, the tiniest microscopic thought that she'd somehow pulled through in order to have sex with me, it's really been burning you up, hasn't it?'

'No,' I said.

'Liar!'

'Fuck off!'

'Liar liar pants on fire!'

'Grow up, Davie.'

'I had her – you didn't, I had her – you didn't!'

'Fuck you, arsehole.' I shook my head. I chewed my lip.

'Gotcha.'

He had fucking got me. The bastard. I'd get him. I'd get him back, with bells on. I fucking would.

'Dan?'

'What?'

'A word of advice.'

'Fuck off.'

'Okay.'

Another mile.

'What then?'

'I think we missed our turn.'

We'd managed to make our way onto the 75, but it was a blessing in disguise really because we were able to follow its loop back round to the 275 and cross onto Long Key and St Pete's Beach via the Sunshine Skyway, a huge finger of a toll-bridge which straddled Tampa Bay and gave us epic views of the sea and ships and beaches beyond. It served to settle us both down, for it was our first real glimpse of majestic America.

'Fan-tastic,' Davie whispered.

'Brilliant,' I added.

'Epic,' he said.

'Just like a movie.'

To mark the occasion Davie produced a large bag of crunchy M&Ms and shook it at me. I hesitated for a moment. My name is Dan Starkey, and I am a chocoholic. He opened the bag, I put my hand out and he poured. I squeezed about fifty of them into my mouth at once. He set the bag on the dash. We crunched for a while, then washed them down with warm Diet Pepsi. Life doesn't get much better. But still, I had to know.

'Did you . . . you know? Ever?'

'With Karen Malloy?' I nodded. 'Of course not. She wouldn't touch me with a barge-pole. Or you, for that matter.'

'I saw her the day she died.'

'Did you?'

'More or less saw it happen. That's why I'm so touchy about it.'

'Oh. Christ. Sorry. Didn't know. I was only raking.'

'Yeah. Well. Forget about it.'

'She was gorgeous though.'

'She was. Even more gorgeous all grown-up.'

'I know. She got better. She was going out with some bank manager, lucky bastard.'

'Dead right there. Lucky bastard. So who was she then?'

'Who was who?'

'Your fiancée.'

Davie shrugged. 'Not a patch on Karen Malloy, that's for sure.'

'So why'd she run off?'

'Who said she ran off?'

'Your mum, for one.'

'Yeah, well.' He turned a little in his seat and his eyes flitted out over the water.

'You don't want to talk about it?'

He nodded. Which was confusing.

'You do want to talk about it, or you don't?'

'Don't,' he said quietly. 'Not now.'

'Fair enough.'

He was a pain in the neck, but I had to feel a bit sorry for him. I'd been through the mill a few times, but at least I'd found true love at a relatively early age. I'd lost it, found it, lost it over the years, but it had always been there, if not exactly within my grasp then certainly not much beyond it. But as far as I could determine, it had always eluded Davie. Now as he sat staring out over the water, a faraway look in his eyes, I knew that he had been hurt, hurt badly. Here was a man who'd been given his first taste of reciprocal love at the age of forty; who'd been brave enough to grab it with both hands, and then been burned for his trouble. He deserved a few moments of quiet contemplation.

'So, was she any good in bed?' I asked. 'Was she a ride?'

There were four or five different resort communities on Long Key, but Davie was quite specific about our destination: the Hotel del Mar on St Pete's Beach. We came off the 275 and crossed the Pinellas Bayway toll-bridge then turned right onto the town's main drag. Initial impressions were good, although ultimately deceptive. The first hotel we came to off the bridge was a huge Spanish-themed castle which flourished under the nickname of 'The Pink Palace'. It was actually called the Don CeSar, and it dominated the skyline. We weren't even within spitting distance of it, yet we could smell the money. Cars were queuing up to avail themselves of its valet parking, international flags fluttered in the sea breeze, and our car groaned with embarrassment.

'You sure know how to treat a guy,' I said.

'Yeah, dream on,' said Davie and directed me on down the strip. It appeared that the Don CeSar was the only building of significance or distinction in the whole area. It went: hotel, hotel, burger joint, hotel, ice-cream parlour, hotel, McDonald's, hotel, hotel for about three miles, leading all the way to Downtown, which wasn't much more than a jumble of antique shops, Chinese buffets and drugstores.

'Well,' I said, 'this looks like fun.'

We managed to miss the Hotel del Mar on our first pass, but found it quickly enough on our second. It was the flashing neon sign and FREE -DULT MOVIES that attracted our attention. It was more of a motel than a hotel. We parked the car and looked around the facilities before we went to check in. Correction: we looked around the facility. The facility was the pool and it either hadn't been cleaned in weeks, or they'd suffered an extremely localised dirt storm that morning. Davie shook his head. 'Looked better in the brochure,' he said.

We pushed through swing doors into reception. At least the air conditioning was working. We could tell that by the frost on the moustache of the Cuban behind the counter. He might not have been Cuban at all, but he looked a bit like Castro and was smoking a cigar, so it seemed kind of appropriate. We Irish are quick to give people nicknames, so he was the Cuban, Davie was Big Davie and I was the fucking loser saddled with the heartbreak kid for three weeks, although as that was a bit of a mouthful I was prepared to answer to Dan.

The Cuban slowly removed the cigar from his mouth.

'Kincaid,' Davie said, 'checking in.'

'And before you say anything,' I added, 'we don't want the honeymoon suite.'

The Cuban looked from me to Davie. 'We don't have no honeymoon suite.'

'Fine,' I said.

'But I booked a honeymoon suite.'

I glanced at Davie.

'We don't have a honeymoon suite, Mr Kincaid. All our rooms are exactly the same, sir. They all cost the same.'

'But . . .'

'Davie,' I said. 'Just sign us in, will you?'

'Hold on Dan, that's not the point. I booked a honeymoon suite. What would have happened if I hadn't been cruelly dumped at the altar, and I'd arrived here with my blushing bride expecting three weeks of luxury in the honeymoon suite, only to find there isn't one? What way would that have been to start our marriage?'

I put my hands on the counter and smiled at the Cuban. 'Don't worry about him,' I said. 'He's a head the ball. I'm sure the room will be fine.'

He looked at Davie. 'I'll need a swipe of your credit card.'

'It's paid for already.'

'Nevertheless, I need a swipe of your credit card. For incidentals.'

'What sort of incidentals?'

'Phone calls. Room service.'

'Davie, will you just give him the fucking card?'

Davie reluctantly removed the card from his wallet and handed it over. 'I did request a honeymoon suite,' he said as the Cuban swiped his card. 'Honestly.'

The Cuban nodded. 'Happens all the time. Travel agents are such wankers.'

I smiled appreciatively. 'Where does someone like you get to learn a word like *wanker*?'

'From British tourists,' he said. 'Looking for the honey-moon suite.'

He put the cigar back in his mouth and handed us our keys.

9

People with freckles don't get a tan. They just look a bit dirty for a few weeks.

Of course in order to get to the dirty look they have first to pass through the burned phase, in which a pasty-skinned Irishman sits out in the sun for about twenty minutes without any kind of protection at all. He then spends the next three days rolling around in agony, sun-burned, sun-stroked and generally swearing never to venture out in daylight again.

On the second day at the Hotel del Mar I wouldn't leave the room because of the intense pain in every part of my body.

Patricia was screaming down the phone, 'What sort of an idiot are you?!'

'I got drunk and fell asleep.'

'Jesus! I suppose Davie's just as bad?'

'No, actually he's . . .'

Davie was fine. He stood and laughed at my pathetic cries for help. 'Did your mother never learn you about sun creams?' he asked.

'My mother never got west of Portrush, there was no need to.'

'Dan, there were hot days when we were kids. I remember.'

'Days? *Day*. And then we got sent out to get a bit of colour. Only fruits bothered with sun creams.'

He rolled his eyes as he rubbed Factor 30 on his face. 'Well, if you don't want to go to the beach, come on out for a drive then.'

'You don't seem to understand. I cannot bear anything to touch my skin. And I cannot go out driving naked.'

'So you're going to spend the rest of your holiday in here?'

'No. I will venture out when my skin settles down. It'll probably come off all together, like a snake. Until then, it's me and the remote control.'

Davie shook his head, then lifted the keys. 'Please yourself, Dan. And don't be watching any of those –dult movies.' He winked at me. 'See you later.'

Of course I never had any intention of watching any of the –dult movies, but now that he'd mentioned it, and I was stuck in my room being miserable, and the only part of my body that wasn't sunburned was my groin, the idea began to grow on me. I thought of Patricia and the Quiet Room and how a man was entitled to his private pleasures, and wondered how much they would charge for a 'free' dirty movie and whether it would show up on Davie's credit-card receipt as 'In-Room Movie' or '*Rampant Lesbian Fuckers* – $15'. But before I could make my mind up there was a knock on the door and a woman shouted that she wanted to clean the room. I shouted for her to come back later, or in a couple of weeks, but she kept banging and when I did open up, gingerly holding a towel around my midriff, her mouth dropped open; she looked like she'd just stumbled on the set of *The X-Files*. She said mamma-mia or something equally exotic and forced her way in for a proper look. She said mamma-mia again and said I should see a doctor.

'It's okay,' I said, 'it's only sunburn.'

'Mamma-mia!' she said again, then strode out into the corridor and summoned the rest of the cleaning staff.

Four of them, four big black women, stood around my skinny mostly naked frame going oooh and aaaah. I was in too much pain to tell them where to go.

'What you need,' one said, 'is Aloe Vera. It will help your skin. And Tylenol.'

I nodded helplessly. My head was pounding. 'I can't,' I said. 'I can't leave the room.'

I carefully lowered myself back down onto the bed, and lay face down. They could clean the room around me, I didn't care. I was dying. They talked amongst themselves for a while, but I wasn't really listening. I drifted away into a fitful sleep; when I woke they were gone, so I drifted off again; when I woke again they were back.

'Has it been twenty-four hours?' I asked drowsily.

''Bout twenty minutes, mister. We had a vote – you didn't hear us?' I shook my head. 'We said to ourselves, if we had a dog in as much pain as you are, we'd put that dog down.'

I nodded.

'So like I say. We had a vote.'

I said, 'Okay, put me down.'

'We had a vote and we agreed we had to do something to help you – so Beatrice got the Aloe Vera, Martha got the Tylenol and I got my hands; together we're gonna give you the best damn medicated massage you ever had.'

I couldn't move, but I managed to say, 'No, please, don't touch my skin.'

She reached forward and ripped the towel away from my groin.

'Ain't no time for modesty here, son,' one of the other ladies said. 'Ain't nothing we haven't seen before.'

'That sun so strong, it burn your balls off right through your costume, you understand? You gotta protect to survive.'

'I understand. But please don't touch my SKKKKII-IINNNNN!'

I guess you have to be cruel to be kind.

And boy, they were cruel.

'Florida ain't no place for no chalk-white boy, that's for sure,' the biggest woman, Martha, said.

There were four of them, big black smiley women anointing my burned flesh with soothing lotions.

It has been the major discovery of my life that if you look pathetic enough for long enough, somebody will inevitably come along who will take pity on you and help you out. I still felt miserable, but I had absolute faith in their ability to make me feel better because, quite simply, I couldn't possibly feel any worse.

'Only one thing,' Martha said, as she pulled a second massive bottle of Aloe Vera out of an Eckerds bag. 'We doin' this out of sympathy for your situation. You spring a hard-on and we'll snap it off and feed it to the rats. You understand?'

I cleared my throat, and nodded. 'Perfectly,' I said.

My recovery was little short of miraculous. My skin literally drank the lotions, it didn't crack or fracture, merely hurled up a huge wall of protective freckles. The cleaning ladies returned for three days in a row to reapply their medication and we became really good friends. I even offered them a tip which didn't involve sleeping in the subway, but they turned it down. They were Christian ladies doing their best to help a poor suffering individual. On day five of our transatlantic adventure I wandered back onto the beach, bronzed and Adonis-like, to look for Davie. I had on shorts, sandals and a Dunnes T-shirt. I wore my shades and an air of nonchalance.

A bleached-blond beach bum (which is like a work-out at the alliteration Olympics) grinned over at me as I passed. 'You should sit in the shade, you look like you're about to melt.'

I smiled at him and made like he was funny, whereas the correct response should have been, 'Why don't you mind your own fucking business, arse-wipe?'

I asked him if he'd seen my mate Davie.

He said, 'No, what's he look like? Is he as red as you?'

I reexamined myself. I'd looked tanned in the dark of my room, but now in the boiling light of day I had to acknowledge that I probably didn't look quite as much like a sex god as I had imagined. Still, there were so many beautiful bodies about that perhaps the local ladies would fancy a bit of freckle for a change.

The bleached-blond beach bum worked out of a wooden hut halfway down the sand. He was offering parasailing rides, dolphin watch cruises, sun creams and the best drugs on the beach. Of course he didn't quite advertise this last service, and I was quite offended that he didn't think to offer me any, but from my position in the shade, sitting by the Del Mar's pool and watching the steady troop of teenagers to and from his beach hut, I knew he was selling something more than the American way of life. It had to do with the nervous way the kids approached him, and the delight on their faces as they left; with the way he behaved when the Sheriff's Land Cruiser eased past four or five times a day, kind of over-the-top and smiley, high-fiving in an exaggerated manner as if for the benefit of the cops; and it also had to do with the fact that nobody ever seemed to go para-sailing or dolphin watching.

Davie came and sat beside me by the pool. I nodded at the hut. 'He's selling dope.'

'Yeah, I know. It's great stuff.'

'I thought you were a police officer.'

'Was.'

I nodded. 'So where have you been these three days, while I've been dying? Besides smoking dope.'

'Oh, out and about. And I looked in on you. I brought you KFC. The last time I checked, you were being molested by four fat black women.'

'They weren't molesting me. They were anointing me with unctions.'

'Well, they looked like they were giving you a wank.'

'Please. There are children present.'

And there were. The pool and poolside were packed with kids and their parents. They were mostly Americans. There were a few British as well, like me, burning in the sun.

'But you're feeling better?' Davie asked.

'Yeah. Getting there.'

'Good. We can go out for dinner tonight then?'

'If you want.'

'Good. I'll book somewhere.' He glanced at his watch. 'Okay, I'd better get moving.' He stood up.

'Davie – where are you going?'

'Out.'

'I'm trying not to look hurt here, mate, but did you never think of asking me if I wanted to go too?'

'I would – I mean, I would if I was doing anything interesting. I'm just touring around, y'know? You relax, mate, give your body time to recover. We'll go out for a nice meal tonight. Here, I'll get you a Piña Colada. That should help.'

He crossed to the beach bar and ordered me a drink. But he didn't bring it over; he pointed me out to the barmaid and she brought it over. Davie walked off across the sand.

The good thing was that it was a long flat beach, so that even as I sipped my drink and admired the pneumatic breasts of the girls by the pool, I was able to watch Davie's progress. Of course, it was obvious what he was up to. You put sun, sand and secrecy together and you just knew there was a woman involved. He'd met a girl and didn't want to let on because he was supposed to be heartbroken over the break-up with his fiancée. I should have been happy for him, but I wasn't. I wasn't jealous exactly, either. I just wanted some company. I've never been a lonely drinker; I like good company and ludicrous conversations. I wanted to talk about our youth and Strummer and fantasise some more about Karen Malloy and find out what Davie's fiancée had been like, but I was stuck by myself, sitting in the shade by the pool, with no one to talk to and disinclined to strike up a conversation with anyone new in case it led to my early death. My life was like that. But still, I was bored. I'd had more crack with the four black cleaners than I'd had with Davie.

He was getting smaller and smaller. Or in fact he was the same size, he was just getting further away. He was almost at the end of the beach when he began to veer up the sand towards the pink façade of the Don CeSar. I watched as he moved between its rows of private beach-beds and disappeared through a line of palm trees into its grounds.

So that was it.

He'd met someone with a bit of money, and didn't want me embarrassing him.

What sort of a guy did he think I was? Didn't he think I could conduct myself in civilised company?

Patricia and I had been to all sorts of functions in our time and we hadn't made fools of ourselves once. Some of the dinners we had attended had even featured more than one set of knives and forks; I could tell a fish-knife from a fish-wife, and caviar from snail trail. I could be sophisticated when I tried; I just didn't try very often.

Or perhaps he was worried about the competition. Maybe he thought I would sweep her out of his clutches. Maybe she would fancy a bit of rough – well, not rough exactly, a bit of crumple.

I drained my Piña Colada and stepped out onto the beach. I'd acquired a baseball cap by this point – because the sun had already burned my scalp through my hair – so I pulled it down low for extra protection and dandered down the sand so that I could walk with my feet in the sea. The water was pleasantly cool. I would have gone deeper, but it appeared to be infested with sting-rays. People were standing looking at them as they glided past in less than a foot of water. Someone was saying, 'It's their breeding season. If you stand still they won't harm you.'

I wanted to add, 'But they might fuck you,' but decided against it. I had enough enemies in Ireland without creating new ones in a foreign country. People say Britain and America are one country divided by a common language. I have found in the past that they are one country divided by a fucking big ocean. People are the same everywhere. Annoying, generally, and intolerant of obnoxious behaviour. Girls are beautiful and men are stupid. Drink is plentiful and drugs are dangerous. I have a simple rule: if people laugh when I tell them my favourite joke, then there's hope for them; if they look perplexed or bored, then they can shove off.

My favourite joke is this.

In fact, it's not even a joke. I say: 'My wife's a redhead. No hair, just a red head.'

It just happens to be in America that a lot more people say, 'Your wife has a red head?' after I tell it; more people than in, for example, Kazakhstan.

So I kept clear of the sea, but I hummed the *Stingray* theme in case they were preparing to shoot out of the waves and attack me. It wasn't just the stingrays that kept me out of the deep; it was my inability to swim – and the sharks. I had no idea if this was an area where you'd find sharks, but it was sufficient for me to know that sharks eat people, sharks swim in the sea, and a little to my right was a big ocean full of sea. I walked on. I had heard that people could drown in three inches of water, so I was already living on the edge.

The closer I got to the Don CeSar, the more impressive it looked. I knew from our guidebook that it was a Mediterranean castle *sharply chiselled* against the blue Florida sky; it had Moorish bell-towers and imperial turrets. I knew that an Irishman called Thomas Rowe had built it in the late 1920s, and if he was anything like me he'd probably painted it bright pink to match his skin. He'd all but bankrupted himself to build it, but then saw it flourish through the Depression years – in fact it was used as a bolt-hole where F. Scott Fitzgerald could stash his wife while she dried out. Everyone who was anyone stayed at the Pink Palace – even Al Capone. It all lasted for about fourteen years – and then the war came along and it was acquired by the Government as a convalescent centre and then for thirty more years as a Veterans Administration headquarters, before falling into rack and ruin in the early 1970s. A local preservation group saved its sorry ass in 1973. Millions of dollars were spent on 277 rooms and 43 suites. Axminster carpets, Italian crystal and French candelabras helped restore it to its former glory. I knew more about the friggin' hotel than I knew about Davie. Why hadn't somebody given me a book on him? *The Rough Guide to Your Loony Friend.*

I checked my pockets for cash. With my bright red skin and my Dunnes T-shirt I looked like what I was, a refugee from a British package deal. I didn't look moneyed, so I would have to act it, and that would mean spreading some about. It was a longer walk than I had imagined, so that by the time I followed Davie's path up through the private sun-loungers with their nice soft cushions I was soaked in sweat and gasping for another drink. The secret of pretending to be a resident of a posh hotel is not to stand about in shock and awe, so I moved down the steps into the grounds proper, taking in the two large pools, the Jacuzzi, the stunning blondes, the uniformed bell-boys and the sunbeds with their little raised flags for ordering drinks without pausing to admire any of it; I shouted my drinks order at one end of the beach bar and they were practised enough at kow-towing to the rich and famous to know that I would expect it to be ready by the time I reached the other end. As they poured – and it was only a beer – they saw me pause to chat to one of my rich friends, whereas in fact I'd stopped to ask if I could borrow this stranger's cocktail menu. The woman was in her fifties; she had three chins, but luckily two of them were stitched up behind her ears. She eyed me up in case I was a gigolo, and then looked away because I obviously was not. She had an open tab at the bar, I could tell that from the print-out from her last round of drinks which was attached to her menu. I thanked her and went to collect my drink. I put it on the woman's tab, then sipped the cool Budweiser while I toured the grounds in search of Davie Kincaid.

He wasn't lounging by either of the pools or sitting in the

Jacuzzi. I followed several dizzying creatures in the vain hope that they might lead me to him, but instead they led me to their equally dizzying husbands. Tans. Muscle tone. Blue eyes. The women were Victoria's Secret models, the men were Marlboro men. I thought briefly about that old woman, way back in Groomsport, who'd lectured us on the nature of beauty and how it gravitated to big cities. Her field of reference had been too narrow; if she'd been there by the Don CeSar pool she would most certainly have argued that the most beautiful women in the British Isles were plain compared to those in America.

Having exhausted the outside, I ventured indoors. Marble floors and piped music. Dark wood and cocktail bars. There was a lounge with a piano-player. A seafood restaurant where you could pick out your own fish and murder it. There were ballrooms and a conference centre and elevators going to penthouses and grown men in toy uniforms licking the boots of women with hat boxes. There was an ice-cream parlour and a swimwear store where there wasn't a bikini under $200. It was the sort of shop Patricia would have drooled over, which is exactly why she wouldn't have been let in. But there was nothing to stop me taking her a present home. I made eye-contact with one of the assistants and she breezed across. She gave me that very sweet kind of American hard sell, harmless but grating, but I lapped it up. I charged a $275 bikini to the three-chinned woman's room. I was quite pleased with myself. Encouraged, I started trying on sunglasses. I was just checking how remarkably cool I looked in the store mirror when I felt a firm hand on my shoulder. I turned to find Davie glaring at me.

'What the fuck are you doing here?' he hissed.

The shop assistant looked up from behind her cash desk.

I angled the sunglasses at him. I smiled and said, 'I saw them first.'

The woman guessed we were messing and returned her attention to her copy of *Ocean Drive*.

But Davie wasn't messing. 'Listen to me. You get out of the hotel – you get out of it *now*.'

I snorted. 'Davie, will you quit—'

'*Now!* You don't know what you're getting yourself involved in.' He put his other hand on my other shoulder, turned me and pushed me out of the door.

'Have a nice day,' the shop assistant called after us, unaware that I was stealing her sunglasses.

I was in mid-wave back to her when Davie gave me another shove. He pointed down a dark corridor to my right. 'That's a staff exit. Go out that way and don't come back. Do you hear? *Don't come back*. I'll see you later.'

He pushed me for a third time, this time harder, propelling me several steps along the corridor. Then he quickly walked away in the opposite direction.

I watched him go for several moments. I scratched my head. Like I say, alcohol can really mess with your head. And so can sex. He *had* met a girl, and now he was petrified that I was going to steal her.

10

The further I walked along the beach, the more incensed I became. I mean, who did he think he was? We had come on holiday together, and apart from the first couple of days I'd barely seen him. He went out early in the morning and came back late at night, he said nothing about what he'd been up to apart from driving around. Meanwhile I'd nearly died from sunstroke. If it hadn't been for four large black ladies rubbing cream into my bits and pieces I probably would have. And did Davie care? No, he did not. He was out there romancing the stone. I tried to remember what he was like as a kid, whether he'd been as selfish and self-absorbed then; it didn't seem to me that he had been, but perhaps I'd forgotten, perhaps I was looking at our punk youth through rose-tinted plastic wraparound shades. Or maybe he had just changed – life does that to people. It doesn't do it to me because I've got Tupperware skin and marbles for brains, but Davie – he'd been in the police; who knew what he'd experienced?

I stopped opposite the Hotel del Mar, up to my ankles in the sea, one eye on the stingrays, the other on the beautiful ladies; the sun was burning down, the beachside cabanas were packed. I was thousands of miles from rainy Belfast, yet I was missing it. I was missing Patricia. We fought like CatDog, but I loved her more than all the tea in China. I shouldn't have come without her. At least she wouldn't have left me to my own devices for three days. Or not unless I'd done something extremely stupid.

I walked back up towards our room. On the way, I nodded at the guy in the beach hut and wondered when he was going to get around to offering me drugs. I was forty, but I had a mental age of twelve, his prime market. Maybe I should get a T-shirt with *Nirvana* on it or something – that might make me seem like one of the kids. But he just scowled across and I tramped on. Just say no, that's my motto, unless asked.

When I got to our room I phoned Trish. She had her head screwed on. She could give me good advice. I always listened to her.

She said, 'What?'

'As you know, I got sunburned and had to spend three days in bed.'

'What sort of a Clampett are you?'

'A red one. It wasn't my fault.'

'Well, whose fault was it?'

'It was the sun's fault. It's far too hot here for a pale-skinned Irishman.'

'Don't talk balls. And one of these days you're going to have to make your mind up whether you're Irish or British.'

'Yeah – me and about a million and a half others. I think the strict rule of thumb is I'm British unless I'm on a plane that's been hijacked, then I'm definitely Irish.'

Patricia shook her head. Obviously I couldn't see that she was shaking her head, but she's my wife, I know she shakes her head when I talk. She ignored my point and went straight for the kill: 'If he's met someone, you should be pleased. What did you expect him to do, hang around feeding you grapes? It's not his fault you're a complete eejit.'

'Well, I'm glad I called you for moral support.'

'Dan, if anyone needs moral support it's Davie. He was jilted at the altar, his heart's been broken, you should be out there cheering him on, not giving him a hard time.'

'But he sent me out of that hotel like I was . . . like I was a wee kid or something.' There was only static from the other end of the line. 'You can contradict that any time you like,' I said.

'Dan, give him a break. You know, you're a big boy, you're quite capable of looking after yourself.'

'Yes, I am. So I should just get in the car and drive off for a couple of days, give him a taste of his own medicine.'

'Don't do that, Dan. Please.'

'Why not?'

'Because you're always doing rash things you regret later.'

'That's not true.'

'Okay – so you don't always regret them. It's lucky you have me around to pick up the pieces.'

'Well, you're not here.'

'A – I wasn't invited. And B – there aren't any pieces to pick up. You spooked him by sneaking up on him. Leave him be – he'll come round in his own time.'

'So what am I supposed to do? Just get my thong on and hang out on the beach?'

'Dan, please don't mention yourself and a thong in the same sentence. I'll have nightmares.'

I sighed. I told her I loved her. She told me she loved me. I told her I loved her more. She told me I probably did. I hung up. I phoned back to prove I'd only been joking, but she'd put the answer-machine on. I left her a long message of love and devotion, although the recording cut out halfway through. I talked to the static anyway. It felt good to get it out.

Maybe she was right. Davie was just highly strung. I should give him space and time and support. I should get drunk. Everything would look better with a little alcohol. Or a lot. We had some bottles of Bud in the room fridge. There was a cool-bag I'd picked up at the airport. I would get some music and chill out by the pool; I could dip in and out of the water, and in and out of the sun; gradually my freckles would join up into a perfect tan. I would indeed become bronzed.

I had brought a Walkman, but my ears had thus far been too burned to listen to it, but now they were fine and ready to rock. And, like all Ulstermen on holiday, our unpacking had consisted of taking our bags and sticking them in a wardrobe, then rifling through them as need demanded. The Walkman and my collection of CDs were somewhere near the bottom of mine. Some people's musical taste can be described as catholic, but mine is whatever the opposite of that is. Protestant – or so narrow and lacking in imagination that you could call it Free Presbyterian. My choice starts in 1976 and ends somewhere around the early 1980s. Where that could mean Chicago and Cliff Richard in someone else's sad life, in mine it came down to Joe again. I would sit by the pool and listen to The Clash – *Combat Rock*, that would suit my mood just right.

Davie was as bad at unpacking as I was. His underpants and shirts were sticking out of his bag at mad angles; I had to shove at it to get at my own. There wasn't much room in the wardrobe, so I pulled his bag right out of the way. It was made of rather flimsy canvas material, so that when I dropped it and the edge of it landed on my bare foot I shouldn't have needed to shout, 'Aaaooow, *Jesus*' – but I did. He was carrying something hard and heavy, and I knew right away what it was. Cans of beer. It was just another extension of his selfishness. He was quite happily dipping into my supply in the fridge while keeping his own hidden away. Although not for long. I dipped into his bag to remove and consume the offending articles.

But it wasn't beer.

And before I'd unwrapped it from the towel I knew what it was and I just felt sick.

I laid the towel on the bed; then I went to the door and made sure it was locked. Then I unfolded the towel and looked down at the gun.

A *gun*.

Christ.

We were on a fly-drive vacation in sunny Florida, and Davie had a gun in his bag.

I sat down on the edge of the bed. I picked up the gun, then put it down. I wiped at it with the towel to remove any fingerprints. It wasn't a huge Clint Eastwood sort of a gun, but it was big enough to install air conditioning in your head. I've been around guns; I don't always know their makes, but I know what they can do. I picked it up again and checked to see if it was loaded. It wasn't. I breathed a sigh of relief. Maybe he'd just picked it up as a souvenir. Maybe it was a replica. What was he thinking of? How could he ever hope to get it back through airport security? And then I had another sick feeling and I went back to his bag and this time searched more carefully – and sure enough, hidden in a side zip compartment under his socks I found two boxes of ammunition.

I sat heavily down on the bed again.

My first instinct was to run out of the room and throw gun and bullets into the sea.

So was my second and third.

My fourth was: Pack up, get out – now.

My fifth said, There's bound to be a simple explanation.

Like –

Jesus, we were on a fly-drive holiday in Florida. What was he scared of, alligators?

I did what all grown men do in times of crisis. I phoned my wife, but the answer-machine was still on and I wasn't about to leave news about Davie's gun as a message. Mostly because she wouldn't believe me, she'd think I was just looking for sympathy. She'd lecture me about the boy who cried wolf and I'd say, 'But he got torn apart by wolves, don't you care?' and she'd say, 'Served him right.'

I looked down at the gun. I looked down at the ammo.

Davie had bought them after arriving in America: there was no way he could have smuggled them through security, either in Belfast or at Sanford. He'd gone out to a store somewhere in the vicinity of St Pete's Beach and bought a gun, just like that. You can do that in America. You can do it in parts of Belfast West as well, but that's another story.

And then I realised.

It was bloody obvious really.

Davie had just been jilted by his girl. He was an ex-cop, he'd been forced out for drink-driving. Ulster is littered with bitter ex-cops who've spent their best years protecting us from the bad guys, but who now can't get new jobs because of their former employment. Depression is rife – and so is suicide.

Christ, I'd come for a break, and now I was on suicide watch.

There wasn't a girl at all. He was just at the end of his tether, driving around aimlessly or drinking by himself in an upmarket hotel, thinking of all the things he could have had, the women he might have married, depressing himself even further.

I was really pissed off.

We hadn't been friends for the best part of twenty-five years – and now he had dragged me halfway across the world just so that I could be around to clean up the mess when he blew his stupid head off. It would put a real dampener on my holiday.

I opened one of the bottles of beer from the fridge. It was ice cold, just the way it should be, but somehow it didn't taste right. I was picturing Davie by himself in our hotel room drinking himself into a stupor then stumbling across to the bag – *Dead Man Staggering* – and pulling the gun out, loading it, putting it into his mouth, then pulling the trigger. Cue, brains on wall.

Poor Davie.

His mother at the funeral saying, 'But if you knew he had a gun, why didn't you do something about it?'

I drained the bottle. It still didn't taste right, but it wasn't for wasting. I got another and looked at the gun some more. What was I supposed to do? Confront him with it? Say, 'What the hell are you playing at?' Try to talk him out of it? But if he'd come this far to end it and gone to this much trouble, then he wasn't going to be dissuaded by me. Patricia says I couldn't argue my way out of a paper bag. What if I wrote him a letter? Pen mightier than the sword, and all that.

No.

Davie was never much of a reader. He'd scan the first couple of lines, then tear it up and tell me to mind my own business.

He wasn't down over Joe Strummer's death. He was down over his own.

Or what if he wasn't depressed at all? Maybe he had some

life-threatening illness. A huge tumour on the brain, or a wasting disease. Maybe he wanted to go out now while he still had possession of all his faculties.

Maybe, maybe, maybe, maybe. There were too many. Certainly more than four. Only one person could answer all of my questions.

Patricia couldn't, I couldn't, even the man I turned to in times of trouble, my old friend Mouse, couldn't. Only Davie.

I wrapped the gun back up in the towel and squeezed it into his bag. I replaced the ammunition in the zip compartment. Then I lifted it and my own bag, removed the Walkman, two sets of underpants and a spare T-shirt and set them on my bed. Then I re-zipped my own bag and carried it and Davie's out into the hall. I walked down the corridor then waited until the Cuban was busy on a call, sitting down low behind the high reception desk so that he couldn't see me. I slipped past him and out into the car park. Davie had taken the car, so that was out. I continued on out to the footpath and walked about two hundred yards down the street, then crossed the road to a branch of the International House of Pancakes. Behind the restaurant there was a half-full dumpster. I checked I wasn't being watched, then hauled both bags into it. I turned and hurried back to the hotel; I put my underpants and T-shirt away, then collected my cool-bag and Walkman from the room, after which I went and sat out by the pool.

Two hours later I was half-cut and the proud owner of about fifty thousand more freckles when Davie came hurrying up, all wide-eyed and breathless.

'Dan – Dan . . . have you moved our bags?'

'What?'

'Have you moved our bags?'

'What're you talking about? Sit down. Have a beer.'

'Dan! Our bags are gone!'

'Gone?'

'Gone!'

'Relax. The cleaners just probably moved them.'

'They haven't. They've gone. We've had burglars. We've been burgled. Our bags are gone.'

'Davie, for godsake, they can't just have—'

'Well, get up off your arse and come and look!' He spun on his heel. I took another drink of my beer, then got up and followed.

He was right. The bags were gone. I made a big show of searching the room. I cursed a lot. We marched down to see the Cuban together.

'We've been burgled!'

'Our bags have gone!'

'What sort of an establishment are you running!'

All the usual stuff. The Cuban followed us back to the room, as if a third pair of eyes would somehow reveal the missing bags. He tutted and cursed. He said, 'Are you sure they're not in your car?'

'Of course they're not! We've been robbed.'

'And what the hell are you going to do about it?' I said.

He looked down at the door lock for signs of a forced entry. He sighed. 'I'm going to have to call the police.'

'I should think so,' I said, but I was watching Davie for some kind of reaction – however he was nodding in support.

The Cuban shook his head. 'Between you and me, guys, this isn't the first time. We're gonna have to take a long hard look at our staff.'

'That's all very well, but what are we supposed to do?' Davie said. 'They've stolen our pants. Everything.'

'You just follow me, sir. I'll call the police then you'll

need to get a copy of their report, then you'll need to fax it to your insurance company. They'll handle it.'

'But what are you going to do *personally*?' Davie asked.

'On the pant front, and all the other stuff,' I added.

'Well, sir, like I say, you should be covered by insurance. You weren't keeping anything of value in the bags? We do post a warning telling you to use our safety-deposit boxes for valuables. We don't accept responsibility for valuables being stolen.'

It was debatable whether underpants qualified as valuable, but they were certainly important. That's why I'd stashed some. Cleanliness is next to Godliness, especially where there are girls involved. Davie would have to go commando until we got sorted out.

The Cuban huffed and puffed some more. After about an hour two police officers arrived and noted down the relevant details, but they weren't particularly interested. When they'd gone we walked to a beachwear store across the road and bought some emergency supplies of loud shirts and flip-flops. I said, 'So we've been burgled. Don't let it get you down.'

'Who's down?' Davie said. He managed a smile.

But he was down, further down than any man should be. I'd just saved his life, of that I was sure. Perhaps it would cause him to think again, to re-evaluate his decision. To take it as a sign from God that he wasn't meant to end it all. Perhaps it would merely cause him to hide the gun somewhere better next time. Because there probably would be a next time.

11

What Davie needed was a good man-to-man talk. But where was I going to find a man he could talk to? There was only me; empathy and sensitivity and understanding are not my strong points. Never have been.

Not unless there is drink involved.

Drunk I am a chameleon.

Some drunks get maudlin, but I generally take off like a rocket when I've had enough, so maybe getting us both drunk was the solution. Sober, men rarely talk about anything other than football and war. Women, on the other hand, dissect their sex lives at the drop of a hat. And often when there isn't even a hat to be found, when they're standing on an escalator with a complete stranger or ordering those difficult-to-find support stockings over the phone.

Davie had already booked us into the Holiday Inn restaurant. It was a circular effort at the top of one of the tallest hotels on the beach. There were stunning views out over the Gulf. They didn't blink twice when we strode in wearing our shorts and Hawaiian shirts and flip-flops, even though it was gone ten at night. The place wasn't busy, and the steaks were expensive, but what price can you put on a man's life, or indeed a good steak? We had a waiter as camp as a thousand Scouts but we didn't even take the piss, that's how serious we were. Davie sat with his chin in his hand. I ordered us two bottles of Bud each, together with a couple of chasers.

'You're feeling flush.'

'I thought we were splitting the bill?'

He managed a smile. 'Yeah, you wish. This is your treat.'

'And why would that be?'

'Because you scared the pants off me at the Don CeSar.'

'Haven't you got that arse-about-face? I was looking through the women's bikinis.'

He shrugged. The waiter brought our drinks. We lifted the chasers, clinked glasses and downed them.

'So,' I said, 'what the hell were you up to anyway?'

'I just . . . don't like being followed.'

I gave him my hurt look. It's not much different from my normal look, just hurter. 'I thought we were mates, Davie. I saw you go in, thought I'd join you for a pint. I didn't mean anything.'

He nodded slowly. 'I know. I'm just – you know, a bit paranoid. When you used to do what I used to do, you're always, like, watching your back.'

'I thought you'd met a girl.'

He shook his head. 'Yeah. I wish.'

'When you say "when you used to do what I used to do", do you mean when you were a cop? Are they all as jumpy as you?'

Davie glanced at the bar, then at a piano across to the left of it. Nobody was playing it. There was piped music. *Marguerita Time*. Later we would have to find the CD and smash it. But for now Davie leaned forward and said, 'No, Dan, all cops aren't like this. All cops didn't do what I did.'

'And what did you do?'

'Stuff.'

'Well, that's a big help.'

'I can't really talk about it. Besides, you're a journalist.'

'Davie, we're mates. Anything you say is off the record.'

'Yeah. Famous last words.'

We'd already ordered our steaks, but now the waiter arrived with two salads, which American restaurants have a disturbing habit of bringing automatically as a starter. Davie and I looked at each other. For godsake, didn't he know we were from Ulster? We picked at them, looking for the meat. After a few minutes of grazing I went out to the toilet and ordered us some more drinks on the way. When I came back, Davie had moved to a different table. Not that far away, but a different table all the same. He was busy crushing his salad so that it would look as if he'd eaten quite a lot of it.

I crossed to the new table and said, 'What's wrong?'

'Nothing. Apart from this shit.'

'Nothing's wrong?'

'No. Why, something wrong with you?'

'This table okay?'

He nodded. 'Sure. Okay for you?'

I nodded. Davie nodded, then said, 'It's good to have a chance to talk.'

'Yes, it is,' I said.

I wondered what was coming, whether he was going to spill his guts before I'd had the chance to enjoy my steak, or get really drunk. So he'd moved tables. He was entitled to be comfortable in his surroundings. The steaks were expensive enough. So I let it lie.

'I'm sorry if I've been a bit off,' he said awkwardly. 'I'll settle down.'

'You'd need to. It's a holiday, Davie, we should be having a ball.'

'I know. But . . .' He sighed. He looked up to the bar again, then back to me. 'Can I talk to you about something personal?'

Right. Here goes.

'Of course.'

'It's just, I've been a bit worried about you.'

'About *me*?'

'Yeah. It's best to be honest, isn't it? You know, are you okay?'

'Me? Am *I* okay?'

'Yeah. You've been a bit strange since we came away. You know, quiet. That first day out by the pool you were really reckless. I told you to put cream on but you just sat there getting drunk like you were determined to damage yourself. Like you wanted to feel the pain. And then all that time in the room by yourself. Drinking. And even when I'm lying there at night trying to sleep, you're flicking the TV channels until dawn; you've hardly slept. You know, I'm fucked up enough already without having to worry about you. That's why I've been going out by myself. That's why I've been driving around. I guessed you needed the space.'

'Me?'

'Dan, it's okay. We're mates. You can talk to me.'

I nodded. I said, 'I need a pee.'

I went to the toilet. I threw water on my face. My heart was beating hard and I'd that sick feeling in my stomach again. I wondered again what it was that Davie did in the police. Was it some kind of torture or interrogation he specialised in? Did he get hapless terrorists under the disco-lights at Castlereagh and grill them from dawn till dusk? Did he twist what they said? Did he get them to admit to things they couldn't possibly have done? What sort of game was he playing with me now? Me? *Me?* He was the one with the gun in his bag.

When I finally emerged from the bathroom Davie had moved to a different table again, this time on the other side of the bar. He was tucking into his steak. He looked up and saw me and waved me over. I crossed the floor somewhat hesitantly. What was he playing at? I took my seat. He didn't say anything. Mind games. He was trying to mess with my head. My steak was looking pretty good. I cut myself the first piece off it, but then I put my knife and fork down and said: 'Bit too breezy for you over there, was it?'

'What?'

'I said, bit too draughty over there? Too near the kitchens?'

'What are you talking about?'

'What do you think I'm talking about?'

'I've no idea. Eat up Dan, steak's great.'

'Is it now? That's nice. Should I start, or are you going to up sticks again?'

'What?'

'You know, should I tuck in or should I lift my plate and walk over to the other side? I see there's some tables over there we haven't tried yet.'

'Dan, what the fuck are you talking about?'

'I'm talking about you, you Clampett.'

'Dan, are you feeling okay? Look, I'm sorry, I didn't mean to upset you, bringing up all that stuff. I spoke to Trish about it and—'

'You spoke to Trish about what?'

'About what happened. About Little Stevie. Grief mani-fests itself in different—'

'Shut the fuck up, Davie.'

He put his knife and fork down. 'Dan . . .'

'Just shut the fuck up. It's got nothing to do with Little Stevie. That's low and mean. It's not me that's all fucked up. Now all I'm saying is, what is it with the tables? Why do you keep moving from one to another? What sort of fucking game are you playing? I don't mind talking to you, Davie. You can tell me anything you want – if you're happy or sad or you have problems or you're thinking of doing something really stupid, I'm your friend – but what is it with the fucking tables?'

'It's a revolving restaurant, Dan.'

'What?'

'It's a revolving restaurant. I haven't moved tables. The restaurant has just revolved.'

'Eh?'

'Look out the window, Dan. You see the way we can't see the Gulf any more, but we're looking out over St Pete's? That's because we've moved. They haven't moved the Gulf, they've moved the restaurant. It's revolving. Look at the floor, Dan. You see those tracks? That's where it moves – that's how the restaurant moves.'

I cleared my throat. 'You never told me it was a revolving restaurant.'

'I didn't think I needed to. Why else would I bring you to a fucking Holiday Inn to eat? And I thought you might have noticed the big sign, *The Holiday Inn Revolving Restaurant*. But no.'

'We're revolving. It doesn't feel like we're revolving.'

'No, Dan, it doesn't feel like we're revolving. Because we're not on a fucking spinning top. It's gradual. You'd hardly notice. Correction, you wouldn't notice at all.'

'Oh,' I said. Then added, 'Sorry. Now I'll eat my steak.'

That was about as personal as the conversation got. He

talked some more, but not about anything of consequence. It certainly wasn't the time to raise the subject of the gun or his suicide. I'd made a tube of myself over the revolving restaurant, but it was an easy mistake to make. I've been in revolving restaurants before, but it's usually a by-product of too much alcohol. So I concentrated on getting hammered and repairing fences. He didn't raise his distorted view of my personal problems again. We talked about Joe and girls and music and girls; he seemed to be in better form.

It was only a few hundred yards back to the hotel. When we entered reception the two cops from earlier were standing at the desk talking to the Cuban, who saw us first.

'Gentlemen!' he exclaimed as the cops turned towards us. 'Good news! Your bags have been found!'

Davie immediately clapped his hands together. 'Excellent!'

The larger of the two cops smiled and said: 'Chef at the IHOP found them in a dumpster out back. Had your ID tags still on board.'

The Cuban lifted them out from behind the desk. 'Look! Good as new!' They were stained and smelled of dumpster, but he wasn't far wide of the mark.

One of the cops said, 'Sir, if we could just take them to your room then you could check and see if anything's missing.'

I lifted my bag off the counter. Davie took his. He was going to have to be careful when he checked the bag. The cops followed us up to our room and I unlocked the door at the third attempt. We were still pretty drunk. They grinned at each other.

'Now if you could just check those bags for us.'

I lifted mine onto the bed, unzipped it and made a show of searching through it. Davie was more reckless. He unzipped his bag, then emptied the contents out on his bed. It only took me a moment to realise that the towel in which the gun had been wrapped was missing. If Davie noticed, there was no visible reaction. He merely nodded down at the array of clothes on the bed then turned and smiled at the police.

'Nope, it's all there,' he said.

'Excellent,' said the cop. 'Then if you don't mind, we won't bother with a report.'

'No problem,' said Davie. 'I used to be a cop back home. I know what it's like.'

The other cop, the smaller one with a thin moustache said, 'Oh yeah? And home is where – Ireland?'

'Belfast,' said Davie.

'Cool,' said the cop. 'Plenty of action there?'

'Too much,' said Davie.

The other cop said, 'And what about you, sir, you a cop as well?'

I shook my head. 'No, I don't think so.'

'Don't mind me asking, what are you?'

'Well, I started out in journalism and built up a bit of a reputation but I kept getting into trouble so I chucked it in and started writing biographies and stuff that doesn't sell so I'm thinking of going back to the journalism. At the moment I'm working on a website for the Northern Ireland Tourist Board called *Why Don't You Come Home for a Pint?*.'

They looked like they were about to arrest me for boring them to death. Instead they made hurried excuses and left. Davie shook his head at me, then started to put his clothes away in the cupboards. I stashed my bag back in the wardrobe.

'Well,' Davie said, 'that was a stroke of luck.'

'You can say that again. You sure there's nothing missing?'

'Nah, it's all there.'

'Brilliant,' I said.

I laid down on the bed. Davie had had a gun. Now it was gone. He didn't seem upset about it, but that was probably an act. What was he going to do next? Acquire another gun, or choose some different means of topping himself? I was going to have to watch him like a hawk. Starting tomorrow, of course – I was too drunk at the moment. Davie climbed into his bed. I thought about turning the TV on, but decided against it. Davie was right on one count, I hadn't been sleeping properly. I would try now. I closed my eyes. Sleep came surprisingly easily. But I should have known better. I had a long and involved nightmare about a heavily armed pancake chef.

12

As far as Davie was concerned I spent the next three days sunning myself by the pool. He made a show of joining me for the first hour or so, but as the sun climbed he made excuses about not being a sun baby and said he was going off for a dander or a drive. But where he walked, I followed. Previously I had not been making any effort to mask the fact that I was keeping an eye on him, but now I stalked him like a private eye. I didn't look a hell of a lot different, but I walked like a crab and kept to the shadows. When he drove, I also followed. I had my own wheels now, thanks to a deal with the Cuban. I'd asked him about renting a car, he'd asked about my licence, I asked about renting a motorbike and he said I could borrow his for a hundred bucks a day. It was daylight robbery, but he could tell I was in a bind. I also had to hire a helmet off him, which he eventually rooted out of a closet. It smelled like ducks had laid eggs in it. That cost me an extra ten a day, but I didn't quibble; you didn't need a helmet in America, but I did.

You can buy anything in America – motorbikes, helmets, people. As before, Davie trudged along the sand to the Don CeSar and then disappeared inside. I followed at a discreet distance with a straw hat pulled down low over my eyes, then hired a sunbed on the beach in front of the hotel. I asked the boy in charge if he could recommend someone who could tail a person round the hotel. He looked a bit shocked, but I reassured him that the man in question wasn't a guest and so I wouldn't be intruding on anyone's privacy but the unwelcome intruder I was after. He said he'd see what he could do; it was a hotel which prided itself on service, and although I wasn't strictly speaking a guest, I was a paying customer.

I had no alternative but to hire someone. It was a big hotel, but not so big that you could follow someone into a corridor or into an elevator without being spotted. A bus boy with a tray was the perfect cover, and that's pretty much what Mikey was. He was nineteen, on a summer break from college, and eager to please. He thought I was some sort of private eye, and I didn't correct him. I gave him a perfect description of Davie and set him loose with an advance of twenty dollars and the promise of lavish financial rewards. Then I put up the flag on the back of my sun-lounger and ordered a drink. Getting a tan, enjoying a drink but still managing to track a head the ball with suicidal thoughts. It was a tough life, but somebody had to do it.

Mikey was as good as gold, not that he could expect to see any. He watched Davie as he sat in the piano bar on the ground floor. He fetched him water as he sat in the seafood restaurant and ate lunch. He didn't get in the same elevator as him, but watched what floor he went to, then followed up, tray of drinks in hand like he was doing room service. He followed him to the seventh floor, where Davie walked from one end to the other without knocking on any of the doors. Then he went out onto the fire escape, which was really a set of partially enclosed steps leading down one of the pink towers that made the Don CeSar look like a castle. Davie pushed the door open at the bottom and emerged behind the pool, then waited for the door to close and tried to open it again from the outside, but couldn't. It locked automatically. A couple of minutes later Mikey pushed through the fire-escape doors and spotted Davie at the pool bar having a beer.

He reported all this, then looked at me like a dog expecting a treat. If he'd had a tail he would have been wagging it. I took out twenty dollars and paid him a second instalment, then gave him an extra ten for a tip. That was fifty dollars for about an hour's work; maybe the high rollers tipped like that all the time, but more than a few days of it would bankrupt me. We both turned away as Davie came down the sloping path to the beach, and then cut through the sun-loungers a dozen yards away from me and began to walk back towards the Hotel del Mar.

I told Mikey he'd done a good job and did he ever think of becoming a private eye? I shook his hand warmly, then followed Davie. I stayed pretty close behind; he was walking with his head down, lost in thought, not taking in the sights at all. I held back as he approached the Del Mar; he made a quick circuit of the pool to see where I was, then headed for our room. When he came back out again I was standing at the beach bar ordering a drink.

He came up, smiling. 'All right? I was looking for you.'

'Just catching a few rays, checking out the talent. I'm starting to get into this holiday. Do you want a drink?'

He thought for a minute, then nodded.

'So,' I said while we waited, 'what'll we do this afternoon?'

Davie shrugged. 'I was thinking of going for a drive.'

'Do you want me to come?'

'Nah, you relax, mate. I'm just gonna drive about a bit.'

I nodded. 'Whatever you want, your holiday too.'

We had the drink, then he went out driving. A minute later I pulled out of the Del Mar car park and took to the highway in pursuit. In my own head I was Steve McQueen in *The Great Escape*, even though I was probably more Donald Pleasance. But Davie wasn't driving a speed wagon, he was in a rust-bucket. If he went over forty, bits would fly off.

He seemed to know where he was going. He passed over the Corey Causeway then turned right on Central and within a few minutes we'd entered the outer environs of the city of St Petersburg. He didn't head for the harbour or the shops like a tourist would, but instead turned north into a low-rent retail strip. He pulled into a car park which mainly fronted a Publix grocery outlet but which also featured a Walgreens drugstore and a video shop. I cruised on by, then turned left at the next intersection which ran along the side of the video store. Davie stopped the car opposite a separate neon-lit entrance for shy customers wanting to peruse a basement selection of adult videos. I thought, Great, we're on the porn trail again, but as I circled back around and entered the car park I saw that Davie hadn't gotten out of the car, but instead two black guys had emerged from the video store and climbed into the back. Davie set off again. I followed the car for another couple of miles, then lost them at a set of traffic lights. I tried to jump the latter, but nearly got cleaved in two by a huge truck for my trouble.

Back at the hotel, I stashed the helmet behind the counter. I was annoyed with myself for losing him, and confused as to what he was up to. I collected a couple of Buds from the fridge and wandered out to the pool. Davie was standing at the beach bar, drinking a beer. There was no sign of the black guys.

He said, 'Dan, where you been?'

'Ah, just went and wandered round the shops.'

'What, you're that bored?'

I nodded. 'I was thinking, maybe we should hit the road again. We've kind of done St Pete's.'

'Sun, sand, what more could you want?'

'Seems a shame not to see more of the country.'

Davie looked thoughtful for a moment, then nodded. 'Yeah, maybe you're right. But I'm just starting to relax myself. Give it a couple more days, eh? Then we'll go on a trip.'

'Fair enough,' I said.

I ordered a beer. He was just buying time. My suspicions were confirmed when I went back to the room and checked his bag. Sure enough, as badly hidden as before, a gun. While out on one of his drives he'd made contact with a couple of shady characters who'd agreed to sell him another one. Once again I was on suicide watch.

Except, I was still intrigued by his visits to the Don CeSar. It was the only thing which didn't quite gel with my suicide theory. If he was so keen on doing himself in, then why did he keep going back there? Did he want to go out in a blaze of glory? What if he was thinking about going in there and shooting the rich and famous, then topping himself? He'd talked some nonsense on the plane over about bombs and how he could make them, but I hadn't taken him seriously. My original theory that there was a girl involved didn't play out either. Mikey saw no evidence of a girl the next morning, or the next, the third day of observing my friend. Each time Davie had a drink in the piano bar, ate in the seafood restaurant, and then took the elevator to the seventh floor, which he walked the full length of, then exited by the fire escape.

I said, 'And you're sure he didn't see you?'

Mikey looked pleased with himself. 'I sub-contracted. I got another guy to follow him.'

'You're one smart cookie,' I said.

He smiled bashfully.

'So what's so great about the seventh floor, Mikey?'

'That's where they have the suites. More expensive. Thousand bucks a night.'

I had a thought. Which is rare, and deserved to be framed. 'Can you find out who's staying there right now?'

'In all of them?' I nodded. Mikey thought for a moment, then shrugged. I gave him some more dollars. I was peeling them off while he watched eagerly. 'Stop me any time,' I said jovially, but he didn't. I called a halt. Much more and I'd have to eat at McDonald's. But he was pleased enough. 'That's great, Mr Petrocelli,' he said. 'You know, I'm kind of enjoying this.'

He was a good kid, eager to please, but with aspirations, which is an annoying combination, unless you want to become President.

'Well Mikey,' I said, 'I'm glad you are.' I started in on the small talk, figuring that if we became mates I wouldn't have to pay him so much. 'You have a girlfriend, Mikey?'

'I'm not gay.'

'I didn't ask if you were gay. You have a girlfriend?'

'Not at the moment.'

'Good-looking boy like you?' He was handsome, blond, muscled.

'Are you gay?' he asked. 'Because I'm not into all that shit.' I wasn't sure if he was being literal or metaphoric, or if he was capable of understanding either concept.

I shook my head. 'No, Mikey, I'm not gay. But if you get me that info about the suites, I'll shag your butt off.' He looked at me with blank-eyed confusion. I punched his shoulder and said, 'Relax, I'm only raking. Joking.'

He laughed hesitantly. 'I like *Monty Python*,' he said.

'That's good, Mikey, that's good. Now what about that list?'

'Coming right up.'

He bounded happily away. I was back on the beach, enjoying a cocktail and trying to work out what Davie was up to. Maybe the list would give me some answers. At the back of my head I was thinking, what if Davie's ex had held onto the honeymoon tickets, and come out by herself to recuperate from the break-up? Or what if she'd come out with another man? What if they had squirrelled themselves away on the seventh floor for a couple of weeks of exciting new-relationship sex and Davie had got wind of it? Out of a job, and now having his face rubbed in the sand by his ex, he'd concocted the whole story about being left with the honeymoon tickets in order to follow her out here. Now, overcome with jealousy, he was building himself up to not only shooting himself, but her as well, and maybe her lover too.

It was a plausible enough explanation, given the crazy world I often found myself living in, but where did I fit in? Why drag me across the ocean just to implicate me in the carnage?

I was coming up with a different theory every day, one to suit every move Davie made. They say history is bunk. You can bracket theory with that as well. It's like doing surgery based on a textbook: it means bugger all until you're out there putting it into practice. So far I'd had Davie secretly meeting up with a girl, planning to commit suicide, planning a massacre and now preparing to execute his ex. It couldn't go on. I needed answers.

By the time I finished my cocktail Mikey was back, clutching a piece of paper. I scanned the half-dozen names but none of them were familiar.

'Do you know any of these people?' I asked.

Mikey shook his head, but then pointed to the third name down the list.

'But this guy, he's from Ireland. He has the same accent as you. Sort of whiney.'

I let that one pass, and took a look at the name. Robert Quinn. Never heard of him.

'I've only been here a few weeks this summer – but he's been here the whole time. Tell you the truth, Mr Petrocelli, most of the people who stay here aren't really high rollers at all – they splash out on honeymoons or special anniversaries, bring their wives down here, give them a few days of luxury, then relocate to somewhere cheaper along the strip. If you really have money you don't come here. You go to the Caribbean or Hawaii.'

'So this guy Quinn being here . . . ?'

'Three weeks, in a suite by himself? More money than sense, Mr Petrocelli.'

It didn't matter to me how people spent their money, but it seemed like quite a coincidence that someone from a goldfish bowl of a country like Northern Ireland should be staying on the very floor that an ex-cop like Davie Kincaid was patrolling on a daily basis.

'Where's Davie now?' I asked.

'He's sitting at the pool bar.'

'And this Robert Quinn?'

'He's in the pool.'

'You think he's watching this guy?'

Mikey shrugged. 'He's facing away from the pool. But he could be watching him in the bar mirror. Kind of less obvious, I suppose.'

I was feeling a buzz in my stomach, an odd mixture of excitement and terror. Davie was watching someone from back home. It seemed suddenly perfectly clear that he hadn't stumbled upon him, he had deliberately sought him out. That was why he'd been so keen to stick to the itinerary, that was why he'd spent so much time out of my company, and clearly that was why he'd gone to the trouble of getting a gun, and then replacing it after it had been stolen. He was planning something, something terrible. I had to talk to him. I had checked his travelling bag that morning and the gun was still there – so he wasn't going to do it right away. But it was only a five-minute stroll back down the beach if he wanted to collect it. It was time to get up off my lardy arse and do something positive, get him away from the bar and talk some sense into him before he did something really stupid.

I was just in the act of standing up when Mikey hissed, 'Here he comes.'

I pulled my hat down sharpish and turned away. Scuffed feet in the sand. I thought he was talking about Davie, but as I chanced a glance after him the figure that passed by barely fifteen feet away was both smaller and rounder than my friend. I could only see him from the back at first. He was well tanned, short, slightly overweight but wearing a swimming costume a couple of sizes too small for him which made him appear fatter than he was. He was looking for a sunbed to lie on, but it was the hottest part of the day and they were all booked up. He started giving off stick to one of the beach boys; Mikey was right – his voice was Northern Irish, whiney and familiar. But it was only when he turned to point to where he wanted a sunbed put, right now, that I finally saw his face.

And immediately the power went from my legs.

I sat back down heavily on my bed. Whatever colour I'd managed to attain drained away into the sand.

'Mr Petrocelli, are you okay?' Mikey asked.

But I couldn't answer him. I reached for my drink, but my hand was shaking so much it slipped from my grasp.

I knew him.

Not only did I know him, I hated him with every cell in my body.

He wasn't Robert Quinn.

He was Michael O'Ryan.

The Colonel.

The man who had murdered my son.

13

I never saw the body of my son. Couldn't face it. In the long cold nights since, I've often debated whether I made the right choice; whether to see his cold dead face in actuality, or imagine it a million different frozen ways for all eternity. I think maybe I got it wrong.

He was not my son by blood, but my son by love. It did not matter that his cells were not mine, but that they were Patricia's, the love of my life. He was my boy from day one and I doted on him. I thought that whatever mess I got into he would always be fine, because Patricia had her head screwed on as tightly as mine was loose.

And then one day in a Dublin hotel a terrorist, a gangster, a hood of the highest or lowest order had laid out Polaroids showing my wife and son being held hostage. If they were to survive I would have to murder a film star who was making a biopic about him: he had picked upon me, my wife and my son, for no other reason than I had temporary access to that star. I was writing his biography. So I killed him. Or thought I did. The news that he was dead was communicated to Michael O'Ryan, by now sitting in a police cell, and he finally revealed the location of the bunker where my wife and son were being held. But it was too late. My wife survived. My son died. They buried him in a little white coffin and they sent The Colonel away to prison for life.

Now he was sunning himself on a beach in Florida and I felt as if the heart had been ripped from my body all over again.

My instinct was to attack, attack, attack. To pound his head with sticks and stones. But instead I staggered away, back up into the grounds of the hotel.

Davie was sitting at the beach bar. He was no longer watching the pool in the mirror, but had turned in his seat to keep an eye on the sloping path down to the sunbeds on the beach. The moment he saw me, a look of surprise and then anger crossed his face, just as it had before, when he'd caught me perusing swimming costumes in the hotel shop. But this time the anger was matched and bettered by my own.

Davie started to come off his seat, but I was upon him.

I headbutted him hard, once, across the bridge of his nose.

He reeled away.

I reeled away.

I'd never headbutted anyone in my life. In fact, I hadn't headbutted him at all. I'd nosebutted him, and it felt like I'd broken it. His and mine. The barman was standing with his mouth hanging open while Davie and I bled on the ground.

Davie was saying, 'Ah, oh, Jesus, ah Jesus.'

I said, 'Christ, fuck, ah . . .'

Mikey had followed me up. He lifted some napkins off the bar and held them out to me. The barman was in the act of calling for security, but Mikey assured him everything was okay.

Davie glared at me.

I glared at him. 'You bastard,' I said.

'Dan, I—'

'You fuckin' fucker.'

'Dan—'

'You fuckin' *fuckin'* fucked-up fucker.'

Mikey took hold of my arm and said, 'Not here, Mr Petrocelli.'

Davie looked from Mikey to me and said, 'He's right, Dan. Come on. Come on inside. I can explain everything.'

'You'll never explain this in a million years, you fuckin' headcase.' I stormed off into the hotel.

Behind me I heard Davie say: 'And who the hell are you?'

'I'm Mikey.'

'Well bugger off.'

I didn't look back, but Mikey must have buggered off because when Davie finally caught up with me inside there was no sign of him.

His nose had stopped bleeding, mine hadn't. He came up and said, 'Do you want me to pinch it?'

'I want you to *fuck off.*'

'Dan – please. Let me explain.'

'Yeah. Right.' I continued on past the piano bar and into the lobby.

As we approached the front doors the concierge appeared to recognise Davie. 'Sir, would you like your car brought round?'

'And you can fuck off as well,' I snapped.

Davie dropped back a pace and slipped the concierge a twenty. 'He's upset,' he said.

'I'm not upset!' I yelled back. 'I'm fucking livid!'

I was on the hill which led down to the main hotel strip. Davie hurried up behind me. 'Dan . . . Dan . . . wait.'

I didn't. I ploughed on down the hill, then turned left.

Our hotel was half a mile away along the hot asphalt. There were a million questions that Davie would have to answer, but there and then I couldn't speak to him. I walked on. Davie dropped back. *'Dan!'*

And then he stopped walking. He turned back towards the Don CeSar.

Three hours later, with the beach cabanas stacked away, and dozens of people sitting on the sand to watch the sun set, Davie arrived back. I was sitting at a table beside the pool. I had brought half a dozen Buds from the fridge, but I'd only had three. I felt sick to my stomach. I had gone to the room and taken Davie's gun out of his bag. I had thought long and hard about marching back up the beach to shoot The Colonel. I thought about what Patricia would say. 'That would just make you as bad as him, Dan.' To which the appropriate response could only be: 'So what? He killed our son.'

Eye for an eye, tooth for a tooth.

Davie approached my table and cautiously pulled back a chair. 'Anyone sitting here?' he asked.

I just looked at him.

'Dan, I—'

'Just tell me what the fuck you're playing at, and what the fuck *he's* doing here.'

He unzipped the cool-bag and took out a beer. He opened it and drank and stared out towards the sea for a while. Then he looked back and said, 'Okay. Truth. But it's kind of complicated.'

'Not from where I'm sitting.'

'Dan . . .' He took another drink. Then a deep breath. 'Okay. The Colonel. Michael O'Ryan. The—'

'What the fuck is he doing here?' I demanded. 'He's supposed to be in prison, he's supposed to be banged up there for life

and now he's sitting out there like he owns the fucking place! What's going on! Why are we here? Why am *I* here? Why do you have a fucking gun, Davie?'

He started to smile, and then thought better of it. 'Let me explain.'

I sat back in my chair and sighed. 'Okay,' I said. 'Shoot,' and gave him a sarcastic look.

He glanced around to see how close the nearest tourist was. Satisfied that we wouldn't be overheard unless we started screaming at each other, he clasped his hands before him and leaned forward.

'Dan, they're *all* out, you know that. Every terrorist, every hood who ever shot someone just for the sake of it then called it a political assassination, everyone who ever slit someone's throat just because he was a Catholic, everyone who ever bombed an Army base, everyone—'

'I get the point, Davie. Except The Colonel got put away for killing my son. My toddler. There was nothing political about *that.*'

'Well, he would claim that there was – they always do. But that's not the point. The point is that The Colonel was doing the double for years: he was killing and shooting his way to the top, and all the time MI5 were paying him eighty grand a year to squeal on his colleagues. MI5 say he actually saved dozens of lives. He worked for them for twenty years, Dan, he had the codename Wheaten Loaf and he was the highest ranked mole in the whole Republican movement. They were scared to death of him; he moved between the various factions with impunity, he was the last person any-one would ever have thought of as a tout. But he was. MI5 told us to leave him alone, but we couldn't. We had him, we nailed him, we put him away – that's all we could do.'

'So why is the bastard putting on factor twenty up the beach?'

'Because it works both ways. Everything got peaceful but O'Ryan was rotting in solitary. He saw all the people he betrayed getting let out and he wanted out as well. So he threatened to spill the beans about collusion between the security forces and him, about the killings he says were officially sanctioned, about the people he killed to cover his tracks with the full agreement of MI5. That's a can of worms they don't want opened. So they got him out. They can do that. Far as I can tell, it came from the very highest level.'

'They just let him out?'

'No, of course not. Too many old enemies wanting to chop his head off. He was placed in a witness protection scheme.'

'In the fucking Don CeSar?'

'No. In Canada – Toronto.'

'So what's he doing down here?'

'Exactly.'

I lifted a fresh beer from the cooler. It showed how messed up things in Northern Ireland still were despite the supposed peace, that nothing Davie had told me surprised me. But we'd still hardly skimmed the surface of what this was all about.

'So what are you doing here, and why do you have a gun?'

'Dan . . .'

'You weren't turfed out of Special Branch at all, you didn't split up with your girlfriend. You're here to keep an eye on The Colonel. You're here on a special mission.'

'No. Yes . . . sort of.'

'Good, I'm glad we got that sorted out.'

'Dan, I *was* turfed out of Special Branch. And I didn't really mind. You know, it's not the RUC, it's the PSNI and

I didn't know who the hell I was working with any more. Do you know what I mean? The half of them used to be on the other side.'

I shrugged. I had thought I was one to forgive and forget, but then I'd seen Michael O'Ryan on the beach and all that was now out the window.

'Dan, I wasn't involved in it, but I knew all about what happened with you and Patricia and your boy, your Stevie. I was absolutely gutted for you. I was at the funeral, man – I've never seen two people more devastated. You don't recover from something like that.'

I hadn't seen him at the funeral, but then I hadn't seen much. 'I've done okay,' I said.

'No, Dan, you haven't. You're all over the place.'

'And how would you know?'

'Dan. I know. And Patricia told me.'

'Patricia?'

'That day you came home and she was crying her eyes out and you wondered what the hell was going on. We were talking about you. She's so strong, Dan, she loves you to bits, but you've driven her to the brink so many times that eventually she's going to break.'

'I can't believe I'm hearing this. I'm fine. *We're* fine. I've got a job.'

'It's not about a fucking job, Dan. It's about the pain you're in.'

'What are you now, a psychiatrist? Well, psychiatrist – heal thyself.'

It wasn't quite right, but he knew what I meant. Who the hell did he think he was, talking to me as if he knew *anything* about what was going on in my head. All I thought about was football, music and sex, although not necessarily in that order. Stevie was the past. I was past it. We were past it. We had moved on. We were happy.

'You're still not telling me anything, Davie. You're not telling me what any of this has to do with you.'

'Do you know how many close colleagues I've lost over the years?'

'No.'

'Nine.'

'I'm sorry. But what has that—'

'They're still out there, the fuckers that killed them. We know exactly who they are. Some of them got sent to prison and are now out. Some we could never touch. Some we pass in the street every day. Some are still doing it, some just shrug it off as something they did when they were kids. Half a dozen of them are politicians now. One of them sits on the fucking policing board, do you hear what I'm saying?'

'I hear what you're saying, Davie, I just don't know where it's going.'

'I'm saying I lost nine people I knew and I couldn't do anything about it. When you pass them in the street you can't just take out your gun and shoot them. At least, that's what I thought.'

He let that sit for a moment. His eyes flitted towards the sun which was now a huge orange ball just sinking into the sea.

'What do you mean, that's what you thought?'

'After I got out, some people I used to work with came to me. They were the same – they'd been phased out, they were too old, too reactionary, too set in their ways. They were sick, sick to the back teeth of seeing those guys out there walking about when our guys were pushing up daisies. So they decided to do something about it.' His eyes came back round onto me again and held steady. 'Do you know what I'm saying?'

'They started a letter-writing campaign.'

Davie smiled ruefully. 'No. They didn't.'

'They went after some of those guys.' Davie nodded. 'They killed them?'

'They *disappeared* them.'

'What's the difference?'

'No body, no evidence, no charges.'

'How many?'

'I don't know, Dan.'

'And you – you've been doing this as well?'

'No. God, no. That's not how it works. There's a . . . how can I put this? There's like a personal angle to all of them. They approach you and say, "Look, this guy's out there walking about, he did this to your best mate or your brother or your family – do you want to do something about it?" They let you take your revenge, Dan. They either set it up so that you can do it, or they do it on your behalf.'

'So they came to you.'

'They came to me because they found out that The Colonel was out.'

'But why you?'

'Because I was your biggest fan, Dan. I had all your columns from the paper stuck up in my locker. I used to say you were my best friend, I never said I hadn't seen you in years. It's . . . kind of childish, I guess. But I was proud of you, your stuff – funny, you know.'

'Davie, I wrote crap in the paper, but you were out there protecting us. I was proud of *you*.'

We nodded awkwardly for several moments. Davie took another drink, then said: 'They knew how much I was affected by Stevie's death. I didn't know him, but I knew you. I always thought those punk years were the best of my life.'

I nodded. They probably were. His and mine.

'So they came to you and said, "We know where this guy is – do you want to do something about it?" That's why you're out here. That's why you have the gun. You're going to kill him.'

Davie shook his head slowly. 'No, Dan. You don't understand. That's not why I'm here. That's not why I have a gun. That's why *you're* here. That's why we've set this all up, the boys, me – even Patricia: Dan, she knows about it. We're here because you have the chance to do what you've been dreaming about ever since it happened, since that fucker killed your son. The gun's for you, Dan. You're going to kill The Colonel.'

14

Davie looked at me and said, 'I think this calls for a good stiff drink.'

'It calls for a good stiff mallet, you bloody head the ball.'

But he wouldn't have it any other way. He went to the beach bar and ordered up Smirnoff vodka in big plastic cups with a Coke between us. He didn't even get Diet Coke, so I could tell he was serious. While he waited to be served I concentrated on stopping my head from rolling off my shoulders into the pool. What was he thinking of? More to the point, what was Patricia thinking of? Davie was within his rights to be as mad as a brush, but Patricia – she was my wife, and therefore had to be more responsible than any normal human being was expected to be. How could she even contemplate what Davie was proposing? How could she even consider dispatching me across the ocean to kill someone?

'I know what you're thinking,' Davie said as he brought the drinks back.

'Do you?' I snapped. 'I don't think so. I'll tell you what I'm thinking. I'm thinking about murder, and not The bloody Colonel. I'm thinking you. I'm thinking Trish. I was thinking about two weeks getting drunk in DisneyWorld, not blowing someone's head off.'

Davie nodded for several moments, then said quietly, 'He's not just someone.'

'I know who he is.'

'Then what's the problem?'

I slapped the table. 'Jesus, Davie, *what's the problem*? What's the fucking problem? What sort of a world do you live in where shooting someone while you're on holiday isn't a problem?'

'He isn't just someone,' Davie repeated. His voice was higher, he was starting to lose his temper. 'He killed your son. He's sitting out there on the beach. Would you just walk away? Would you just go home to Trish and say, "Guess who I saw on holiday"?'

I stared at the pool. 'This is crazy. This is fucked up.'

'This is real life, Dan. You only get one chance.'

'You obviously don't know me that well then. I get hundreds of chances. I have done many stupid things in my life, but murdering someone on holiday just because I have the opportunity is madness. It's wrong, Davie. And even if I thought it was right, I couldn't do it. I really couldn't.'

'You could, Dan. When you look him in the eye, when you see what a monster he is, you could do it.'

'You're wrong, Davie.'

'Then I'll do it.'

'No.'

'It won't be a problem.'

'I'm sure it won't, but *no*. No thank you.'

'You should take some time to think about it. I've just kind of sprung it on you.'

'Time to think about it? I'm not buying friggin' life cover, Davie.'

'Well, maybe you should, considering what we're about to do.'

'I'm not doing it!'

'Sleep on it, Dan.'

'Sleep? You think I'm going to be able to—'

'I mean just take some time, talk to Trish.'

'That's Patricia to you. You don't know her at all. You haven't earned the right to call her Trish.' I pushed my chair back and stood up.

'Where are you going?'

'None of your fucking business. You just wait here. And try not to assassinate anyone while I'm gone.'

Davie nodded glumly. I lifted my drink and hurried away. When I got to the room I phoned Trish. It rang for nearly three minutes before she picked up and mumbled a groggy, 'Hello?'

'Hi.'

There was a pause, and then: 'Have you any idea what time it is?' She yawned. 'It's three o'clock in the morning.'

'Not here it isn't.'

'Dan, I'm tired. Is something wrong?'

'Wrong? No. Nothing's wrong. I'm having a drink, I'm enjoying the views out over the Gulf, I'm looking at thirty years in the joint for shooting The Colonel.'

'Oh.'

'Oh. Is that it?'

'Well, what about, uh-oh.' She sighed. 'Dan, I'm sorry. I didn't know what else to do.'

'You didn't know what else to do? *You didn't know what else to do?* What about saying to me over the kitchen table that some mad bastard wanted me to murder someone? What about that for a start?'

'Because if I'd said that to you, you wouldn't have gone.'

'Too bloody right I wouldn't! Every time I turn my friggin' head Davie's buying another gun. Whatever made you think in a million years that I would even consider murdering someone?'

'He's not someone, he's—'

'I know who he is! I know he should be in prison! But I'm not Charles Bronson!'

'And I don't want you to be, Dan. I just want you to do whatever you have to do so that when you come home I'll be getting the real Dan Starkey back. Because he hasn't been around for a while.'

'What're you talking about?'

'The Dan I know is full of life and fun and jokes and stupidity and love. Not a shadow. Not a ghost.'

'I'm not a ghost.'

'Yes, you are, Dan.'

I sighed. 'What happened, happened. It's always going to be there, Trish. You can't just turn the clock back.'

'I don't want to turn it back, Dan. I just want it to work. I want to wind it up so that it tells the right time. I want the old you back.'

'Well, I'm sorry. I am what I am. We don't all cope with things as well as you.'

'Cope? You think I'm coping? Christ, Dan, open your eyes. It's not just you. That man has ruined our lives. He killed our boy. He's out there on holiday while our son is mouldering in the ground. This isn't about revenge, it's about justice.'

'Can you hear yourself? Can you bloody hear yourself? *This isn't about revenge, it's about justice.* I've stumbled into *Groundhog Death-Wish Day*! Christ, Patricia, have you and Davie been grazing at the same fucking psychotic drugs or something?'

'Dan, I'm only trying to—'

I hung up. We had been through hell together, but we'd never volunteered for it before.

I lay back on the bed and drank my vodka. My head was throbbing as I heard again Davie's words by the pool: 'It's not rocket science, Dan. I've done the legwork. We go up to the seventh floor, we knock on the door, he opens it, we push him inside, get him down, put a pillow over his face and you shoot him. Nice and quiet. We come out of the room, go down the fire escape and run on down the beach in the dark. We lay low in the hotel for a couple of days then we get out of here.'

'Great,' I'd said. 'Nothing can go wrong with that.'

He was right, in some small way, because I had imagined it. Killing The Colonel. At night. In bed. In the dark. And only about a hundred million times. But it was like fantasies of sex with girls you hardly know, thrilling but with the full knowledge that it's never going to happen; that if ever you were presented with the opportunity you would blush and enquire about the weather. Now Davie was by the pool, plotting murder. My wife was quite happily going along with it – not only going along, but positively endorsing it.

The world was mad.

Or was it only me? Was this what now passed for normality?

I opened my wallet and found Dr Raymond Boyle's card. There was an office number, but it was gone three at home so that wasn't much use. There was also a mobile, which was an invitation to disturb his sleep – otherwise, why print it?

It rang for about five minutes. Eventually a voice as groggy as Patricia's said, 'What is it?'

'Dr Boyle? It's Dan Starkey. I hope I'm not disturbing you.'

'What? Who? It's . . . three o'clock! Christ, man, of *course* you're disturbing me. Christ, it's three! What . . . ? This had better be . . . I mean, is someone dead or something?'

'Not yet,' I said.

'I . . . wait, just let me get . . . lamp . . . glasses . . . Sorry, dear – work . . .'

The line went dead and I thought maybe he'd hung up, but then he came back on and he sounded slightly more alert. 'Dan, what's the matter?'

'You said to phone any time, day or night.'

'Well, of course – but I wasn't being literal. Any time day or night, but preferably between the hours of nine and five. Now what is it that's so import—'

'Everything I say to you is off the record, right?'

'Well, yes. Up to a point.'

'What do you mean, up to a point? It either is or it isn't.'

'Well, Dan, I'm court appointed. So I have to report back to them. But I don't have to give them all the juicy details. Why, what's the problem?'

I took a deep breath. 'Well, I have this friend—'

'Stop right there.' He was definitely alert now. 'We know each other well enough for you not to have to give me all that bullshit about having a friend with a problem. Be straight with me.'

'No really, I have this friend—'

'Dan, please, we're grown—'

'WILL YOU JUST FUCKING LISTEN TO ME?'

'Okay, Dan. Settle down.'

'Right. Right. Sorry. I'm just upset.'

'That's okay. You're allowed to be upset. Now tell me all about your imaginary friend.'

I sighed. I should have hung up. I didn't need a psychiatrist, I needed *Dear Abby*. A problem-page solution to a problem-page problem, simple and to the point. Yes or no. Do it. Don't do it.

'You know I'm on holiday, that I came away for a break.'

'Yes I do, Dan.'

'I thought I was helping a mate over his splitting up with his girlfriend. But it turns out he has me here under false pretences.'

I let that sit in the air for a moment. So did Dr Boyle. Then he said, 'You know, Dan, an attraction between two men can be a wonderf—'

'He wants me to kill someone.'

'Oh.' There was a tick-tick-tick sound, like he was drumming a pencil on a table. 'Someone in particular?'

'You don't seem unduly shocked that this should be my predicament.'

'I've seen your CV, Dan. I'm frankly surprised that you waited this long to call.'

I cleared my throat. 'I know you're trying to humour me, Doctor, but I really don't need it right now. I need some advice.'

'I'm not going to advise you to murder someone, Dan.'

'Even if he's the man who killed my son, and he got let out of prison and he's lying on the beach here soaking up the rays while my boy is in the ground?'

'They let him out?'

'They let him out.'

'And he's sunbathing on the beach?'

'Well, not right now, but that's about the long and the short and the tall of it. My mate wants me to kill him, he has a gun. My wife wants me to kill him. She thinks it will sort out our lives.'

'And what do you want, Dan?'

'I want you to tell me what the right thing to do is.'

'I think you know already.'

'Well, how can I know it, yet he can't, and she can't?'

'Because half of the world needs lithium, Dan – they're all just undiagnosed. The other half phones me in the middle of the night with rhetorical questions.'

'Rhet . . . ?'

'You knew my response before you phoned.'

Yes, of course I had. 'And if it was your son?'

There was a pause then. The tapping sound started again. 'Is this off the record?' he asked. 'I mean, you're a journalist. A writer. You're not taping this, or intending to use it?'

'No, of course not. The relationship between a journalist and his contact is sacrosanct. Unless of course there's money involved. But you're the exception to the rule. You're my psychiatrist. I know what answer you have to give. But as a man, as a man who had lost a son in the most painful way possible, what would you do? If his killer was presented to you, in the flesh, and you could do it and get away with it, what would you do?'

Tick tick. Tap tap.

'And get away with it?'

'Yes.'

'And you're definitely not taping this? And I'm addressing this as a purely hypothetical situation, and nothing I say can be taken to condone or encourage an act of violence?'

'No. Yes. You know what I mean.'

'Well, in that case – yes, I'd go for it. I'd do it. I'd shoot him. With a huge amount of pleasure.'

'But what about the psychological damage you might do to yourself?'

'Oh, bugger that. Frankly, I'd be on a high for weeks. Hypothetically speaking.'

I was getting the impression that with very little further

persuasion he might jump on the plane to Florida in the morning to give us a hand.

I thanked him for his time, and he told me to be careful. He said there was theory, and then there was real life. The desire for revenge was understandable. That the problem with turning the other cheek was that invariably you got whacked there as well. As a psychiatrist he could understand my predicament but not possibly advise me to carry it out; as a man he was already applauding.

I put the phone down and returned to the vodka. I sat and thought for another twenty minutes, then went back outside to Davie. His drink was sitting untouched. There was a cool breeze now off the Gulf which made it really rather pleasant. The beach bar was beginning to close up. Nobody in Florida drinks after nine o'clock at night.

'Anyone sitting here?' I asked.

He didn't smile, but he blew air down his nose like he appreciated it. I pulled out a chair and sat down.

'I've talked to Trish. I've sat in there and thought about it.'

Davie nodded. 'Good. That's all I ask.'

'I've thought about doing it. I've dreamed about it, Davie. About stabbing him, cutting his head off, gutting him. It's what he deserves. But I can't do it, because it would make me as bad as him, and I'm not. It's as simple as that. You've gone to a lot of trouble setting this up, getting me here. But no. No thanks.'

'You want me to do it?'

'No, I don't. I want you to leave him alone.'

'You want to let him just walk out of there?'

'Yes, I do.'

'Because I had Mikey check the register . . .'

'You had *Mikey*?'

'Yeah, the gay waiter.'

'He's not gay.'

'Just because he doesn't fancy you, doesn't mean he's not gay. Anyway, he'll work for anyone. He checked the register and The Colonel's only there for two more nights. This is our only chance, Dan. He could disappear and you might never find him again. You might regret it for the rest of your life.'

I took a deep breath. 'I know that. I probably will. But I just can't do it. And if I can't, and I have more reason than anyone in the world, then you can't either. I don't want you killing him, Davie. I came here to have a holiday, and that's all I want to do.'

Davie gave me a long, hard look. Then gradually his features softened. He winked and raised his glass. I hesitated for a moment, then raised my own.

'Okay, mate,' he said. We clinked. 'I think you're making a big mistake, but it's your decision. So let's forget about that bastard and enjoy the rest of our holiday. All right?'

'All right.'

And that was it. All sorted out. Nothing more to worry about. Really.

15

Ah, relaxing on holiday, with nothing to worry about apart from the knot in your stomach and the pain in your head and the certain knowledge that although everything appeared to be back on an even keel, it most certainly was not. There was no evidence beyond the circumstantial, there was no proof beyond the absolute conviction that nobody could go from being a double-dealing son of a bitch to best mate laughing on the beach in the blink of an eye.

He did his best, Davie. He got the beers in the next morning. We charged into the sea and blatantly challenged the stingrays to war. They chickened out straight away. He borrowed a Frisbee and we chucked that up and down the beach for an hour. He ordered hot dogs and fries from the beach bar, he played with kids in the pool. We looked through a new set of leaflets for the theme parks. I still had one eye on the Spiderman at Universal; unfortunately the other eye was on Davie, wondering what he was up to. He was too good to be true. Nobody changes that quickly.

A voice in my head was going, Go on, give him the benefit of the doubt. He's strange and delusional and somehow tied into a gang of revengers who make old Death Wish Charlie look like a Boy Scout, but it doesn't mean he can't change. He respects you, Dan, he loves your work, he was only trying to help you and Patricia. It was a very talkative voice and it was really starting to annoy me.

Davie was looking at me. 'We're young, free and single, matey,' he said, 'with the exception of you. What say we go look at the babes on the beach.'

'We did that about twenty minutes ago.'

'So?'

We wandered up and down the beach looking at the girls. When we started out, Davie began to walk in the direction of the Don; I made sure to turn him around and walk the other way, which he accepted with a wry 'can't blame a boy for trying' smile. The beach was lovely, the sand was warm, the sea was cool, the girls were beautiful, apart from the huge ones and the ancient reptiles with leather skin. We had a debate about thongs and came to the conclusion that they were last year's thing. After half an hour of cruising, we flopped back down on the sand outside the Del Mar. Davie opened his cool-bag and got each of us a beer. We lay back on the sand and looked up at the sky. We watched the same thing: someone was up there, parasailing, a tiny blot against the big blue.

Davie jabbed a finger up towards him. 'There, that's what we should do.'

'Aye, that's right.'

'No. I'm serious. What's that, about a thousand feet up? Views'll be magnificent.'

'As Oscar Wilde said, you can stick your views up your hole.'

'Ah, come on, man. Where's your sense of adventure?'

'Tucked up in bed where it belongs, thank you.'

'Look at it. The peace. The quiet.'

'The danger. The death.'

'I'll go and check out the price.'

He was up and scampering away across the sand to the bleach-blond beach bum in the kiosk before I could say, 'Stop or I'll kill you.'

I stared up at the sky, and then down to the sea. It was a long way. One man with a parachute attached to a speedboat by a piece of string; outer space above him, water full of sharks, stingrays and little fishies below him. It wasn't peace and tranquillity, it was sheer bloody terror.

Davie came bounding back after five minutes. 'Struck a deal. Usually it's fifty bucks each, but they'll do the two of us for that. Business is slow.'

'That's because people keep dying.'

'Would you ever wise up? They haven't lost anyone this week yet.' He punched my arm. 'Come on, Dan!'

'I hate things like that. Dangerous.'

'It's not dangerous! Get a grip! Come on!' He lifted his cool-bag and started walking down to the sea. 'Come on!'

He had supported me and my decision, now I had to show some gumption and fall in with something he wanted to do which didn't involve murder. So, very much against my better judgment, I followed. When I was a thousand feet up and about to die I would scream, 'See, I told you it was dangerous!' which would look good on my gravestone, although of course there'd be no actual body beneath it, because the sharks would have eaten it. Or the little fishies.

We cooled our heels at the edge of the water for ten minutes until the speedboat came in. The bleach-blond beach bum stood with us, but didn't say much. He didn't try to sell us any drugs, which was a pity because it was one of the few times I'd ever needed them. He did smile at me once and say, 'You're as white as a ghost.'

'And that's with the tan,' Davie commented.

'Don't worry,' said the BBBB. 'We haven't lost anyone this week yet.'

I gave him my steely grin. I wondered how many times he'd said it in his short sandy life.

The speedboat came in within a few feet of the beach and dropped a short ladder, and the last poor sucker they'd sent into space climbed down.

'How was it?' Davie asked.

'Fantastic!'

He was a boy of about fourteen. He scurried off up the beach, yelling, 'Dad! I want to go again!'

I swallowed and waded out after Davie to the ladder. Eager hands pulled me up. There was a pilot, and someone to look after the harness, parachute and line. Davie had been offered the option of a photographer for an extra twenty bucks, but I finally put my foot down. I had this image of the bodies plunging out of the Twin Towers after it was struck – you wouldn't wish those photos on your worst enemies. Davie finally conceded a point, and we set off.

The sea was calm.

I wasn't.

The harness guy said, 'There's nothing to worry about.'

I nodded, and gagged.

Davie said, 'I'll go up first, all right, mate?'

I wasn't going to argue. I kept one eye on the rapidly disappearing beach. I wondered how long it would take me to swim back there, and then how long it would take me to learn to swim.

'Way-hey!' Davie shouted with glee as he lifted off the small platform at the front of the boat. 'Way-fucking-hey!' he yelled as he gradually began to rise, the parachute billowing out above him. His ascent seemed slow and contained, but within thirty seconds he was up there, right up there, a thousand feet above the ocean, closer to the moon than any man I'd ever had a pint with. His 'way-fucking-heys' faded into nothing, there was only the pulse of the speedboat, the flap of the waves and the beat of my heart, which was loudest of them all.

After five minutes the harness guy said, 'Okay, let's bring him in.'

'Is that it?' I said. It was the only good news I'd had this decade.

The harness guy smiled and nodded. The pilot shouted, 'Any longer and the lack of oxygen could kill you.'

He was bull-shitting. I knew that, even though he kept his face straight. Ridiculous. Everest was higher and they'd climbed that all right.

Davie landed perfectly, all beams and smiles. 'You'll love it! You'll love it!'

They removed his harness and strapped me into it. There was a little plastic seat to sit on, there was a life-jacket, there was a thick cable to keep me tethered to the speedboat. Nothing could possibly go wrong. Davie clapped me on the back and said, 'It's fantastic, you'll have a ball.'

They were just about to release the parachute behind me. I shouted at Davie: 'If anything happens, tell Patricia I love her.'

He came as close as he could and said: 'You'll be fine.'

'Can I have that in writing?'

He smiled at me for a moment, then abruptly it faded. He came close and suddenly hugged me. 'I love you, man,' he said.

My mouth dropped open slightly. 'Davie . . .'

'And sometimes a man's got to do what a man's got to do.'

'Toffo,' I said as a matter of reflex. It was an old TV ad featuring a cowboy about to . . . 'Davie?' I said.

But he turned and nodded to the harness guy. Then there was a sudden lurch, and before I could think about what Davie meant I was off the edge of the boat and rising. At least part of me was. My stomach was still back on the platform. I managed a very half-hearted, 'Way-heh,' just to show that I was a good sport.

I was rising, rising, rising, just like the bile in my throat. The speedboat was already Matchbox size. I was closing in on a thousand feet.

And then, suddenly, it was okay. It was fine. The bile sank, my spirits soared. I was flying. Floating. I was safe. It was truly breathtaking. Beautiful. Completely quiet. Surprisingly calm. Look at me, King of the World. I wanted to phone Trish and tell her how much I loved her and suggest that perhaps I should have a career change and volunteer for the Parachute Regiment. I could jump with my 'chute three or four times a week, when I wasn't busy shooting civilians.

There was another lurch, and I didn't even blink. A bit of turbulence. So what? I could deal with that. I was *Dan Dare*. They could tell I was doing well below, because they were cutting me a bit more slack, I was floating higher. Funny how you can meander through life without ever being aware that there are other things out there besides drink and arguments. But there I was, not only literally, but metaphorically, on a higher plane. I could see why people believed in God or Van. I could see where the hippies were coming from. Peace, man!

Davie, you were right, this is great!

I gave him a wave.

In fact, I would have given him a wave if he'd been down there. If the boat had been down there.

But he wasn't, and it wasn't.

It was racing back towards the beach.

The line was cut and I was floating helplessly in the sky.

In fact, not floating.

I was now drifting.

It was not a windy day, but I was still drifting further and further from the beach. No, not the beach – the *coast*. That's how far out I was. Next stop Hawaii. But no, I was descending as well. The boat was disappearing and I was slowly coming down towards the water.

I couldn't understand it.

Had there been an accident?

Were they rushing to get help?

No, of course not. If they needed help they would radio for it; they were all equipped up for that. The inescapable conclusion was that someone had deliberately cut the line. And that someone was Davie.

Sometimes a man's gotta do what a man's gotta do. I'd dismissed it as Davie taking the piss over my fears about going up, but now I knew different. I could see that the speedboat was now close to the beach and that a figure was wading ashore. It was Davie. I recognised the blue canvas cool-bag and realised as soon as he turned towards the Don CeSar why he'd kept it so close to him all morning; the gun was inside it.

But at that moment, I really didn't care.

The sea had looked calm and lovely and blue from way up there, but now I was coming down on it fast. I may have had on a life-jacket, but I couldn't swim. I was half a mile out to sea and the water was teeming with many interesting varieties of marine life intent on eating me.

I hit the water hard.

It seems stupid to say that, water being hard; it wasn't, of course, but it was cold and deep and as much a shock to the system as hitting a concrete wall. The parachute folded in around me and the water surged over it and began to suck it down, and even with the life-jacket I was dragged down with it. I plucked at the harness, trying to release the catches, but my fingers were shaking and at first I couldn't work them loose; my mouth and eyes were full of water. I was being buried at sea, I had an appointment in Davy Jones's Locker, a lunch date with Sponge Bob or Square Pants.

The catches came loose. The parachute wasn't sucking me down. It had settled on the surface of the water. It was now just a case of floating out from under it. I couldn't swim for toffee, but I could kick my legs. I wasn't drowning. I was panicking.

I emerged shaken, stirred, and got smacked in the face by a wave. I coughed and spluttered and then drank another one. They weren't particularly high, they were just constant. I bobbed as best as I could.

They wouldn't leave me like this.

They *couldn't* leave me like *this*.

My God, it would be dark in another six hours.

I hated the water. It was dark and scary.

A million possibilities raced through my head, nine hundred and ninety-nine thousand nine hundred and ninety nine to do with sharks, the other to do with the fact that Davie had paid them to fake an accident and was now hurrying along the beach to kill The Colonel. That he had felt the need to do it this way, when he could just have gotten me drunk and left me sleeping. He *was* barking.

And I was crying, because something touched my feet.

Something *nudged* me.

Something *big*.

I'd been in the water for less than ten minutes, but already the word was out.

It touched me again.

My legs flailed.

If I had any legs.

Perhaps it was just the nerve-endings reacting like they were still there, whereas some shark was already off, putting them in a bap for lunch.

There was no blood that I could see. Probably because a million little piranhas were greedily sucking it out of my stumps.

Nudge.

Fuck!

I had a glimpse of fin. Then another. Cutting through the waves close by. Christ. A herd. A school. A whole fucking pile of sharks coming to fight over me!

I screamed and screamed. I didn't want to die like this. I didn't want to die at all, but this was definitely my least favoured option.

I thought of Trish and never being able to hug her or bicker with her again. I thought of Little Stevie and his gurgles and his first words and the bill for the little white coffin I had repeatedly failed to pay.

I thought of Joe dying at fifty. I thought of great rock'n'roll and how it made you feel alive.

And that was where I wanted to be.

Alive.

I would not let them just fucking eat me! I would not go without a fight! I had some pride!

I started to thrash out all around me. I pummelled the water with my fists, I kicked with my feet or my nerve-endings. I screamed and screamed and screamed.

'Come and get me, you fuckers! I'm not scared of you! Come and get me! I see you! Come on!'

Nudge, nudge.

Please God, just make it quick.

And then suddenly there were hands on my shoulders, and I was being hoisted up into a boat – a different boat. A bleach-blond of a slightly different hue pulled me over the side and laid me down while I yelled, 'My legs, my legs!'

'You're okay, you're fine, settle down.'

'My legs . . . Oh thank God, thank Christ.' I counted them. I counted them again. I checked inside my shorts. Everything present and correct. I sat up, then threw my arms around the blond and said, 'Thank you so much, you saved my life!'

He said, 'No worries. The other boat called me in, said they'd had an accident with your chute.'

I sat up on the deck, breathing hard. I was drained and elated at the same time. I put my hand out to my saviour. 'Really. You're brilliant. I could have died.'

He kind of shrugged, then shook my hand.

'No problem,' he said. 'Though next time, try to avoid punching the dolphins. We depend on them for a living. They'll report you to their union.'

He winked, let go of my hand, then turned to steer the boat back towards land.

16

My rescuer was called Konrad and I promised him I would name my next child after him. This seemed to satisfy him. Plus the soggy fifty-dollar tip I fished out of my shorts. He brought the speedboat up close to shore and I jumped off. The other boat was floating empty on a short anchor just a few yards away, but as I waded ashore the pilot, the harness man and the bleach-blond beach bum came hurrying panic-stricken down the sand towards me.

'Are you okay? Are you all right?'

'He pulled a gun on us! He made us cut the line!'

'You're going to sue us, aren't you!'

'You signed a disclaimer, you can't touch us!'

'Word gets out, we're ruined!'

'We haven't phoned the cops!'

'We thought you'd like to negotiate!'

But I couldn't afford to get caught up with them now. I had to stop Davie. I pushed through them. I said, 'My lawyer will be in touch! My lawyer will be in touch!' and started to run down the sand towards the Don. I glanced back once and saw that the BBBB and his colleagues were now gathered around the wooden beach hut. They appeared to be arguing amongst themselves about their options. Call the cops, get rid of the drugs they were selling or buy me off. Possibly all three.

My T-shirt and shorts were soaked and stained with sand and salt, my sun cream had been washed off and my forehead was burning red again. I pounded along the beach with a stitch in my side and a lump in my throat and grit in my eyes in pursuit of Davie Kincaid, my friend, my revenger.

I bounded up through the sunbeds and the sloping path to the swimming pools. Nobody tried to stop me. Nobody cared. I cut between the pools then up the steps to the set of wide doors which formed the largest of the rear entries to the Don. I hurried down through the empty piano bar and across to the lifts. A few moments later I stepped out on the seventh floor.

Everything looked normal. The Don had wide corridors, the kind you just had to run down. There were large mirrors mounted on the walls at either end which gave me a distorted view of myself as I progressed. Or maybe that was the way I looked – elongated and slightly out of focus. It was certainly the way I felt. I was running to meet my fate, and my fate, in my own hands, was running towards me.

I hesitated. Things were happening too quickly. I had been snatched from the mouth of *Jaws* – well, *Flipper* – and then hit the shore running. I had not stopped to think this out. My only concern was to stop Davie from doing what he was going to do. He was an ex-cop with a gun and a not so hidden agenda. But The Colonel was a monster who surely would not be taken by surprise wherever in the world he was resting his reptilian soul.

I had had enough of death, of cold stinking murder. I wanted it over. I wanted home to Trish and eggs and bacon and eggs and fertilisation. I would be a new Dan, same as the old, *better* than the old. I had promised this before, but this time I meant it, now that I knew how she really felt. I had to accept that she knew more about me than I ever could. She had the keys to my head.

And I had the keys to hers.

She had admitted herself that she was messed up over Stevie, and it was to my eternal shame that I had failed to properly recognise it. Now I knew why she'd gone along with Davie's bizarre plot to exact revenge on Michael O'Ryan, The Colonel. Because she wasn't well – she wasn't the real Patricia. I loved her. She didn't plan murders. She just needed help. We needed to help each other. But not like this. Not like this.

There was sand on the richly patterned carpet. What had the leaflet said, English Axminster? It wasn't quite formed into footsteps, but I was able to follow it along the corridor and then left at the mirror and into a smaller corridor leading to the suites at the very front of the hotel.

The tracks led along it for just a few metres, and then stopped abruptly outside Room 707. The sand was Davie's and the room was The Colonel's. What if I banged on the door and Davie wasn't there at all and it was just The Colonel? What would I do, what would I say? Would he even remember me?

I knocked on the door. There was a pause, and then: 'Go away! I'm sleeping!'

The voice was rough and disturbed, and Davie's.

'Davie! Don't do this!'

'Fuck off, Dan!'

'Davie! I swear to God, I'll turn you in if you do this!'

'Get the fuck out of it, Dan!'

I banged on the door hard, and kept at it. 'Let me in! Let me in!' It was spoiled child as saviour. 'Davie, please! Please! Let me in!'

Then a bolt went back, and the door was opening, and there was a flush-faced Davie Kincaid, gun in one hand, trained somewhere beyond him, and beckoning me in with the other.

'Davie, please God you haven't—'

'Shut up.' He closed the door after me and locked it. I walked on into the suite, my body pulsing with dread. There was a short corridor which led into a lounge. Two men were on their knees with their hands folded behind their heads. One of them was Michael O'Ryan. If he recognised me, there was no indication. I walked up and kicked him hard in the stomach. He let out a groan and keeled over. The other guy was a lot younger, maybe in his late twenties, with prematurely receding hair and a thick black moustache. He looked scared to death.

'Who the hell's this?' I said.

'Assistant Manager.'

'Great,' I said.

'I haven't done anything,' the Assistant Manager said.

'Yeah, right,' said Davie, and gave him a kick as well. As the AM went down, The Colonel rolled back up like a Weeble, and he was just as attractive. He said, 'If you're going to fucking kill me, just do it.'

Davie snorted. I knelt down beside The Colonel and stared into his eyes. 'Do you know who I am?'

'The Angel of Death? The Toxic Avenger? Save the speeches, Redskin, and do your business.'

I stood. 'You don't then.'

The Colonel shrugged. 'You're just another boyo with a chip.'

'You killed my son. You put him in a bunker with my wife and you starved him to death.'

'Ah.' The Colonel nodded slowly.

'Is there anything you want to say to me?'

'What, like Last Will and Testament? I don't think so. He was a casualty of war. You don't apologise for war.'

Davie came up beside me. 'And you want to let him live?'

The Colonel's eyes had been cold and dark and resigned, but at Davie's words the merest spark of hope flitted across them, and then left, chasing his vicious response.

I didn't nod, but neither did I shake my head.

Davie was right. Now that I was face to face with him, my desire was to shoot him. No – to cause him the maximum amount of pain for a long, long time, and then shoot him.

But it was nothing more than an instinct, like hunting and procreating and supporting Liverpool. A man thing. Something you were born with but which you didn't necessarily have to follow.

There is instinct, and then there is right and wrong.

Davie was breathing in my ear. 'I got you here, old son. I knew I'd get you here.'

I nodded. It was obvious now. It was all part of his plan. He had lured me there in a ridiculously roundabout but nevertheless perfectly calculated way. 'Look at him,' he hissed. 'Look the fuck at him, Dan. Look what he did to you, look what he did to your son. This is your chance. Do it. Here, take the gun. Take the fucking gun.'

But instead I said, 'What about him? What's he got to do with it?'

'Nothing. Forget him.'

'I can't forget him, he's a witness, he's—'

'We have to kill him as well, Dan. You know that.'

Terror peeled down the AM's face like a botched wallpaper job. 'You don't need to kill me! You don't! Take it – just take it. I wish I'd never heard about it!'

I glanced at Davie. 'What's he talking about?'

'Nothing. If you don't do it, I will.' He raised his gun.

'No, please!' the AM shouted. 'Take the gold! I was just greedy – I didn't mean to harm anyone. I didn't know about a baby . . . I'm sorry – just take it.'

'Davie?'

Davie sighed. He had the gun trained on O'Ryan still, but he said, 'Go look in the other room,' and nodded his head back slightly.

I walked down a small corridor to another door and hesitantly pushed it open.

It was a bedroom, but if I'd been The Colonel I'd have complained to the management. There was a huge King-sized bed, but you could hardly see it for bricks, plaster and loose masonry. Behind and above the dust-covered mattress a large hole had been drilled into the wall. I could tell it had been drilled because there was a huge drill sitting to one side of the bed.

I shouted back into the lounge: 'What the fuck is going on?'

'There's a case on the floor,' Davie called back. 'Open it.'

There was a battered-looking old case sitting on its side on the ground on the other side of the bed. It wasn't exactly Louis Vuitton – more like the kind of string and cardboard effort my old dad would have stuffed his de-mob suit into and hidden away in a cupboard. I bent to lift it up onto the one clear spot in the bed; but I couldn't, mostly because it weighed a ton. And clinked.

I bent to it for a closer look. The flimsy locks had already been punched, so the lid just lifted up.

I blinked. I closed the lid. I opened it again. I closed it.

Gold bars.

Thirteen of them. I counted.

'Davie? What the fuck is this? Who robbed the bank?'

'Nobody did,' he called back. 'Well, at least not for seventy years.'

'What the hell are you talking about?' I walked back into the lounge.

Davie continued to stand over The Colonel. 'Ask him. He's the criminal mastermind.'

I looked at The Colonel. 'I don't want to ask him anything. I don't want to get into a conversation with him. I want you to tell me what's going on.'

'What's going on is that The Colonel here is just like us in one respect. He has his heroes. We had Joe, he had Al.'

I was confused. 'Jolson?'

'No, you Clampett, Al Capone.'

'The gangster?'

'No, the washing-machine repair man. Of course the fucking gangster!'

'I don't follow.'

'I studied Al Capone all my life,' said The Colonel.

'Shut the fuck up,' I said. 'Davie?'

'Let him speak, Dan. He's not going to talk me round. He's tatie bread.'

I stared down at The Colonel then gave the slightest nod. 'What's it all about, fuck face?'

He ignored the abuse. It wasn't big, and it wasn't clever, but it was right.

'I studied him all my life because he was the best. That's what I wanted to be. And I am.'

'You don't look so hot from here,' Davie snapped.

The Colonel ignored him. He wanted to talk. He wanted to impress us with how clever he was. He knew he was going to die, but he didn't want his story to die with him. 'You remember Geraldo Rivera?' He looked from me to Davie and back.

The AM was nodding. 'Trash TV,' he said.

161

'Twenty years ago Geraldo staged this live show on TV, supposed to be the opening of Al Capone's secret bank vault behind a wall in a Chicago hotel. Millions watched, but those were the only millions involved. Nothing in there but dust and rat shit, but it got me thinking about what he'd done with his money. It had to be somewhere. He travelled a lot, he was a superstar, he had the best of everything, stayed in the best hotels, *lived* in the best hotels.' He was talking quickly, sweating freely. 'So when I was left stuck in prison last year when every other son of a bitch was being let out, I had to do something with my time. So I started tracking him down.' He was smiling now, full of his own cleverness. 'How, you ask?'

'Get fucking on with it, Agatha,' Davie snapped.

'The Internet. Prison provides it free of charge. There's so much info out there, so many newspaper reports, I could practically trace Capone from day to day over the last couple of years before he got put away. The net was closing in, he had to stash it all somewhere.'

'If I wanted to listen to *Jackanory*,' I said, 'I'd have stayed at home.'

This annoyed him. I detected a redness through his tan. 'I swear to God, I worked it all out from my cell. Where the money came from, why he wouldn't keep it in notes, why he suddenly took off for here but didn't take any of his women with him. I checked the local papers, knew for sure when I found out the Assistant Manager here turned up shot dead a couple of days after Capone left town. Don't you see? He was in on the secret, helped him to hollow out the wall in there, then Capone offed him to make sure he didn't help himself to the gold.'

'Assistant Managers,' the AM said, 'we're always getting shit upon.'

'You shut your mouth,' Davie said.

The AM sighed, but he wasn't to be stopped. The adrenalin was running. 'And we get no pay to speak of. I was weak! Mr O'Ryan bribed me. I'm not proud, but he bribed me to let him stay in here, to keep the cleaners out, to enter it on the computer that we were having repairs done so he could rip out the wall without anyone complaining. It was stupid. I shouldn't have done it. I'm sorry. Please don't kill me. I swear to God I'll never tell another living soul.'

'No,' Davie said, 'you probably won't.' He raised his gun.

'Davie?' I said.

'It has to be done.'

'Both of them?'

'Both of them.'

'But why?'

'You know why.'

'I can't be a part of this.'

'Then go.'

I cleared my throat. 'What about the gold?'

'We take the gold.' He smiled down at The Colonel. 'If it was a war crime, you warped fucking bastard, then consider your death and that gold as reparations. Except it's not one tenth enough.'

'Please don't kill me,' the AM whispered.

'Davie . . .'

'It has to be, Dan.'

'One is revenge, two is murder.'

'Just go and get the gold. I'll handle this.'

'Davie?'

'*What?*'

'I probably should have mentioned this earlier. I kind of forgot.'

'Dan – will you let me do this?'

'Yes. Of course. I'm sorry.' But I stood my ground.

'*What?*'

I moved closer. I whispered to him, 'Thing is, when you were in the shower this morning I was looking for your gun. I didn't want you to do anything silly. So I found it and, like, you know, took the bullets out. Just in case there were any accidents. I presume you checked? I presume you replaced them?'

The colour drained from his cheeks. And then he made the fatal error of letting his eyes fall to the gun.

It was the merest of looks, the slightest of glances. But it was enough for The Colonel. He dived suddenly to one side. Davie pumped the trigger twice in the vain hope that I was bull-shitting him, but I wasn't. The Colonel rolled and either from within his shirt or from beneath the sofa he retrieved his own weapon. He was up onto his knees in an instant. He fired once and Davie let out a yelp as he flew backwards. The Colonel was just moving his gun across to me when the AM shoulder-charged him hard from the side and the gun flew from his hands.

I dived for it.

I picked it up and raised it, and as The Colonel launched himself towards me I shot him once through the eye and he fell dead at my feet.

It was a good shot for an amateur, but a perfect one for a father.

17

Davie was lying flat on his back, The Colonel was dead on the ground, the AM had taken off like a jet, the smoke alarm had been activated by the shooting and there was several million dollars' worth of gold bars sitting in the next room. I had been in better situations. Also, I had been in worse.

'Will you stop day dreaming about the fucking state of the planet and help me?'

I turned to find Davie struggling up into a sitting position. Blood was flowing freely from his arm, which he was holding tight against his chest. I hurried across, took hold of his other arm and eased him to his feet.

I said, 'Are you all right?'

'Does it look like I'm fucking all right? Christ.'

It was a stupid question, but the kind we all ask. 'We need to wrap it in something. Let me tear a sheet or—'

'Leave it! Just get the gold.'

'What?'

'Dan, for crying out loud, *get the gold*. This place is going to be swarming in a minute.'

I hurried into the other room. I tried to lift the old suitcase, and where I hadn't quite managed it before, this latest rush of adrenalin added something to my strength and I was able to raise it almost to waist-level before the bottom of it gave way and the gold bars tumbled out; if I hadn't been feather-footed they would have broken my feet. I dropped the bag with a curse and ran to the wardrobe. I found The Colonel's case and heaved it out. It was good and sturdy. He too unpacked like an Ulsterman. I emptied out his clothes and then fitted the gold back inside the empty case. The good thing was, it was on wheels. If we walked out of the hotel with it we would just look like a couple of tourists, although one of us might be bleeding to death.

Davie wrapped a small towel tightly around his arm, then took a larger bath towel and threw it over his shoulder as if he was heading for the beach. It covered the smaller towel, which was already soaked in blood.

Davie nodded down at The Colonel. 'Good shot,' he said.

I had killed him. It was the exact opposite of my intentions at the start of the morning, but that is also the pattern of my life.

'Come on,' I said.

I wheeled the suitcase to the door then turned right to go down the corridor, but Davie hissed at me to go the other way, and he led me left towards the fire-escape door. He pushed through it with his good arm, then held it for me as I manoeuvred the case through. I looked at the flights of steps leading down from the mock bell-tower. The wheels were no good: if I had to bump the case down every step it was bound to split. We needed the elevator to get the gold down to ground level.

'Davie, we—'

'I can help.' He reached down with his good arm and lifted the front of the case; I took most of the weight at the back, and cautiously we began to descend. The smoke alarm was still sounding above us, and in the distance I could hear several sets of sirens – police, fire, ambulance, ice cream.

Sixth, fifth, fourth . . . We were drenched in sweat; at the third Davie set his end of the case down and staggered against the railings gasping for breath. It was just too bloody heavy. We turned suddenly as the fire-escape door behind us opened, but the half a dozen people who hurried out weren't interested in us, they were interested in saving their lives. The hotel was being evacuated. I looked at Davie and he nodded, and we wheeled the case back into the hall and then with the advantage of the wheels, raced along the corridor to the elevators.

There was a sign inside that said *Do Not Use in Case of Fire*. We ignored it. There was no fire. Just murder and mayhem.

We reached the lobby and were relieved to find it teeming with anxious guests. We passed through them unnoticed and were just approaching the front door – we agreed it was crazy to try dragging the suitcase along the sand, it would just sink – when a voice said: 'Excuse me, sir?'

We froze. We turned slowly.

It was Mikey.

'Can I be of any assistance?'

He glanced at Davie's arm. The blood was now seeping through to the bath towel. Davie quickly covered it up and said: 'We need a ride.'

'I'll bring your car right round for you, sir,' Mikey said.

He hurried away. Good old Mikey. He would liberate a vehicle from one of the valet-parking guys, and worry about the bloodstains later.

More and more guests were starting to arrive in the lobby. The concierge was flapping around and shouting over the high-pitched wailing of the alarm, 'If you could all just move out of the building, ladies and gentlemen, and let the firemen through,' but he was largely being ignored. There was no smoke, no obvious fire, and these people hadn't paid over the odds to waste their time standing out on the sidewalk.

Davie was pale, and now that we'd stopped moving he was again having trouble staying upright. He leaned against the case. I asked my stupid question again. 'Are you okay?'

But this time he was too past it to do anything other than nod. I looked to the doors for Mikey. Nothing. My attention was drawn to a retching sound, and through the crowd I saw the balding head of the Assistant Manager behind the front desk. He was sitting on a stool, being comforted by someone while he threw up into an empty flower pot.

Heavily equipped firemen hurried through the front doors, shouting instructions for everyone to vacate the premises; a moment later police officers followed them into the building and made straight for the stairs. They knew where they were going, but not what they would find.

Then Mikey arrived back. 'This way, sir,' he said. Davie nodded appreciatively. 'Let me help you with that,' Mikey said, and reached down to give us a hand with the case.

'Leave it!' Davie snapped.

'We're all right,' I said.

Mikey just nodded, like he understood, and then held the door open for us. Davie visibly wavered again as we wheeled the case out, as if the sun had reached down out of the sky and slapped him. Again he steadied himself against the case.

'We have to get you to a hospital,' I whispered.

'No. Fucking. Way,' he said.

Mikey led us across to a Sedan and opened the back door.

Davie was reluctant to let go of the case. I said, 'It's okay, Davie, it's okay.'

He nodded and released his grip. When I touched the handle it was soaked in his sweat and blood. Mikey helped him into the back, then opened the boot. I tried to lift the case into it, but couldn't get it off the ground. Mikey was already in behind the wheel, but when he realised I hadn't moved he jumped out again and hurried back to see what the problem was.

'Story of my life,' I said. 'Packed far too much.'

He raised an eyebrow, and nonchalantly took hold of the case. He was a big guy, muscles on his muscles, but you have to be prepared to use them; when he yanked at the case and it hardly moved he let out a yelp like he'd sprung a leak in his sixpack. He rubbed at his stomach and said, 'What the hell you got in there?'

'Kitchen sink,' I said. 'Let's just get it in.'

He set his legs to a better position, then took hold of his end of the case. I lifted mine, and together we heaved it into the trunk.

The car sank about a foot as it hit the floor.

Davie said, 'Christ,' from the back seat.

I slammed the trunk and climbed into the passenger seat. Mikey got behind the wheel and said, 'Where to?'

'Hotel del Mar,' I said.

'You're sure?' He looked a little disappointed, like we should have said Cuba or Arkansas.

He started the engine and we moved down the hill just as an ambulance came racing up. Davie needed one, The Colonel didn't.

'Do you want to tell me what happened?' Mikey asked.

'Nothing,' I said.

'You met that guy, I know it. Someone said they heard shooting on the seventh floor. Is he in the valise?'

'You've been very good to us, Mikey,' I said, 'but now we need you to mind your own business. It's done, it's over, just get us to the hotel.'

He nodded. It was only about half a mile to the Del Mar so I wasn't quite sure why he was driving so slowly. Perhaps it was out of concern for Davie's comfort. Or because he wanted to chat to an old friend.

'They track this back to me, I'm in deep shit,' he said.

'I know. We appreciate it.'

'They track this back, I'll be fired. And maybe sued. I need this job. It's paying for college.'

'You'll be fine.'

'No, you don't understand. I really need it. It's the best paying job on the beach. I'll be fucked without it.'

I glanced back at Davie, but he had his eyes closed. I took out my wallet. I'd about three hundred dollars in cash. I offered him two.

'That won't buy me shit,' he said.

This was a definite shift in his attitude. The ready smile was gone. He was no longer the happy-go-lucky servant. He had the upper hand now, and he knew it.

'What're you saying, Mikey?'

'All I'm saying is, you know, help me out.'

He finally pulled into the car park at the Del Mar. He sat behind the wheel. He'd done his helping, he'd set out his case. I drummed my fingers on the dash for a moment. It came to me that I still had The Colonel's gun in the pocket of my shorts, and that I could just shoot Mikey, just off him the way I'd offed The Colonel. It was a scary feeling, how easy it would be, and I didn't like it. Even the thought of taking the gun out and threatening him with it, it was just too much. Instead I just said, 'Wait here a minute,' and jumped out of the car.

I opened the boot, unzipped The Colonel's case, made

sure there was nobody passing, then opened it up and removed one of the gold bars. I rezipped, closed the boot and slipped back into the car.

Mikey looked a bit jumpy, as if he'd suddenly had the same thought about a gun, that I might have been getting the murder weapon out of the trunk. But then he saw what I had in my hands. His eyes widened.

'Here,' I said. 'Buy the whole fucking college.'

There are sleepless nights, and then there are sleepless nights.

There are nights when you toss and turn a bit and wake up the next morning and tell your wife, 'Gee, I had an awful night.'

And then there are nights when your psychotic best friend is dying in the bed next to you and all you can think about is how you're going to get rid of his body and how you're going to avoid going to San Quentin and how you're going to smuggle Al Capone's gold back to Belfast.

Davie groaned through the night; he alternated between lucidity and mad-eyed shouting. I went across the road to the Eckerds and bought bandages and antiseptic cream and treated him as well as I could, but I had no idea what I was doing. I might have been making matters worse. I had never been a Scout and learned First Aid. I had been in the Boys' Brigade and merely learned how to kill people by boring them to death with scripture. But in the darkness I said a prayer for him and God responded pretty quickly by reaching down and knocking him into the kind of heavy sleep which is just a hair's-breadth short of a coma.

There wasn't anything more I could do. He had expressly forbidden me from calling a doctor or taking him to a hospital. He was in no position now to stop me from doing either, but I didn't. And it wasn't all out of respect for his wishes. It was out of fear for what would happen to me if I did.

I didn't want to be caught.

I didn't want to go to prison.

And it seemed that I was prepared to let Davie die if it meant staying free.

I set it up as a kind of moral conundrum in the darkness, as if it was one of those big life-defining decisions, but it wasn't really. I have mentioned instinct before: hunting, procreation and Liverpool. Add another to that list. Self-preservation. Like the boxing referees say, protect yourself at all times.

Besides, Davie couldn't die. He'd been shot in the arm. I'd seen that enough in movies to know that you didn't die from that. You got a bit of a fever and a friendly woman applied a cold poultice to your brow and in the morning you felt better, and she spoonfed you soup, and you fell in love. So I soaked a flannel in cold water and placed it on his brow and Davie came round enough to glare at me and spit, 'Would you *fuck off*,' at me.

I backed away. He fell back into his sleep and I switched on the TV and watched the news coverage. America is great for news. Dozens of channels saying exactly the same thing, that a wealthy Irish tourist had been shot dead in an apparent robbery at the famous Pink Palace, the Don CeSar on St Pete's Beach. Several of them made references to the fact that the hotel had once played host to Al Capone, which might have seemed fatuous and irrelevant if I hadn't had twelve of his gold bars stashed in the cupboard. They said police were following several lines of enquiry, but that nobody had yet been arrested.

Good. That was a relief.

In the morning Davie was awake before I was. He shook

me and I sat up real quick. He said, 'Relax. Just thought we'd better get moving.'

He had some colour back in his cheeks. 'How're you doing?' I asked.

He laughed, then showed me his arm. He had obviously been up to the bathroom and cleaned it. It was still raw, but it wasn't bleeding.

'I think the bullet might have gone straight through,' Davie said.

'You still need it seen to.'

'I know. But not here.'

I nodded. I went out to get coffee, though mostly it was just to see if the coast was clear. There didn't seem to be anything amiss. Tourists were out getting breakfast, the road was busy with people going to work or heading off to the theme parks. I bought the coffee and some doughnuts in the Publix across the road. When I got back, Davie had his bag out and packed.

'We should hit the road,' he said.

I nodded. 'Where to?'

'I don't know. Lose ourselves for a few days.'

'I want to go home.'

'I know. You did brilliantly yesterday.'

'I killed someone. I don't call that brilliant.'

'Dan, don't you feel like a huge weight has been lifted from your shoulders?'

'Just the opposite.'

Davie shook his head. 'Well, you will. I swear. Soon. You have done the right thing.'

'I did it by accident.'

'That doesn't matter. And you saved my life.'

'After you tried to end mine.'

He tutted. 'I didn't try to kill you, Dan. For godsake – we're mates. You were never in any danger.'

I glared at him. 'I still want to go home.'

'I know. But we can't fly back with the gold. I think it might exceed our baggage allowance.'

I laughed in spite of myself. 'That and about ten thousand laws.'

He nodded. I nodded.

'We'll sort it out,' he said.

'You'd better,' I added.

18

We had just crossed the Pinellas Bayway toll-bridge and were entering the outskirts of St Petersburg City when the car picked us up. I noticed because I was noticing everything – the love bugs copulating on our bonnet, the hum of lawnmowers, the sweet mix of cotton candy and exhaust fumes in the air, the glances of people waiting to cross roads, the perceived looks from drivers going in the opposite direction, the way the traffic-lights ran against us and the way cars seemed to conspire to hem us in. The devil was in the detail, and now the devil was on our tail. We weren't yet wanted men, but we felt like it, and the longer the car remained resolutely on our tail the more jumpy we grew.

We knew it was after us, but we kept denying it.

'It's just the traffic,' Davie said.

'They're just going the same way,' I said, and our eyes flitted nervously back to our mirrors.

It wasn't like you could miss it; it was a big black Land Cruiser, and it followed us with the callous indifference of a warhead.

I was wearing T-shirt and jeans and shades and a baseball

cap pulled down. Davie had squeezed his hurting arm into a long-sleeved shirt. Far as we were concerned, we looked like a couple of shit-kickers in a beat-up car. Nothing unusual about that.

I slowed when I could, I went faster when I could. I switched lanes at the merest hint of a break. We intended to hit the Sunshine Skyway again, cross Tampa Bay and head south on the 275. Davie reasoned that if by some miracle the cops did find out who we were, it wouldn't take them long to discover that we were due to fly home out of Sanford. It was the only airport in Florida with a direct flight to Belfast. So he suggested cutting across to Miami; there was a better chance of losing ourselves there and then working out how to get home. It would mean going east either along the Everglades Parkway, also known as Alligator Alley, or heading further south and accessing the smaller FL31, which would take us through Big Cypress National Preserve. We settled on the latter. No particular reason, except that I hated alligators even more than I hated sharks.

Not that it mattered whether we took the 31 or the Yellow Brick Road because the Land Cruiser was suddenly right up behind us.

'Who the fuck is it?' Davie hissed.

'I don't know! How the fuck should I know?'

'You did kill him, didn't you? He was dead? It wasn't just a flesh wound?'

'It went through his eye and out the back of his head, Davie. If it was you it might have missed your brain, but not him.'

Davie sighed and then winced. His arm was hurting and someone was following us. No – they weren't following, they were intimidating us. They were now so close that if I did anything beyond just brushing the brakes, they'd be right into the back of us.

'What do you think the chances are of outrunning them in this thing?' Davie asked.

'Zero,' I said, with absolute certainty. It might once have been a decent motor, but it now barely retained the engine capacity of a milkfloat. It was old and rusted and would fall apart if spoken to harshly.

'*Fuck*,' said Davie. 'You still have your gun?'

'It's packed in the boot,' I said.

'*Fuck*.'

'Do you think they'd give me time to get out and find it?' Davie didn't even shake his head. 'What about yours?'

He opened the glove compartment and showed me it. 'But the bullets are in my bag in the boot.'

'Well, that was fucking stupid.'

'Shut the fuck up – you're one to talk.'

I sighed. We weren't Butch and Sundance. We weren't even Thelma and Louise. We were a whisker away from Laurel and Hardy. Yet Davie had been a cop. He should have known better. Maybe he'd been thrown out for being a tube.

There was a sudden blast of sound from behind, and we both turned to see that a flashing police light had now been affixed to the top of the Land Cruiser.

'The cops,' Davie said needlessly.

'Is that better or worse?'

'I don't know. I don't fucking know.'

'Well, what do I do?' I hissed.

Davie thought for a moment, then shook his head and said, 'We pull over.'

'What if they *know*?'

'What if they don't, and it's just a dodgy brake-light? Bluff it, Dan, bluff it.'

I pulled into the side of the road and the Land Cruiser stopped close behind. I made to open the door and use my charm, but a megaphoned voice boomed, 'Please stay in your vehicle. An officer will approach you – please have your licence ready.'

Of course, we didn't *have* a licence, not even one to kill.

'Fuck,' Davie said.

'Fuck,' I said.

The police officer was coming up behind us now. He knocked on the window. I turned as nonchalantly towards him as I could and gave him an Ireland of the Welcomes smile.

'Well, hell,' he said. 'Look who it is.'

For a moment I didn't recognise him – he was out of uniform. It was one of the cops who'd returned our bags to us a couple of days before. He was wearing blue jeans and a tan jacket over a black T-shirt. Smart casual. Miami Nice.

'Hey,' I said, 'how're you doing?'

Davie looked across and waved.

The cop smiled, stepped back a bit and looked at our car. 'Noticed you were riding a bit low in the water there.'

I smiled. 'Yeah, I know. I think we bought half the trinkets in Florida. Kids can't get enough.'

He nodded, then glanced back at his own vehicle. The other cop was now climbing out. It was the same partner. He was in black jeans with a white shirt and there was a chain of white gold around his neck. He came up along Davie's side of the car.

'Hey, Cody, look who it is,' the cop beside me said.

Cody dipped down to look at Davie, who by now had his window down. 'Hey, man, how are you?'

'I'm fine,' Davie said.

'Just saying,' my cop said to Cody, 'saw them riding kind of low, thought maybe they had a problem.'

'Looked kind of low to me,' Cody agreed.

'Well thanks,' I said, 'but there's really no problem.'

'We're just heading east,' said Davie, 'spend the last few days on the other side.'

My cop nodded. 'Well,' he said, 'I hope you enjoyed your stay.'

'We had a blast,' I said.

'Well, that's fine,' my cop said. Then he withdrew a gun from his jacket and placed the barrel against the side of my head. 'Now put your fucking hands where I can see them.'

On the other side Cody was doing the same.

I put my hands on the steering-wheel. Davie put his on the dash. Under his breath he said, 'Fuck.'

A moment later the back door opened and Cody climbed in. 'Now,' he said, 'we're going to go for a little drive.'

I said, 'We're really tired, we were thinking about stopping for a rest.'

He said: 'Shut the fuck up.' He reached forward and ran his free hand over Davie's body. Davie didn't wince when he touched his arm, though I could see his lips tightening against his gums. Cody couldn't quite reach the glove compartment without making himself vulnerable to attack, so he told Davie to open it. He did.

'Reach it out, barrel first.'

Davie did as he was told.

My cop opened my door and searched me. There was nothing to find but sweat. Satisfied, he closed the door again and turned back to his own vehicle and climbed in. He took the police light down from the roof, and then pulled out onto the highway to follow us.

'Are we going anywhere in particular?' I asked.

'Shut up and drive.'

Cody's instructions were strictly of the right-left-right-left variety; there wasn't even a brief history of the area we were driving through, though I knew from following Davie around that he was taking us deeper into the suburbs of St Petersburg.

'This where the station is?' Davie asked.

'Shut your mouth.'

'I'm guessing because you're out of uniform, because you didn't call this in, because you didn't run our plates, I'm guessing you've gone freelance.'

'I told you to shut up.'

'I'm guessing when our bags turned up you went through them and found my gun. I'm guessing you've been watching us ever since.'

'Left here.'

It wasn't an admission, but it wasn't a denial. I would have to apologise one day to a dreamily maligned pancake chef.

'I'm guessing—'

'Will you shut the fuck up!' He pushed the barrel of the gun hard into Davie's head.

I glanced back. 'Look, mate, we're willing to split it with you.'

'It's not about what you're willing to do, *mate*.'

'You don't even know what we have,' Davie said.

'You have gold bars. A lot of them.'

'Yeah, right. And we'd be driving this heap of shit.'

'That's what Mikey said as well, until we beat the crap out of him.'

I glanced at Davie. He blew air out of his cheeks.

'Big guys,' Cody said, 'always cry like fucking girls.'

'Is he okay?' I asked.

'Oh yeah. It's not like he'll need skin grafts or anything.'

I sighed.

'Right here.'

'So where *are* you taking us?'

'Somewhere nice and quiet. Somewhere things can go

bump in the night and the neighbours don't call the police. Oh – I forgot. We are the police. Now shut the fuck up and pass me the candy.' He nodded forward. Sitting on our front dash was the long-neglected bag of M&Ms. They'd probably melted and set a dozen times in the heat since we'd driven out of Orlando. I passed them back.

Davie said under his breath, 'And I hope you choke on them.'

'I heard that,' Cody said, and struck Davie on the back of the head with the barrel of his gun. Davie ducked forward and cursed. He rubbed at his skull with his good hand.

Cody laughed. He lifted the bag with his gun hand and poured the sweets into the other one, keeping his eyes trained on Davie the whole time. 'You think you're so fucking smart, but you stick out like sore thumbs. Minute the Don went down we had you pinned for it. You are so fucking amateur.'

He laughed again, then filled his gob with sweets.

A moment later there was a sudden eruption of spit and vomit from the back; Cody keeled over, gagging and screaming. The shock of it caused me to swerve on the road; I straightened the vehicle and glanced back just as Davie reached back with his one good arm, grabbed the retching Cody by the hair then dragged him backwards between our seats.

'Fucking hit him!' Davie screamed.

I hesitated for just a moment as I saw Cody's face. There were ants crawling all over it.

He was on his back but he was spitting up, trying to get them up, but they were racing everywhere. Down his throat, across his tongue, now up his nose. Maybe they were mad on sugar. Maybe they were just mad. But I fucking loved them. I brought my left elbow down hard on Cody's face and his nose split and broke under it; hurt my funny bone too, but I wasn't complaining. Cody groaned and started spitting blood as well as ants. Davie let go of his hair and grabbed Cody's arm as he tried to bring his gun up. I hit him again. Davie wrestled the gun from his grasp and then cracked it into his mouth, breaking his front teeth.

Vomit, ants, blood from his nose and sliced gums covered the barrel; Cody's eyes were crossed in horror as he looked at it, but he finally stopped struggling and lay there like a wild horse that had finally been broken.

I looked in the mirror. There was no indication from behind that the other cop had noticed anything. He'd missed my swerve, and the action in the back seat had been low enough to fall under his radar.

'What now?' I said.

'Well, we could call by the local dentist, make sure Cody here gets some good treatment.'

I smiled. It was good to have a sense of humour. It was pure Irish sarcasm. Cody probably didn't get it. He was probably wondering if he had the medical cover and what nice robbers we were. I slapped at my thigh, squashing half a dozen of the ants that were still racing around. It wasn't much of a reward for saving our lives, but Mother Nature's like that; she gives with one hand and takes away with the other.

Davie said, 'Indicate, pull in here.'

'Here?'

It was just an ordinary road with bungalows. I indicated. Davie removed the gun from Cody's mouth and said, 'Sit up, you bastard. You do exactly what I say. Understand?'

Cody nodded.

I pulled in. A moment later the Land Cruiser stopped behind us. I watched in the mirror as the other cop got out and hurried up. He had his hand inside his jacket, ready to pull out his gun.

I rolled my window down as he approached.

'We're outta gas,' I said.

'Aw, shit,' he said, then peered in to get confirmation from Cody.

'And you're out of luck,' Davie added, and raised the gun. I'm not sure what the cop saw first, the state of Cody's mouth or the outline of Davie's gun, but they each had the same effect. He froze.

'Take his gun, Dan.'

I took it. It didn't seem odd to be taking it. I'd been handling guns a lot lately.

Davie turned to Cody. 'Get out of the car. Dan – open the boot.'

I kept the cop's gun trained on him while I opened it. Davie got out, protecting his arm as best he could, then prodded Cody towards the rear.

'Get the gold out,' Davie said, 'and our bags.'

'Davie?'

'Just do it.'

I reached in, moved our bags out. The gold was harder to shift.

Davie said, 'Help him.'

The other cop helped me lift it out. He gasped when he felt the weight of it. 'Christ,' he said, 'there must be millions.'

Davie nodded. 'There is. So close, and yet so far away. Now get in the fucking boot.'

'In the . . . ?'

'Just fucking get in.'

The cop climbed in.

Davie indicated for Cody to follow.

'We'll suffocate in there,' he said.

Davie nodded. 'That's the plan.'

Cody climbed in. Davie slammed the boot.

'We're not going to travel about with them in the boot, are we?' I asked.

'Of course we're not, you fucking bonehead.' He nodded towards the Land Cruiser. 'From now on in, we travel in style.'

19

I thought Davie was being remarkably calm about it. But then he wasn't doing the driving. I was behind the wheel of a stolen police car. Next time we got stopped he'd claim to be a hitch-hiker called Norris and I would go straight to San Quentin without passing my lawyer's office.

'Relax, will you,' he kept saying.

'That's easy for you to say.'

'Look Dan, the only two people who suspect us of involvement in killing The Colonel are those two clowns, and they're not even interested, they just want the gold. They won't even report that they've had their car stolen. It's not a police car – look at it, man. It's not equipped like one, is it? Where's the radio, where's the cuffs and all the crap we carry? They carry the siren about to impress people. What would they say anyway? First of all they wouldn't be able to handle the shame of having their car stolen, second of all they'd have to explain exactly what they were doing, and third even if they did call it in and the cops caught up with us and shot us dead, someone else would get the gold. So relax. We're home free.'

'No,' I said. 'Home is where the heart is.'

He smiled. 'You old romantic.'

'They're not really going to suffocate, are they?'

'Of course they won't. I came out here to help you get The Colonel, not to become a serial killer. They'll flounder around in the dark for a while, but eventually they'll work out there's a catch on the inside of the boot. They'll be fine. And look, they don't go away empty-handed. They get a free car out of it. It's worth over *five hundred* dollars.'

'As opposed to the millions we have in the back.'

Davie shrugged. 'Millions to someone. At the moment it's worth nothing to us. We can't go into McDonald's and slap one of those babies down on the counter and say, "Give us a Happy Meal." We have to find someone to sell it to.'

'You're right. How hard can that be? We just stand on a street corner like Del Boy. Shouldn't take long.'

He gave me a filthy look but didn't respond. He was right about one thing though. We were travelling in style. We were up high, the air conditioner worked without belching fumes at us, we were ant free and there was a great sound system, although it was kind of wasted on the Kris Kristofferson CDs in the multi-player. However, they made wonderful Frisbees. We trawled the radio for something suitable and ended up with a 1960s station whose every other record seemed to be Van's 'Brown-Eyed Girl'. When I was fourteen and suffering either from flu or puberty, lying in bed all miserable or ecstatic, I asked my dad to buy me the 'Brown-Eyed Girl' single from Aquarius Records just down the road from our house. He brought home 'Brown Girl in the Ring' by Boney M instead. I wasn't greatly surprised. This was the man who called Sylvester Stallone 'Victor Stallion' and thought George Formby had been the World Heavyweight Champion.

'What *are* we going to do with it?' I asked. 'The money? The millions.'

'We'll divide it up. Split it in two. Fifty-fifty.'

'And what's the first thing you're going to buy?' It was a dangerous game to get into, but irresistible.

'Nice car. Aston Martin. Big house. For my mum. Holiday home somewhere. Mauritius . . . I hear that's nice. Invest in the stock market, kind of fancy that. And I'll put a bit aside just for gambling. Monte Carlo. What about you?'

I shrugged. 'I think Trish has her eye on a new table for the kitchen.'

Davie smiled. 'You're not really cut out for this, are you?'

'Never claimed to be.'

'Yet trouble seems to follow you around.'

'That is indeed my destiny.'

'Yeah, Obi-Wan.'

We had left St Petersburg far behind and were continuing our journey south. We turned off outside Naples and ate lunch at a restaurant overlooking one of its beaches. We laughed and we talked and we wandered across the sand. To anyone who even noticed us we probably looked like just an average gay couple on holiday.

It was only when we got back on the road that the stormclouds really began to gather. Literally. There's nothing subtle about Floridian weather. Back home you can have grey clouds for days, weeks or months, it might rain every day or it might not rain at all. It can spit for *years*. In Florida, you see grey clouds, you start to batten down the hatches.

'I don't like the look of this,' I said.

'Spot of rain's not going to hurt us,' said Davie.

At about this time, lightning started to crackle across the sky.

In Florida they don't do their lightning by half measures either. At home, lightning looks as if a couple of fairy-lights have short-circuited. In Florida it's the end of the world.

BOOM BOOM BOOM, went the thunder, CRACK CRACK CRACK, went the lightning. And then the rain started. I know you're getting sick of this, but at home – rain? Well, it can get you a bit damp. Occasionally you might get soaked. In Florida, on that road, in the sudden dark, it felt like we were under artillery attack. The rain pelted out of the clouds in thick sheets which smashed us, hammered us, flooded the roads and reduced visibility to fuck-all squared in a box in the time it takes a normal individual to chew an Opal Fruit. I kept driving, thinking we would pass through it, but it just went on for ever. We were crawling along, lights on full; my face was almost pressed against the windscreen, trying to make out the cars in front.

'This is crazy,' Davie said.

'Tell me about it. Christ, look at it.'

'We're going to get written off,' Davie said.

'We're going to be the richest corpses in America.'

Somewhere in front of us there was a sudden flash of light and a loud crack as a lightning bolt narrowly missed a car. Or else it really was artillery. I knew the Yanks were jumpy since September 11, but shelling us seemed a bit over the top. I would have given myself up at a polite, 'Excuse me.'

'Dan!'

I slammed on the brakes and just managed to stop us rear-ending the car in front. I'd been too busy admiring the lightning. Horns sounded from behind. To our left a massive truck roared past inches from us, impervious to the conditions or the danger. Big places have big weather, but this was Mother Nature's spectacular revenge for crushing her ants, or introducing them to E numbers. Either way I'd had enough.

'We have to get off the road, Davie, this is madness.'

'Just pull over onto the hard shoulder, wait for it to pass.'

'No. You can't even see the bloody markings – someone'll

slam into the back of us. We need to get right off this road. I'm turning off at the next exit – we'll hole up somewhere for a couple of hours.'

I managed to keep us alive long enough to reach the next exit; I was expecting a motel or a McDonald's, but there were only farms and shacks and trees. If anything, it was even more dangerous because the road was narrower and there was no division between us and the oncoming traffic. Several times we were pressed heart-stoppingly close to flooded ditches as cars veered unintentionally across the invisible divide.

'You do know where you're going, right?' said Davie, wiping sweat from his brow. His hair was sitting dank on his head. He'd been as cool as a cucumber with a gun. He'd been in control. But this was beyond anyone's control, apart from Gandalf.

'South,' I said, 'then east.'

'I *know* that,' he snapped. 'But here and now, you know where you're going?'

'Of course I do.'

'It just looks to me like you haven't a clue.'

'Of course I know. We're going – straight ahead.'

'Where are we, Dan?'

'We're south of where we were, and we'll shortly be turning east. For fuck sake, Davie, I can't see the fucking signs.'

'Well, why don't you stop and ask someone?'

'Who? They're all in their fucking bunkers. Besides, I know where we are.'

'Ask directions.'

'You ask directions.'

'You're fucking driving.'

'And you're fucking doing nothing. You ask.'

'Ask who?'

'I don't fucking know.'

I drove on. He probably had a point, but I wasn't willing

to concede it. It was Northern Irish politics in microcosm. I just drove. It didn't really matter where we were. The big weather was everywhere.

'It's getting heavier,' Davie said.

'Yes, I can see that.'

'How can it get heavier? It makes what we had earlier seem like a light shower.'

'I can see that too.'

'I'm only pointing it out.'

'Well, you don't need to.'

'Is it my imagination, or is the road getting narrower?'

'It's your imagination.'

'It is, you know.'

'Okay, so what do you want, a fucking framed certificate?'

'I just want to know that I'm on a road not a fucking dirt track.'

'It's not a dirt track. It's a road.'

'I just want to know we're not going to get stuck and some fucking big alligator isn't going to crawl out of the Everglades and bite my one good arm off.'

'Would you ever wise up? We're nowhere near the Everglades.'

'Oh yeah? Weren't we going south, didn't you start driving east about twenty minutes ago? Have you seen a sign? Hold on, I'll roll the window down and ask those fucking flamingos.' He mimed the action with extravagant arm movements. 'Hey mate, we're nowhere near the fucking Everglades, are we?'

I sighed. 'This is madness. Whose bloody idea was it to pull off the interstate?'

Davie cleared his throat.

'Well, it seemed like a good idea at the time.'

'Then turn back, get back on it.'

'I can't. I've no idea where we are, and this road is too narrow, and it's starting to flood and *I'm* starting to worry about getting eaten by alligators, and I'm not entirely sure our insurance covers us for being dismembered by crawling fucking handbags.'

'Great,' Davie said. 'Fucking great.'

'It's not my fault.'

'Well, whose fault *is* it?'

'Yeah. I'm responsible for the rain. That's right. Don't be such an arse.'

'Huh.'

'Huh.'

We drove on. The rain got heavier. The road *was* getting narrower. Davie cursed and moaned and made sarcastic comments while I tried to maintain the stiff upper lip, mostly for his benefit, or to annoy him, because I was frantic inside. I've never been any good at physical manly-type things, like changing a light bulb or wiring a plug. The last time I had a flat tyre I put the car up for sale. Negotiating Mordor on a bad night was way beyond the limits of my experience or ability.

'Really, now, finally, turn back,' Davie said, 'or we're going to die.'

'We're not going to die. Just a little bit more,' I said.

'It's a fucking *Land* Cruiser, Dan, not a boat.'

'We'll be fine.'

'Oh yeah,' he said. 'Have faith.'

He rolled his eyes, then pressed his forehead against the glass. I drove for another five or fifty minutes, then finally stopped. 'Okay,' I said. '*Now* we'll turn back.'

'You just had to,' Davie said, 'go that extra mile. Just to make it *your* decision.'

'Don't be so childish, Davie. You get your way, and I still get criticised. I can't bloody win.'

'Yeah, right.'

The thing about Land Cruisers is they always advertise them on TV in much the same way as they advertise tampons: no matter how crap you're feeling, you can still go out show-jumping and water-skiing and mountain-climbing. The Land Cruiser could leap over volcanic rock, ford suddenly raging streams, negotiate snowdrifts and conquer sand-dunes. Unfortunately, it could do bugger all about being driven backwards into a water-filled ditch. It could do sod all about the back wheels slipping into six feet of floodwater and then upending the rest of the car. It couldn't toss life-jackets to us as we scrambled out of the windows and dragged our sorry arses through the muddy water. It couldn't give us a hand or a round of applause as we hauled ourselves up the mucky, slippy bank to some kind of safety. It couldn't do anything but sit there filling with water.

Finally we stood on the bank, soaked, caked in mud, miserable, the rain teeming down around us, the lightning still cracking out of the sky and the farts-of-God thunder rolling angrily around us, looking down at our stolen vehicle filled with gold and floodwater.

'Fuck!' Davie exclaimed angrily.

I joined him.

'That's just fucking brilliant.'

'I did my best, Davie.'

'Oh yeah.'

'Well, how was I supposed to know there was a ditch there? You didn't exactly get out to check.'

'You didn't fucking ask me to!'

'You could have volunteered. You knew I couldn't see anything.'

'You seemed to know what you were doing. *Now* I realise you didn't have a fucking clue. Now I realise what a wanker—'

'Aw, shut up.'

'No, *you* shut up.'

'Oh yeah, you're the big man, sank our car.'

'I'll fucking sink you.'

'Aye, you and whose army?'

'What age are you Davie, twelve?'

'Old enough to beat you, you stupid fucker. You've just driven millions of dollars' worth of gold into the fucking river.'

'I didn't do it on purpose.'

'Yeah, sure.'

'What's that supposed to mean?'

'I don't know what it's supposed to mean. Take a guess.'

'What the fuck are you talking about? You saying I drove in there deliberately? Like any sane individual would do that, out here, the weather like this?'

'I rest my case.'

'You can rest your case up your hole, you wanker.'

'You're the wanker.'

'No, *you're* the wanker.'

'Is that right?' He came up to me and gave me a push.

'Fuck off,' I said and pushed back.

Then he pushed me again.

And I pushed him.

He took a swing for me with his good arm and missed. I swung for him and he ducked. He kicked out and I grabbed his foot and walked him backwards until he fell over into the water. I went with him. I landed on top of him. He pulled my hair and I punched his shot arm. He let out a howl and poked me in the eye with the finger of his good hand. I grabbed my eye and screamed; at the same time he punched me in the stomach. He tried to buck me off, but I stayed where I was. I got one hand round his throat and pushed him down into the water. With the other hand I scrabbed his face. He got a hand free and pulled my ear hard.

Then he pulled my cheek out and twisted it. I screamed and brought my knee hard down on his balls. He yelled and let go of my cheek, but then he thrust his pelvis up and managed to throw me over his head. I landed with a splat and a splash. I was winded; before I could raise myself he was on me, trying to punch my face, but I kept moving my head from side to side. Every time he missed my face, one of my fists shot out and punched him on the bullet wound.

It was a good fight, and could have gone on all day, or until one of us drowned, but it was ultimately interrupted not by fatigue or tears or by one of our mothers arriving, but by a shout.

'Hey! Fellas! You okay over there?'

We stopped, and groggily turned to stare into the rain: there was a tractor with its full lights on twenty yards away, and just visible around the glare and rain, a farmer type waving at us.

Davie and I exchanged glances, then helped each other up. I stumbled across to the farmer shouting without any dignity at all: 'Help us, we're lost, we don't want to drown.'

As I reached him he smiled indulgently. 'Looked like you boys were having a fight.'

'We were just helping each other up. We went off the road. We had an accident. We're both a bit shaky. Thank God. You hear about people getting lost in the Everglades for ever.'

The old guy smiled with his cracked yellow teeth. 'Everglades? Those aren't Everglades.'

'Well, what are they?'

'Fields.'

I nodded. It didn't matter what the hell they were. We were safe. Davie arrived at my side. He was covered in mud from head to toe. So was I, for that matter. His shirt was ripped and I could see blood and dirt mixed on his shot arm. 'We need help to get our car out,' he said, and nodded back at the ditch. 'Do you have a chain or tow rope?'

The farmer was about seventy years old, his face pinched and weatherbeaten, his yellow oilskins cracked and ancient, but he was game for anything. 'Reckon I have,' he said, and began to climb down from his tractor. He splashed his way over to the ditch. Davie and I followed, glaring at each other behind his back. The farmer looked down at the car, which was about three quarters submerged. He nodded to himself. 'Reckon I can get it out all right, but it ain't gonna work. You'll need to take it to town to get fixed up.'

'That would be great,' I said.

'I'll go bring the tractor closer.' He splashed his way across to it.

Davie looked at me and hissed, 'Wanker.'

'Fucker.'

The farmer drove the tractor up, then jumped down and secured a tow rope to a hook at the front. He held the other end out. 'Now I need one of you boys to go in there and secure the rope. That or we can come back tomorrow when the rain's off. Course, not sure the car will still be there.'

Davie looked at me, I looked back. Davie's lip curled up. Mine curled down. Davie stepped forward and took the rope out of the farmer's hand. 'I'll do it,' he said, and jumped back down into the ditch.

The farmer was just climbing back up into his tractor when I said: 'So where is the nearest town?'

Davie was just preparing to submerge himself in the water.

The farmer turned and pointed in the direction we'd been travelling. 'About a hundred yards that way, just around the bend.'

I nodded down at Davie, vindication enveloping my face. 'Told you, told you,' I sang.

'Fuck off, wanker,' Davie replied, then dived beneath the oozy muck-coloured water.

20

Everglades City had no real right to call itself a city. It would hardly have qualified as a village back home. It had a population of 321. That's what it said on the cracked green sign we passed on the way in, sitting on top of Farmer Giles's tractor. He wasn't really called Farmer Giles. We didn't know what he was called. More to the point, we didn't care. We were cold and damp and miserable. We hated each other. If we'd been two hundred years older, or younger, depending on how you look at it, we might have fought a duel. And I would have won, because I had right on my side.

When we weren't glaring at each other we noted the small school, the bank, the half a dozen guest-houses and dozens of small tourist-trap businesses exploiting the city's position on the edge of the western Everglades. It probably looked okay in the sunshine.

Farmer Giles towed our Land Cruiser to an auto-shop on the far side of the city, although you could have walked back to the nearside in about three minutes. It was still raining heavily, but it was all a question of degree: at home it would have qualified as the worst thunderstorm in history;

standing at JJ's Auto-shop waiting for JJ to finish ramming a four-tier sandwich into his bake, it actually looked like the rain was easing off.

When JJ eventually emerged I said, 'Nice weather for ducks.'

He just squinted at us. 'What's that?' he said.

Our accents were as thick as champ. And yet he had an accent and we could understand every word. It was a conundrum. I thought about raising this point with Davie, but instead I gave him the fingers. He had turned me into a murderer and a thief, but much worse than that, he was being really mean to me. I was his oldest friend and he was subjecting me to torrents of abuse. He was a fucking fucker.

JJ took a look at our vehicle. 'Nice wheels,' he said. 'You give it a bath or somethin'?'

'That's right,' Davie said.

JJ smiled. He was wearing oil-stained overalls and a Miami Dolphins baseball cap. Some people suit baseball caps. JJ didn't. His head was too wide; his ears were bent down by the sides of the cap and sticking out at each side like handles. His hair was voluminous and naturally curly. He looked like he'd failed the audition for the Hair Bear Bunch. But he was going to get us out of a hole, so we wouldn't take the piss until later. And then only if Davie and I were speaking.

'I'll have to dry this mother down 'fore I can see how much damage been caused. You gentlemen planning on sticking around for a while?'

'How long's a while?' Davie asked.

'Difficult to say. I'm not too busy. Reckon I'd have her ready for you some time tomorrow, presuming I can get her ready at all.'

Davie glanced at me. I shrugged. We had no choice really.

'Is there a hotel in town?'

'Guest-house. Tell them I sent you.'

We stepped out of the auto-shop and stood stunned for a moment on the hot asphalt outside. Sky – blue. Sidewalk – dry. Sun – blasting.

'How do they do that?' I asked, even though I wasn't speaking to him.

'God knows,' said Davie, and He probably did.

We started to walk down the street marked Broadway – and then I stopped and said: 'Aren't you forgetting something?'

Davie thought for a moment. 'I'll count to three, and then we both apologise at the same time.'

'I was thinking more of the gold bars we've left in the boot.'

'Oh, fuck!'

We turned and hurried back into JJ's. He was back at his sandwich, so we shouted to him about our cases, and he waved us on. We opened the boot and hauled the gold out of the back. The soaked bag was even heavier than before. Davie winced. We were still caked in mud and slime, which couldn't have been good for his arm. My repeatedly punching him on it couldn't have helped either. I delved back into the car and pulled our travelling bags out. I draped one over either shoulder.

'Cheers,' Davie said.

'No problem.'

It was a small peace gesture on my part, although at the least provocation I would hurl his bag into the nearest swamp. I took hold of one end of the gold bag, Davie took the other with his good arm, and we heaved up. We began our walk back into the city.

It was hard going.

The sun was now so strong that the mud was drying

out on our clothes and hair and faces, causing us to walk with a stiff gait like an arthritic version of the Wild Men of Borneo. If I'd been the local Sheriff, cruising past, I would have stopped for a nosey. So I can quite understand why he did – Sheriff Sterling Baines. It said his name on the side of the car. Under his name someone had painted two neat little rows of x's. He eased along beside us for several metres, then pulled the car into the kerb. He rolled down the window and smiled out at us. He was about sixty. His hair was thick and white. He was old, but he didn't look like someone you'd want to mess with. As soon as we'd clocked him I'd said to Davie, 'Let me handle this,' and he'd surprised me by agreeing.

'You the guys went for a swim?'

'That's us.'

'You should watch out – when the water comes up like that, that's about the only time we see the 'gators real close.'

'We'll bear that in mind.'

'JJ fixing your vehicle?'

'Yes, he is.'

'Okay – well, anything I can do to help, just let me know. We have a small, peaceful community here, kind of like to keep it that way.'

'Absolutely,' I said. Then I nodded down at the x's on his door. 'Those all the people you've killed?'

He laughed. 'No, son, that's the number of days till I retire. Can't hardly wait.' He winked and said: 'See you boys around.'

Then he drove on.

'Didn't bother about a lift,' I said when he was completely out of range.

'Thank God,' Davie added.

We moved sluggishly on down Broadway. We laboured

past a Spanish-style railroad depot and a frame community church. There was a flaking four-column temple building with a sign that said *Old Collier County Courthouse* and a plaque that told us it was built in 1926. We turned onto Shorter Avenue, moved past the Company Laundry Building, then finally came to a halt outside the Bank of Everglades. It had been built in the same year as the courthouse, which seemed to make sense.

'We have to go in, put this in their safe.' Davie nodded down at the gold.

'What we have to do,' I said, 'is get a room, get cleaned up. We walk in the bank like this they'll push the alarm button.'

Davie shook his head. 'Shit-kicking town like this, they're used to all sorts. They won't bat an eye.'

'Davie – they'll chase us. Or they'll shoot us. I know about places like this. *My Cousin Vinny.*'

'Trust me.'

'Yeah, right. That's what you said in St Pete – now look at us.'

Davie blew air out of his cheeks. Then he reached into his pocket. 'Tell you what, seeing as how we're not going to get anywhere like this, we toss for it.'

I thought about that for a moment. I'd read *The Dice Man* and knew what trouble following the whim of a dice could get you into: this was somewhat the same, only with fewer options. But as the alternative was getting into another scrap with Davie and having to live with the ignominy of being beaten up by a one-armed man, I nodded and he tossed and I called and he won.

We lugged the bags up the steps into the bank. Security seemed a little lax to say the least. There were a couple of elderly women drinking coffee and reading magazines on comfy seats set into a window alcove; a teenager was getting a Mountain Dew out of a vending machine; and instead of a series of windows with cashiers, there was a high desk with a bored-looking man in an open-necked white shirt sitting on what appeared to be a bar stool, reading a copy of the *Everglades Echo*. A small black plastic nameplate was sitting before him. *Mr EC Hamilton, Manager (Owner)*. So now we knew.

'What sort of a bank is this?' asked Davie.

'No idea, Sundance,' I said.

EC Hamilton, the manager and owner, looked up from his paper. 'Bank's across the road,' he said.

'It says bank outside,' said Davie.

'Yes, sir, it does,' said EC, with the weariness of a man who'd spent his whole life apologising for not being a bank. 'Used to be the bank. Now we're a guest-house. Kept the name. Seemed like a good idea at the time. Not so sure now. Like I say, bank's across the road.'

Davie peered back out through the door. 'There's a laundry across the road. The Company Laundry Building.'

'Yes, sir, that's the bank. It's the Company Laundry Building, but it's the bank.'

'So where's the laundry?' I asked.

'Ain't no laundry,' said the desk guy.

Now that we had that sorted out, and seeing as how we were actually already in a guest-house, albeit by default, we decided to take a room, get cleaned up, then deposit the gold in the bank later. Davie signed us in while EC blinked curiously at us.

'You fellas been for a swim?' he asked.

'Car trouble,' I said.

'Figures.' He returned his attention to his newspaper.

'JJ sent us,' I said.

'JJ?'

'JJ of JJ's Auto-shop. That entitle us to some sort of discount?'

'Nope.'

There were no elevators in the guest-house, so we had to lug the gold up three flights of stairs to our room. When I glanced back I just caught EC's eyes flicking back down to the newspaper. Across the lobby, the two old women didn't even show us that courtesy; they watched us until we were out of sight. The only one who didn't show any interest was the teenager struggling with the vending machine. If past experience was anything to go by, we'd be better off killing him right away, because it's always the one you least suspect.

Upstairs we were more than polite to each other. There were single beds. Davie said after you and I said no, after you. So he chose the bed by the window. He said he was going to have a shower, and I said so was I. He said after you and I said, no, after you, and he said, no I got the bed I wanted, you have the first shower. It was going to get really annoying after a while.

I stood in the shower and scraped away the mud. I hadn't had a chance yet to think about the repercussions of what I'd done – killing The Colonel. I did not feel particularly different. I did not feel as if a huge weight had been lifted off my shoulders. But nor did I feel numb. Or racked by guilt. It almost felt like it hadn't happened at all, like it was someone else's memory. As if The Colonel, who had paid such a significant part in my life, was now too insignificant to waste thought upon. He was dead. Gone. End of story.

Or end of *that* story. The complication was now the gold.

Davie had argued that the gold bars were the spoils of war, but they weren't. They were an afterthought. They were a different scene, from a different movie.

While I got dressed, and Davie was in the shower, I briefly debated phoning Patricia.

Only briefly, because I didn't know what to say. She believed that killing The Colonel would help bring back the old Dan Starkey. But it wouldn't. Because he had never gone away. Everyone else had changed, I had stayed the same. It was as if the world was rotating one way, and everyone on it was walking in that direction, while I was going the other way, against the flow, anti-clockwise. I phoned my psychiatrist instead.

Dr Boyle sighed and huffed and puffed while he got to his study. 'How's your friend?' was his first proper question.

'My imaginary one, or the real one?'

'Either.'

'They're one and the same, and they're fine. But thank you for asking. Never mind about me.'

'Dan, I—'

'I did it.'

'You did it?'

'I did it.'

'You . . . ?'

'I did it.'

'Oh. Well done.'

'Thank you.'

'And how do you feel?'

'Rotten.'

'Rotten in what way?'

'Rotten in any way you care to think of. Sick to the core. Feverish. Angry.'

'You're sure it's not smallpox? I hear there's a—'

'I did it and I'm not proud, and I'm not ashamed. Somewhere in the middle.'

'Times like this, somewhere in the middle is the best place to be. Do you know what I mean? It probably won't hit you for another six months. Have you told your wife?'

'No.'

'Do you *want* to tell your wife?'

'Yes. Yes and no. I don't want it to look like she told me to go out and kill him so I did it.'

'But that's how it could be interpreted.'

'Yes. But it's not how it happened. I – shot him, but it was in self-defence. He was attacking me. I had no choice. It was him or me.'

'Dan – that's perfect. You didn't murder him in cold blood then. You've nothing to feel bad about.'

'He didn't commit suicide. If I hadn't been there, he wouldn't be dead now.'

'It doesn't matter. Your hand was forced, you can't blame yourself, you were put in a position, you shouldn't feel guilty.'

'I don't feel guilty.'

I happened to glance up, and Davie was standing in the doorway listening, a towel wrapped around him. 'Give her my love,' he said.

'My imaginary friend sends you his love,' I said into the phone.

My psychiatrist was silent for several moments. Then: 'Dan?'

'Mmm-hmmm?'

'Describe your friend.'

'About six foot two.'

'Yes?'

'White fur. Big pointy ears. Answers to the name of Harvey.'

'Dan?'

'Mmmm-hmmm?'

'You are barking, you realise that?'

I put my hand over the mouthpiece and smiled at Davie. 'She loves you too.'

21

First off, we tried the hotel safe. Said to EC that we had something valuable we needed stored and he said there was a safety deposit box in the room. We said yes, it's hardly big enough to take a shoe. And he said, 'What size of a shoe do you have?' We said, 'It's not about a shoe,' and he said, 'Well, what is it about?' He was as nosy as fuck but we were on our best behaviour so we didn't hurl abuse at him or, indeed, shoot him in the head. Perhaps we were maturing.

'So about this safe?' Davie asked.

EC sighed, folded away his paper – it was only about ten pages long, he must have read it a dozen times since we'd been upstairs and come down again – and turned and opened a small door leading into a storage room behind him. There were a lot of keys hanging on hooks, a big stack of towels and boxes of soap, and beneath them all a small, squat safe. EC bent to it, made a point of blocking our view while he twisted a dial, then stepped back to show us the interior. It was crammed full of papers and files and bags of coins. There was more space in the safety deposit box in our room.

'You should try the bank,' he said. 'They got a strong room. It's just . . .'

'Across the road. Yes, we know,' I said.

'It's in the . . .'

'The Laundry Building,' I said. 'I remember.'

'But don't be misled, it's not a . . .'

'It's not a laundry,' said Davie, ''cause there ain't no laundry.'

EC nodded with the glum resignation of an actor whose best lines have been given to someone else. As we lugged the bag between us EC shouted after us, 'Tell the manager EC sent you.'

We nodded and stepped out into the late-afternoon sun. 'Fucked-up town this is,' Davie said. 'Bank's a guest-house and the laundry's the bank.'

I nodded. 'We'll go to the pub later, discover it's a whorehouse.'

'Well, that would be a tragedy.'

We crossed to the Company Laundry Building and entered the bank. For all the activity inside, it could have run a laundry on the side. There were jokes to be made about money laundering, but we knew from the look on the manager's face that he'd probably heard them all before. He was deeply tanned, his hair was flecked with silver and perfectly coiffured, his body appeared to be thickly muscled: we could tell this because of the excellent cut of his expensive-looking white suit. He would just about have been every woman's dream date if he hadn't had a face like a bucket of spiders. You can tart ugly up a million different ways, but you still get left with ugly. The nameplate on his desk said BJ Harmon, President. He smiled widely at us and said, 'Afternoon, gentlemen. We're just about closing up here – what can I for you do?'

'For you do?' I said.

'We'd like to put something in your strong room. Kind of valuable.'

'You gentlemen have an account here?'

'No, sir, we do not.'

'Do you wish to open an account?'

'No, sir, we do not.'

'Bank rules say you can't use the strong room 'less you have an account. But it's no trouble to open one – that I can for you do right away. Even if you only make a small deposit, just to keep things right and above board. All I need,' and he produced a small form from beneath his desk, 'is for one or other of you to fill in this form. Your name here, your permanent address here . . . and your social security number here.'

I glanced at Davie. He shrugged. I said, 'We're tourists, we don't have social security numbers.'

'Then I can't open you an account. No, sir, that I cannot for you do. It's against the law. No offence, gentlemen, but we get a lot of illegal aliens these parts – Cubans, Mexicans – but they don't have no social security number, then they don't get no bank account, and they don't got no bank account they don't get no credit card, checkbook, they can't borrow money, buy a house . . . it's a way of keeping it all in check.'

'We don't want to borrow money,' I said. 'We don't want to buy a house. We just want to use your strong room.'

'I understand that, sir, but rules are rules.'

'EC sent us,' Davie said.

'And JJ.'

'JJ?'

'From JJ's Auto-shop.'

BJ nodded. 'That's as maybe, nevertheless . . .'

Davie sighed. He reached into his back pocket and produced a wallet I hadn't seen before. 'Hoped I wouldn't have to do this,' he said, in what seemed to me to be a passable American accent. He flipped open the wallet and showed BJ a police badge. 'Cody Banks,' he said, 'St Pete Beach Police.'

'Oh my,' said BJ.

And I thought something similar.

'We were transporting vital evidence back to head-quarters when we got caught in that shower.' He leaned forward to whisper conspiratorially. BJ leaned forward as well, his brow furrowed with curiosity and age. Much closer and Davie could have planted a smacker on his lips. If he'd been that way inclined. There was no need for any of us to be whispering. The bank was still empty. Davie glanced back at me, 'And this is Officer . . .'

He hesitated for a moment, allowing me in to dig my own grave. I stepped forward and leaned into the circle of enlightenment. I put out my hand to BJ. 'Dan . . . DM . . . DM Boots.'

Davie blinked at me.

BJ shook my hand warmly. 'Officer Boots.'

'BJ,' said Davie, 'I can't stress to you enough how impor-tant it is that you keep our presence here in Everglades City under wraps. We've been pursuing a Mafia gang . . .'

'Russian Mafia,' I put in.

'We're pursuing a Russian Mafia gang—'

'Actually they're from Georgia – that's Georgia in the old USSR, not the one up the road.'

I thought the extra detail might help convince BJ. Davie quietly stepped on my toe out of sight of the now perspiring bank manager. The fact that I was wearing flip-flops only added to the pain. The fact that he was wearing them as well was neither here nor there. He was a big bastard, and mean with it. But I grinned nevertheless, although I was crying inside.

'And unless this evidence gets back safely to St Pete's,

then the whole case is all shot to hell. As we will be. We need the use of your strong room, sir. Just for one night.'

BJ stood back from his desk. 'Sir, it would be a pleasure for the Bank of the Everglades to help the officers of law enforcement in their time of need, an absolute pleasure.' He made a come-hither gesture with his hand. 'You just give me that evidence. I'll make sure—'

'We'd prefer to place it in the strong room ourselves.'

Davie was a cop, just not an American one, and he knew how to sound authoritative.

BJ hesitated for just a moment. 'Of course. If you'll just come round . . .'

BJ pressed a buzzer which opened a door at the end of the counter, then led us through an office to the strong room. He yanked a heavy metal door open with some difficulty, then ushered us inside. There were several rows of safety deposit boxes, a medium-sized safe and several large filing cabinets within. BJ eyed up our bag.

'Looks kind of big for the safe,' he said. 'Unless we could squash it down.'

'It doesn't squash,' Davie said.

'That case, just leave it there in the corner. Be safe enough. Haven't had a robbery here in thirty years.' He blinked for a moment. 'Unless of course you're bank robbers. Guess I let you in here kind of easy.'

Davie smiled. For a moment it put the fear of God into BJ.

But then I smiled, and he relaxed.

Two smiles, totally different reactions. It said a lot about Davie, and it probably said a lot about me.

'Relax,' I said. 'Bank robbers don't wear flip-flops.'

'And besides,' Davie said, 'I spotted the security cameras. What sorts of fools would we be, comin' in here without masks?'

BJ swallowed. 'I guess,' he said. He ushered us quickly out of the vault and re-secured it. It worked on some kind of time-lock principle, with a combination thrown in – I didn't know or care. Egg-timers confuse me.

As he walked us towards the front door BJ said, 'You want I should tell the Sheriff, he could keep an eye?'

Davie shook his head. 'Appreciate the thought, but no thank you. Less people know about it, the better, you understand?'

'Yes, sir.'

'These Georgian Mafia,' I added, for colour, 'their tentacles reach far and wide.'

BJ nodded as if it meant something.

'We'll be back tomorrow,' Davie said. 'We're just across the road if you need us.'

BJ nodded and hurried back inside his bank. A moment later a Closed sign went up and he locked the front door.

Davie blew air down his nose as we walked across the road to the bar.

'Cody Banks,' I laughed. 'Where'd you find that?'

'Left it in the car.'

'Very thoughtful.'

'Georgian Mafia – what are you like.'

'Trust me,' I said. 'The devil's in the detail.'

'Security cameras!' scoffed Davie. 'They're about as real as his hair.'

'Really? It's a wig?'

'Yes, it's a wig – and yes, they're fake. Just thought you'd like to know.'

I patted my hair down for reassurance. Forty and not a bare patch in sight. I was doing all right for an old drunk guy.

* * *

The Mountain View Bar and Grill was pretty much what it said on the tin, except if you wanted to view a mountain, then you'd have to move to a different state. There were decent views of the beach and the handful of tourists down to watch the sunset. It was the kind of bar the locals used and the tourists avoided. There was nothing particularly dark or dangerous about it, it just lacked the finesse tourists expected. The barman was the first person we'd met in a while who didn't have his name emblazoned on some kind of badge, but we knew soon enough that he was called DJ and that he owned the place. 'Hey DJ, set 'em up!' 'Hey, DJ, gimme a shot!' DJ was an impressively large figure in his late forties, muscled up like BJ but with a face to match – chiselled, rugged. He wasn't the kind of guy who slapped moisturiser on before going to bed; he probably wrestled alligators for fun and caught marlins with his teeth.

Davie got the beers in and we sat at the bar and talked about nothing interesting or deep, which was a relief. As the evening wore on and the beers went down we both began to relax. There were difficult times behind us, and difficult times ahead of us, but for now we were just a couple of off-duty cops getting wasted. Actually, we didn't bother with the Yanky accents. Only BJ knew we were cops, but he also knew we were posing as tourists. Our story was as watertight as our car, but it was only for one night. JJ would have us on our way in the morning, we were sure of that. Well, I was. Davie thought he'd better check, especially when he spotted him sitting at the bar later on, pissed as a skunk.

'Leave him be,' I cautioned. 'He's off-duty.'

'Ah, sure he won't mind.' Davie was pretty drunk by this stage. JJ was sitting with five or six of his cronies. I didn't know if they really were cronies, but they looked how cronies should look. A bit like JJ himself, but slightly less sophisticated. They were laughing and drinking and laughing and shouting and clapping each other on the back and giving each other bear hugs and yelling at the TV because there was a baseball game on. They'd been watching it for a while. The TV was set high up behind the bar, and the longer the night wore on, the more excited they became about the game. The way they were sitting, they'd all have sore necks in the morning. And the way they were drinking, sore heads as well. I finally had to acknowledge that this didn't bode well for our car being ready. So Davie wandered across and stood behind them for a while, pretending to watch the game. JJ, in turning to punch one of his friends on the arm, noticed Davie, but said nothing; he just turned away slightly in his seat in the vain hope that Davie wouldn't recognise him. But in truth, he was as hard to miss as a wanker in a convent.

'Get you another beer?' DJ said.

I nodded and he set one up.

'You here on vacation?'

'Here by accident. Car got caught in the flood.'

DJ nodded. 'Right. You're that guy.' I laughed. He laughed. 'Bush telegraph. You gettin' it fixed?'

I nodded across the bar. 'JJ.'

DJ rolled his eyes. 'Good luck,' he said, and retreated into a back room to change a keg. I watched Davie for a while. He was still standing there, waiting to be noticed, and JJ was sitting there, determined not to. I turned the other way and saw that there was now a girl sitting a couple of stools away from me. She was a real stunner; tied-back blonde hair, small sharp eyes, slightly turned-up nose, immaculate skin, perfect figure, white cut-off T-shirt under a white denim jacket which was draped loosely over her shoulders. I'm pretty good with detail when I need to be.

I'm not that good with age, but she couldn't have been more than sixteen years old. She was drinking either a strawberry milk-shake or some kind of a cocktail through a straw. She wasn't using her hands to hold the glass. Instead she leaned forward and sucked it up. It was perfectly innocent, and at the same time the most sexually suggestive act I'd seen since the last one.

And working on the principle that she was probably sick of tanned muscle freaks, and that I hadn't flexed my freckles in a while, and that I loved Patricia more than anything but that there wasn't any harm in talking to someone, I smiled across at her. It had nothing to do with the fact that she was ravishing. If she'd been a pig in a wig I would have smiled, although I probably would have followed it up with, 'Shift your big arse, fat chops, I'm going for a piss,' rather than the much more sophisticated, 'What's that you're drinking? Looks nice and cool,' I released on this beauty.

Her eyes flitted towards me. And her lips. She licked them, then sat back on her stool.

'Why, are you offering to buy me one?'

'No, just curious.'

She smiled. Probably everyone in the state had offered to buy her a drink at one time or another. I was a refreshing change. With that and the freckles, I was on a winner.

'But I've nearly finished this one,' she purred.

'Well, how much are they?'

She smiled again. Cheap and ignorant. Gets them every time.

'I really don't know.'

She was like royalty. She probably never had to dirty her hands with money.

DJ was back behind the bar again, but he was down at the other end watching the baseball with JJ, his cronies and Davie, who still hadn't made his move. I didn't mind so much now, he could stay as long as he liked. It would give me time to turn on my cheeky-chappie Irish charm. For the moment I was Irish, even though there was no immediate danger of being hijacked.

Of more immediate concern was how to bridge the gap between my bar stool and hers without looking like a lounge lizard. Or just a lizard.

'You on vacation here?' she asked.

'Sure am.'

'You like our little city?'

'Sure do.'

'I think it sucks.'

'Well, that's what I was thinking, just didn't like to offend.'

She smiled again. Gorgeous white teeth, and all her own. There was a sudden roar from down the bar as someone hit a home run. They were all cheering. Even Davie. I said, 'Friends of yours?'

She made a face. 'They like to think so.'

'I met JJ. He's fixing my car.'

'JJ.' She nodded along the line of them and sighed. 'I know them all. JJ. CJ. LJ. DJ and MJ.'

'Well, they seem okay to me, but that's only an initial impression.'

She laughed this time. 'You're pretty cute, mister.'

I swallowed. She'd said cute. Not funny. *Cute.* I blushed, although with the sunburn it was probably difficult to tell.

It was time to take my chance. I eased off my seat. I moved up the three stools to where she was sitting. I smiled as cutely as I could and put out my hand.

'Dan Starkey,' I said.

She blinked at me for a moment, then shrugged off her denim jacket.

If she'd had any hands I'm sure she'd have put at least one of them out.

But she didn't.

She had –

Flippers.

No hands, no *arms*, just small, slightly fleshy flippers, about six inches long.

My hand just kind of hung in the air in front of her.

Time seemed to stand still. She was looking at me, gauging my reaction, the way she must have done a million trillion times in her life. If I'd had time to think about it I could have dealt with it as well as anyone, I could have shook that flipper as if there was nothing different about it at all – but I was drunk, and she could see from the look of bug-eyed shock on my face that I was a single drink away from yelling, 'Holy fuck – look at those flippers!'

I tried to say something, but it wouldn't come out. She raised an expectant eyebrow. Her mouth was set passively but her eyes were narrowing, an odd combination which suggested both laidback resignation and the possibility of a headbutt.

Luckily, Davie saved the day.

As the baseball fans sat with bated breath waiting on the swing that could win the game, he finally made his move.

'Baseball,' he said into the temporary void. 'It's a pile of fucking shite, isn't it?'

22

Davie had been a cop for twenty years. He had undoubtedly been highly trained in unarmed combat. He probably had certificates and medals to prove it. But this was a type of fighting they don't teach at school; this was bar-room brawling of the highest calibre. Or lowest. Eye gouging, ear pulling, Chinese burnsing, bottle breaking, stool wrapping, ball squeezing, hair pulling, tongue twisting bloody mayhem. Naturally I sat offside, trying to protect my armless young friend from flying glass. That lasted all of about a minute. DJ, behind the bar, finally remembered his responsibilities and bellowed, 'Michelle! Get upstairs!' before leaping over the counter and weighing into the fight.

Michelle said, 'Bye, bye, Dan Starkey,' and walked round the other side of the bar.

'Bye, bye, Michelle,' I said.

I watched her as she walked slowly up a set of stairs, and only took my eyes off her when a glass flashed past my head and crashed against the bottles of spirits behind the bar. It was too late to duck, but I did it anyway. When I raised my head again, she was gone.

It was a fairer fight than you might imagine. If it had been

Davie versus DJ, CJ, JJ, MJ and LJ I would have sprung to his defence, or at least phoned the police, but shortly after the first punch was thrown, or the first eye gouged, it became a free for all. They were all fighting each other. For no reason whatsoever, as far as I could see. For fun. To pass the time. For sure, it was more interesting than baseball, although they could have achieved that by taking up knitting. Five minutes after it started, it was all over – and they were laughing about it. Even Davie. It was like *Fight Club* for drunks. Davie was buying them drinks at the bar. Or he was trying to. They insisted. Then DJ put them on the house and suddenly everyone was happy, and much drunker. Davie twice waved me over to join them, but I just nodded and kept to my own drink. I didn't know if the fight represented some sort of weird initiation, or was just their way of letting off steam, but with my luck, the moment I walked over there and disparaged their national sport they'd inflict the same damage on me as they had tried to inflict on Davie. The difference was he was physically and mentally built to take it. I was not.

So when they were all looking the other way I finished my drink and slipped outside into the cool night air. I stood looking out over the water, wondering why I hadn't joined in with Davie and his new pals. Normally I didn't need a second invitation to get drunk, or indeed a first. Perhaps it was the company. Perhaps it was a newfound maturity. Perhaps it was Michelle and the shock of seeing her flippers and the shame of my reaction to them. She reminded me of Little Stevie and the life he had not had the opportunity to fulfil. Nothing could change that. Not a psychiatrist or a court nor putting a bullet in his killer's head. He was dead. Michelle was one of the most beautiful girls, women, I had ever seen. Yet she had no arms. She had flippers. Did that mean she wasn't beautiful? No, it did not. Did it mean she wasn't a proper girl? No, it did not. Those were the correct thoughts to have. And yet. How good a man would you have to be, to accept her the way she was? Could I?

These are the sort of deep thoughts a drunk has when he has time on his hands, and no real friends to speak of. I smiled to myself. I had spoken to her for ten seconds, and I was already imagining how we'd get on on our honeymoon. Fantasy, once again, as the justifiable preserve of the married man.

I hadn't been standing there more than a couple of minutes when I realised there was someone behind me. Just a subtle clearing of a throat and the quiet setting of a coffee cup on a glass table. I turned and saw a figure sitting in the semi-darkness of the wooden veranda which fronted the Mountain View Bar and Grill. It was only when he leaned forward to pick up his cup again that I saw it was the Sheriff. Sterling Baines.

'Evening, son,' he said, his voice low, gravelled, but not particularly cold.

'Sheriff.'

'See your friend met up with JJ and the boys.'

I smiled. He had his feet up on the second chair, but he took them down and indicated for me to sit. It wasn't an order. It was an invitation.

'You want a beer?'

He leaned back and produced two bottles of Rolling Rock from an ice-bucket behind him. He reached one across to me and I twisted the lid off. He nodded down at his coffee cup. 'Doesn't look good for folks to see me drinking, so I have to hoodwink them.' He began to pour his beer into the coffee cup.

'And do you?'

'Doubt it,' he said.

I took a sip of my beer. I was taking more sips these days,

whereas I used to gulp it down, then fall over. 'It's not a race, Dan,' Trish used to point out. Although with her, it used to be. I said, 'You didn't go in to stop the fight.'

'Ah, they're just letting off steam.'

'Glad you think so.'

'Well, son, times is hard. This town is going through a tough time right now. Visitors dropped away since September eleven, those that do come head further up the coast, or stick with Orlando. We had a couple pollution spills, didn't help. Now this SARS thing's reared its head, and that was the last darned straw.'

Call me uncharitable, but I didn't know whether to weep or invite Bruce Springsteen down to record an album. In the old days I might have said, 'Stop whining about it, Pop, and tell me what's really on your mind.' Because cops, even old cops, don't sit outside bars coming on like Grandpa Walton for no good reason. But these weren't the old days, these were the new and I was able to hold off on the abuse. I nodded and did my best to look thoughtful. I took another sip of my beer. He'd get to the point soon enough.

'Any news on that ve-hicle of yours?' Sheriff Baines asked.

'The ve-hicle is still in the gar-age.' I wasn't consciously taking the piss. I was just half drunk. 'And JJ's at the bar.' Try as I might, I just couldn't split *bar* into two syllables.

'JJ's always at the bar. You still planning to leave tomorrow?'

'Just as soon as JJ works his magic.'

The Sheriff nodded. 'Hear you put some valuables in the bank.'

'Yes, sir.'

'Valuables as opposed to evidence, like you told BJ.'

He had opened the trapdoor, and I had dived through it,

smiling naively. But I could still argue my case from the darkness of the dungeon.

'Valuables *are* evidence.'

He nodded again. Took another sip of his beer. 'You do realise it's a crime to impersonate a police officer?'

'Is it?' I smiled, and he smiled back. Dig, Dan, dig yourself out of the hole. 'We were only joking, Sheriff. Didn't think he'd take us seriously. We only wanted somewhere to put our stuff.'

He took out a pack of cigarettes and offered me one. I shook my head. He lit up, bent his head back and blew a thin stream of smoke into the air.

'If you did that in there,' I said, nodding at the bar, 'I'd have to make a citizen's arrest.'

'And you'd be perfectly within your rights, son.' He continued without pausing for breath; it was a clash of two tangents. 'Soon as I saw you, I ran your plates.'

'No one ever tell you not to judge a book by its cover? We'd just fallen in a ditch.'

'In my experience,' said the Sheriff, 'it pays to *always* judge a book by its cover. Seems to me that vehicle belongs to a St Pete Beach cop called Cody Banks.'

'Yup. That's my friend.'

'Son.'

'He has a split personality. Some days he's a St Pete Beach cop, other days he's a mad Irish tourist.'

'Son.'

'Only raking.'

'Son, I never saw anyone less like a cop in my life.'

I shrugged. 'I know what you mean. Truth is, we met Cody in St Pete Beach a few days ago, got on like a house on fire, he lent us his car. Those hire-car places are such a rip-off. We're shit scared of taking the car back to him now 'cause we drove it into that ditch. But we'll do it, 'cause we're good honest people and we're sure JJ will do an excellent job.'

'Thing is, son, I was kind of curious, so I gave the St Pete Beach cops a call, and guess who answered the phone.'

'Wouldn't have been Cody Banks, by any chance?'

'Why, that's exactly who it was.' He gave me a long, cool look.

This time I gulped my beer. I spilled half of it. 'So,' I said while I wiped at my trousers, 'do you want to arrest us now?'

Sheriff Baines nodded thoughtfully, and I thought I saw the hint of a smile. 'Thing is,' he said, 'Officer Cody Banks said his car hadn't been stolen, that it was sitting right out front, that I must have misread the tags.'

Once again I'd shot myself in the foot. Par for the course, really.

'So what did you say to that?' I asked.

'I said well maybe he was right and I'd check with the officer who'd called it in. I apologised for wasting his time and I hung up. Now, son, I don't even want to think about why a police officer would lie like that. I told you earlier today, I got thirteen days until I retire. Last thing I want is anything spoiling my run-in. I've been the Sheriff here for seventeen years. Do you know what else I've dealt with this week?' I shook my head, although there was no need, he was going to tell me anyway. 'Monday I helped a guy with a broken hip up at the Trail Lakes Camp Ground. Tuesday there was a vehicle roll-over on the I-75. Wednesday there wasn't anything at all. Thursday, there was a guy suffering from dehydration right here in the city. Do you get the picture? And that's a busy week. Night-times I've spent going to official receptions thanking me for my devotion to duty, accepting awards from the school and the medical centre. Now what I'm leading up to is this: I don't know what in hell you guys are up to, it sure doesn't strike me as anything particularly legal, but as long as you aren't doing nothing in my city, in my last thirteen days of service, then I'm quite prepared to turn a blind eye. Do you understand?'

'Yes, sir.'

'Okay, son, then we understand each other.'

I nodded gratefully and pushed back my chair. 'I appreciate your candour, Sheriff. We won't let you down.' I put my hand out to shake, but he kept his firmly on the table.

'I'm just letting you know, son. I don't want to be your friend.'

'That's quite all right.'

I dropped my hand, then stepped down from the veranda. I hadn't been aware of it, but my shirt was stuck to my back. My head was starting to pound. Delayed panic. I was just about to turn away, but curiosity got the better of me. I put my hands on the rail and said, 'Sheriff?'

He took a sip of his drink, savoured it for a moment, then swallowed. He nodded.

'The girl in there, Michelle, what's her story?'

'She ain't got no *story*, son. She just ain't got no arms.'

'That's what I mean. What . . .'

'Born like that. Nothing more to say. Except you keep away from her. DJ dotes on her. You so much as look at her the wrong way, DJ'll tear your head off and use it for a piss pot. And I'll look the other way. Special girl, that Michelle. Special girl.'

'Yeah,' I said, 'she seems to be.'

I nodded and turned to walk back to the Bank. I'm sure he watched me all the way, but I didn't turn to check. I was too busy thinking about her dad using my head as a piss pot.

223

23

Davie woke next morning with a raging hangover and an arm that was dripping pus.

'Jesus,' I said, 'is that sore?'

'Of course it's fucking sore, you moron.'

'It's not meant to be green, is it?' Davie rolled his eyes. '*Now* we have to get you to a hospital.'

'We can't, Dan. It's a bullet-wound.'

'So what're you going to do, just hang around till your arm drops off?'

'No.'

I could tell by his face – and indeed his arm – that he was worried, but I also understood why he wouldn't go to a hospital. We were a couple of murderers on the run. We had gotten lucky with the Sheriff, but we couldn't expect that luck to hold. Life wasn't like that. Especially mine.

We eventually agreed on a compromise. Everglades City wasn't much more than a village so it didn't have a hospital. But Sheriff Baines had mentioned getting an award from the local medical centre, so there was at least one doctor. He probably made most of his money from tourists with sunburn and kids with ear infections from the polluted water. We'd concoct some bullshit about an accident and hopefully get at least enough t.l.c. to keep Davie on his feet until we could offload the gold and fly home. If it looked like he was going to turn us in we'd try and buy him off, and if that failed we'd make a run for it. I called EC downstairs and said Davie wasn't well and we needed a doctor.

'Medical Centre's just down the road,' he said, with the same amount of concern he'd show if we were ordering breakfast. I could hear him turning the pages of his newspaper as he spoke. 'It's in the old Rod and Gun Lodge. Won't take you more than five . . .'

'I need the doctor to come *here*.'

EC sighed. 'Well, just how sick is he?'

'Can we let the doctor decide?'

There was a pause, and then he said: 'I guess. The number is . . .'

'Could you call him? You being local and knowing him and all?'

He hesitated again. 'I guess.'

Forty-five minutes later there was a knock on the door. When I opened it EC was standing there with a woman who looked to be in her early thirties: about my height, auburn hair, well tanned, brown eyes, white shirt, shorts, doctor's bag. 'You'll be the doctor,' I said.

'Kelly Cortez,' she said. She extended her hand. 'You don't look well,' she said.

'It's not me – it's him.' I nodded at Davie, lying on the bed in his shorts with his Hawaiian shirt open to the waist and a small towel wrapped around his arm.

Dr Cortez raised an apologetic eyebrow. 'Well, let's take a look,' she said, and marched into the room. EC tried to follow, but I blocked his way. 'Thanks,' I said; there was no need to add the *now piss off*. He could tell it by the mean look in my eyes.

I closed the door and turned back to the bed. Davie had already pushed himself upright and was smiling endearingly at the doctor.

'So,' she said, 'there's a sixty dollar call-out fee, with prescription on top of that. Do you have insurance?'

It was probably time to retire the third party fire and theft joke, but I used it anyway. She nodded blankly at me. Davie said we were tourists. 'Well, you pay me when I'm finished, I'll give you a form, you can claim it when you go home. Now then, what seems to be the problem?'

Davie cautiously peeled the towel away. Dr Cortez sat on the bed and took hold of his arm around the elbow, then turned it carefully to get a better look at the wound. Then she made a face.

'We had a fishing accident,' I said.

'Were they shooting at you?'

Davie laughed suddenly, involuntarily, loudly. It was a warm appreciative laugh and it caused the doctor to blush. It was probably what saved us. She was duty-bound to report a gunshot wound, but she was also a laidback Floridian and seemed to share Sheriff Baines's attitude to trouble.

She gave a brief shake of her head, then examined the wound more closely. 'Whatever it was,' she said, 'it seems to have gone clean through. But it beats me why you felt the need to pack it with mud.'

'Wasn't on purpose,' Davie said. 'We really did have an accident. Thought I washed most of it out.'

She lifted her medical bag. 'This,' she said, 'is going to take some time. You should really go to a hospital. But I guess that isn't an option.'

Davie made a little-boy-lost face, and Dr Cortez blushed again. Finally, after forty years, he had discovered a woman who found him charming.

I said, 'I'll go and check on the car.'

Davie winked.

Downstairs in the lobby, EC had his face buried back in the newspaper. I hurried past, but as I reached the door he said, 'Everything okay?' without looking up.

'Fine and dandy,' I said.

The sun was already beating people to death outside. Patricia had once dreamily talked about retiring to somewhere like Florida. I had laughed and said, 'Do you seriously think we're going to make it to that age?'

'You won't,' she had countered, 'but I will. I'll come out here and spend your money.'

Now, standing on the sidewalk, I smiled at the memory, and the irony. My money? The millions in gold bars sitting in the bank? Sure thing. She could have it. But if by some miracle Davie and I did get it home and we were suddenly rich beyond our dreams, the last place we would ever show our faces again would be Florida. Too hot, and in more than one way.

I stayed in the shadows as much as I could as I walked up to JJ's Auto-shop. It was a bit of closing the barn door after the horse has bolted, but at least it was something.

JJ's Auto-shop was all closed up, although there was an Open sign still hanging on the front door. I stepped back and looked up. It was a two-storey wooden frame building. 'Ramshackle' was the word that came to mind. The top left window was half-open and a pair of jeans had been laid out to dry over the sill. So he lived over the shop. I banged on the door again, and kept it up until eventually JJ appeared, rubbing at his face and yawning as he approached the door in his underpants – not that there was a door in his underpants. He was already, or still, wearing his baseball cap. His hair did not look any more attractive for having been slept on. It veered to the side, like Marge Simpson's.

'Yo,' JJ said through the glass, without any of the enthusiasm the word requires.

'Just checking on our ve-hicle,' I said as he wearily opened the door. He was wearing too-small boxers and an odour straight out of the fish-market.

'Oh yeah.' He scratched at his stubble again. He looked behind him, as if the ve-hicle might be sitting on a shelf ready for collection. 'The Land Cruiser, right?'

I nodded.

'Be ready this afternoon.'

'You said this morning.'

'This afternoon. You must have misheard.'

'We really could do with it this morning.'

'Man, give me a break. This afternoon, all right?'

He closed the door and locked it. He stood looking at me for a moment through the glass. If Davie had been with me he'd probably have smashed his hand through the pane, grabbed JJ by the throat and dragged him out and down to the shop to work on our car. But he wasn't, so I contented myself with giving him my disappointed look. It was like my normal look, but more disappointed.

JJ tramped away, probably back to bed, and I returned to the shadows.

Dr Cortez was gone when I got back to the room. Davie was just settling back down into bed. 'Think she's gone to get the cops?' I asked.

Davie smiled. 'I think she's gone to get all dolled up for lunch.'

'She's what?'

'Well, she's really nice, so I asked her out to lunch.'

'And she agreed?'

'On the condition that I get a couple of hours' sleep first. So that's what I'm going to do.'

'Davie . . .'

'What harm can it do?'

'Davie . . .'

'I'm following doctor's orders. That's what you wanted. She's given me an antibiotic, I'm to rest, I shouldn't be travelling.'

'We have to get out of here. We can't afford to hang about socialising.'

'So the car's ready?'

I sighed. 'Not quite.' I told him about JJ.

'Then what's the problem? Relax, Dan. The Sheriff's cool. Kelly . . . Dr Cortez is cool. Our car's getting fixed. We'll leave tomorrow.'

'Tomorrow? What happened to this afternoon?'

'Well, depending on how lunch goes. I mean, if it goes well, what's the harm in . . .'

'Davie!'

'Okay – all right. This afternoon. Later. C'mon, Dan. She's nice. I haven't met a woman who laughs at my jokes in twenty years.'

I shook my head. 'Davie . . .' I began. And then thought, What's the point? I can whine all day, he'll still do exactly what he wants. 'Right. Great. Okay. This afternoon. But that's it. We have to get moving. So, get some sleep, hornball.'

He smiled. 'Thanks, mate.' I turned for the door. 'Where are you off to?'

I shrugged. 'Walk.'

'Dan?'

I stopped.

'Watch out for the sun, you'll get burned.'

'Thanks, Grandma,' I said.

So I wandered back downstairs and out into the sun. I bought a baseball cap that said *Everglades City – Florida's Last*

Frontier from a giftshop. I sat for a while in the Mountain View Bar and Grill and ate breakfast. Possibly I was hoping for another look at Michelle, possibly I was just hungry. But she wasn't around anyway. I stayed off the beer. I read a newspaper and studied some tourist leaflets. I learned that Everglades City was a frontier outpost until 1923 when Barron Collier made it the seat of Collier County and a supply depot for the construction of the Tamiami Trail. Prior to this it had been Florida's last outpost for fur-trappers, plumage-hunters, Cuban fishermen and people with a disdain for modern civilisation. It was fascinating, and I didn't care if I never learned another fact about Everglades City in particular or Florida in general for the rest of my life. I wanted to go home. I could hear Patricia calling me. She was calling: 'Dan, where the fuck are you?' Yet home seemed as remote a prospect as ever. Davie, at the least opportune moment in history, had chosen to start dating again. He was a cop – he would probably malinger his wounded arm out for several more days until he saw where the course of true love or lust led him. That still left us with having to get to Miami and finding someone dense enough to fence the gold bars for us. Going home wasn't getting any closer. If anything, it was receding.

I finished breakfast, then walked around a few more stores. I was offered tours of the Everglades, a trip to an alligator farm, a circus and a flea-market. None of them interested me. A free trip to the moon probably wouldn't have gotten me going either. I wandered out along the beach. The sea was blue and calm and the sweat was soon cascading down my back and I cursed myself for not wearing my trunks. I couldn't swim, but I could dunk. I took my flip-flops off and walked along the edge of the water. There were only five or six other people on the beach. Maybe the Sheriff had a point about tourism being slow. I kept walking. The further I went, the less manicured the beach became; the tourists didn't venture this far along. The sand gave way to a heavy shingle then rocks heavily covered in coarse weeds. I sat down on a rock and stared out across the water. What if I just walked back into town and caught a bus? Caught a flight home. Left Davie and his gold behind. Up until now he had managed to dictate my every move. But our business was finished. The Colonel was dead. There was no law that said I had to stick with him; the gold was madness – just let it go, go home.

No – I couldn't just walk.

I would tell him I'd had enough. He would understand. And even if he didn't, what was he going to do? Besides, it probably made more sense to travel separately. And to dump the Land Cruiser. Yes. Good. Tell him. Tell him *now* while he's in a good mood about his date with Dr Cortez. I stood up and was just starting to climb down from the rock when I noticed a dolphin bobbing in the water a hundred yards away.

Aww, I thought, you don't often see them this close to land.

And then I saw that it wasn't a dolphin, but a human, and not just a human, but a human woman without arms.

Michelle.

Michelle.

She seemed to be looking right at me. I raised a hand and waved. She raised a flipper. She began to move back towards the beach. Her flippers were moving, but they were so tiny they didn't make much impression on the water; it was her legs that were driving her at remarkable speed through the water.

I walked down to the edge to meet her.

'Hiya,' I said.

'Hiya, Dan Starkey.' I blushed. She remembered my

name. And then I blushed again as she stood up. She was naked.

I mean, *completely* naked.

She smiled. My heart galloped. She was like a blonde white Halle Berry but with fewer arms.

'What's wrong?' she purred. 'Haven't you seen a naked woman before?'

'No,' I said. And then: 'Yes.'

24

Michelle had a T-shirt, shorts and a towel secreted behind some rocks just a few yards further along from where I'd been sitting. She sat down beside the T-shirt then lifted it with her toes. She leaned forward and pulled the T-shirt effortlessly over her head. It was, I thought, an amazing feat of physical dexterity and I nodded with the kind of appreciation I normally reserve for people who can change light bulbs or wire a plug. She probably did similar things a hundred times a day. She was probably used to clots like me giving her patronising looks. Although possibly she confused my patronising look for the one I adopt when looking at wet breasts through a white T-shirt. Sometimes only an expert can tell the difference. It was a baggy T-shirt. She didn't feel the need to put her shorts on. Not yet. Perhaps *that* feat of amazing physical dexterity would have entailed her revealing more of herself to me than she intended. Or maybe she wanted to sit there with her pants off. Either way, it was somewhat disconcerting.

I sat beside her on another rock.

She said, 'Are you married, Dan Starkey?'

'No,' I said. 'Are you?'

'What do you think?'

'I don't know what I think. You don't look old enough.'

She smiled. 'Married twice, divorced twice, and I'll be twenty-one next month.'

'Happy birthday,' I said. 'What went wrong?'

'What do you think?'

'It's a lovely day, Michelle, and you're asking me to do an awful lot of thinking.' I made a show of sitting like *The Thinker*. She giggled. It was a nice giggle. Like soft waves on a moonlit beach. Although the sun was out.

'I hardly know you,' I went on. 'You're probably expecting me to say they left you because they couldn't cope with your arms. Or lack of therein. But I think part of the reason you asked is because the answer isn't the obvious one. I therefore advance the theory that the reason why you have two ex-husbands is that you chucked them out because they were dead boring. In fact, it wouldn't surprise me if you were married to MJ, JJ, CJ, LJ or any of the other alpha-betties that hang about in your daddy's bar.' I raised my eyebrows. 'How'd I do?'

'You did good.'

'Just good?'

'You did one hundred per cent good.'

I shrugged modestly. 'Par for the course.'

She gave me a long, searching look, while I stared out to sea. 'You're very perceptive,' she said.

I shrugged again. I was normally about as perceptive as the Normandy Germans on the eve of D-Day. I was just applying man logic. Those eejits probably never left the bar. Michelle was the only woman they ever saw on a regular basis. And DJ was so protective of his daughter he probably never let her venture much beyond the bar. So he looked kindly on his cronies paying attention to her. He thought, Who else is going to marry a girl with no arms? This way his daughter got a shot at married life, plus he keeps her close at hand. Except she wouldn't stick with them. She was a bright girl, but you could see that she was looking for something else. She just wasn't sure how to get it. The long and short of it was, she probably fancied a bit of freckle.

I shifted uncomfortably. Although, not too uncomfortably. I was still looking out to sea, but I was aware of her watching me. She was admiring my chiselled features, the strong cut of my shoulders, the fine line of my backbone which suggested strength yet compassion. I had a lot of other wanky thoughts about how lush I was, but she was actually looking at the skin peeling off my forehead.

'You should get some cream for that,' she said.

'It's only sunburn,' I replied. 'What harm can it do?'

She smiled, and kept looking at me. 'If you had to ask me anything, what would it be?'

'What do you mean?'

'I mean – I have no arms. You're probably thinking about what it must be like to have no arms. There must be something you'd love to ask, but you'd never dare. But you can ask me anything. I really don't mind. About anything at all.'

She leaned forward enough for her breasts to press hard against the damp material of her T-shirt.

'Well,' I said, trying to do the gentlemanly thing and keep my eyes above her shoulders. 'How do you pick your nose?'

She nodded thoughtfully, savouring the question. 'You won't tell?'

'Not unless I'm tortured. Or asked.'

'I use a straw from the bar.' She moved a flipper and bent forward as if to pick something up. The end of the flipper curled inwards, grasped something invisible and then moved back towards her face. 'If I'm feeling mean I sometimes put the straw back in the jug.'

I made a face and laughed.

'Go on then, something else.'

She moved a little closer to me. I was facing the sea and she now was half-turned towards me. Just enough so that her breast was resting against my arm through her T-shirt. This obviously wasn't going to affect me at all, because I'd felt breasts against my arm before. Patricia's, for one. Or two. And clearly, once you've felt one breast against your arm, you've felt them all. Sort of. Kind of. I wasn't sure any more if it was skin peeling off my forehead, or just my blush giving up the ghost because of overwork.

'Well,' I said, 'what about writing? You use your toes, right?'

She shook her head. Her lips parted slightly. 'I use my mouth.' Her mouth opened wider; she formed it into an *O*, then closed it slowly as if she was gripping a pencil. Or something.

'I see,' I said, my voice suddenly several octaves higher. Somewhere in Ireland a sheep dog responded.

She giggled again. 'Of course I don't use my mouth. Not to write. I can paint with it though. You know, with a brush.' She opened her mouth a little further, a little rounder. 'The shaft is much thicker.'

'I see,' I said, and I did. I was picturing it.

'Go on then,' she said, 'ask me something else.'

'I . . .'

'Ask me about sex.'

'I . . .'

'Isn't that what all men think about?'

'Yes.' Although it sounded more like *Yeeeeeaaaash*.

'Well, ask me then.'

'What, about sex?'

'Yes. Anything.'

'Well, what . . . what . . .'

'You want to know what I do, how I manage . . .'

'No, I . . .'

'How I pleasure myself without any arms or hands or fingers?'

'No, really. I, I mean . . . too much information . . .'

'Do you know what I do?'

'No, and I really . . .'

'Do you know what I use?'

'I have no id—'

'I use my feet.'

'You use your . . . ?'

'And a banana.'

At this point I melted onto the rock and oozed away into the sea. There was sultry flirty talk and there was VAULTING OVER THE BOUNDS OF HUMAN DECENCY.

'Christ,' I said.

'There's an image to store on your mainframe,' she said, and laughed. I nodded helplessly. 'What do you think about that, Dan? Me and a banana? A nice, fresh, curved, yellow banana.'

'I . . . I mean . . . great. Whatever turns you . . . I mean . . .' I cleared my throat. 'Aren't you worried about pesticides?'

She nodded. 'You *are* a perceptive man. I put a condom on it. Do you want me to show you how I put a condom on it?'

'I think I can guess.'

I blew air out of my cheeks. My body temperature was off the scale. She made Lolita look like a big thick farmgirl. Half of me knew she was only winding me up. Which leaves half of me that didn't. Besides, you can only wind a man so far before he explodes. Or runs away. Perhaps she sensed this. She said suddenly, 'You're burning up, Dan. Come on – let's go for a swim.'

'I . . .'

She raised her foot and began to peel her T-shirt back up over her body. But it was still slightly damp so it didn't come off easily. It stuck on her breasts. She tugged at it, but it wouldn't come free. She said: 'Help me, Dan.'

So I eased it up over her breasts.

She smiled gratefully. She was completely naked again. 'Swim,' she said.

'I've no trunks,' I said.

'Neither have I.'

'I . . .'

'Come on.' She began to hop confidently down across the rocks and then onto the shingle. She had a small, round, perfectly formed bottom. 'Come on!'

Skinny-dipping?

I had never skinny-dipped in my life. Also I had never run down a beach with an erection before. But I did it – and strangely enough, I did it to recover my modesty. Her back was towards me, she was doing her dolphin swim already. If I could make it to the water and disappear beneath it, she wouldn't see my erection, and hopefully the cool water would hasten its departure. So I could explain to Patricia without any guilt at all why I was swimming with the Venus de Milo.

Although I wasn't swimming, of course. I was up to my shoulders and fearing for my life. My toes were desperately searching for footholds in the sand. Michelle swam up to me and I tried to hide my discomfort, and my erection, because it wasn't going anywhere but north.

'You're very good,' I said, 'at the swimming.'

'I'm like a shark,' she said. 'Gotta keep moving or I drown.'

Right enough, she was kicking her legs furiously while bobbing in front of me. That is, she was kicking her legs furiously until she suddenly surged forward and wrapped them around me. In a general groin-to-groin-type position.

I went, 'Oh.'

She went, 'Ah.'

'Oh.'

'Ah.'

'Mmm,' I said as she bobbed up enough to kiss me on the lips. I caught her and kissed her back. I held onto her for a moment. She was already grinding against me. Her breasts were crushed against my chest.

I enjoyed the crush and the grind and the kiss and her tongue for around thirty-seven seconds; and then I slowly pushed her back. This took a huge amount of mental effort. I should get some sort of a medal. I pushed her back, but her legs remained clamped around me. And they were strong, as they needed to be. I had no doubt that she could flex them and break my spine. Or flex them and force me to enter her. Which was as close as from here to over there.

She gasped, 'What?'

'I lied. I'm married.'

'So am I.'

She used her legs to pull herself in for another kiss. I co-operated, but only for twenty-six seconds.

I pushed her away again. 'You're divorced, Michelle. I'm not.'

She smiled indulgently. 'I'm divorced twice,' she said, 'but I got married again.'

I took a deep breath. 'You're . . .'

'I'm married to DJ.'

'You're married to your *dad*?'

'He's not my dad!'

At times like this I normally rubbed at my brow in frustration. But she'd pulled herself closer again and now

I had one of her breasts in either hand and it would have seemed impolite to release them.

'You're married to DJ?'

'Yes!'

'And yet you're . . .'

'Yes!'

'But why?!'

'Because he's lousy in bed!'

'Then why did you marry him!'

'Because he asked me!'

'If someone asked you to put your head in the fire, would you do that!'

'No!'

She was glaring at me now. Glaring at me, although her breasts were still in my hands and she was using her calf muscles to try and steer me into her nether regions.

Half of me was saying, Go for it.

And so was the other half.

But my third half was made of stronger stuff.

Moral fibre.

More than Davie, but still less than a Shredded Wheat.

She kissed me again and said, 'It doesn't matter.'

I kissed her back and said, 'Yes it does,' when I came up for air. 'I'm in love,' I protested.

'So am I!'

It was no longer a question of guilt. Because I was guilty as charged. It was fear of retribution. At home in Belfast, Patricia suddenly sat up straight and growled. It was called instinct. It was about connection. She could smell my wicked ways at three thousand miles.

I had to make the break *now*.

When I was at the very tip of entering.

It was like turning back one foot from the summit of Mount Everest.

Or less than a foot.

It was like freezing in the World Cup Final on the point of scoring the winning goal.

It was the horse smiling at the camera for the photo finish, and losing the race.

I pushed her back for the final time. 'No!'

And this time I backed suddenly away, breaking the hold of her legs; she flailed helplessly in the water for a moment, then regained her buoyancy. She looked disappointed, but not particularly angry. Maybe I wasn't the first person she'd tried to seduce in this manner. Maybe I was the one hundred and thirty-first. She was the Siren of the Seas and I had survived. I had done the right thing. I had been good, despite terrible temptation. I was suddenly pleased with myself, although I didn't smile.

Michelle surfed away towards the shore.

And I thought: What the fuck am I playing at! Sex in the sea with a beautiful woman! Nobody for miles! Leaving this afternoon! Who could possibly find out?!

'Michelle!' She didn't stop. 'Michelle! I'm sorry! I was wrong! Come back!'

She glanced back for a moment, but she kept moving towards the beach.

'Please! Come on!'

She stepped out of the sea and onto the shingle. I strode towards her through the water, which always looks rather ungainly. Then I followed her up the beach. We were both naked. It was Tarzan and Jane. Or from some points of view Laurel and Jane. She was gaining speed, hopping from rock to rock like a rock-hopping expert. I followed, erect, tough, determined. She was luring me into the long grass. She was playing hard to get. She would have me, but she would now set the rules, call the shots.

As she passed by where we'd been sitting Michelle

scooped up her T-shirt and shorts with her foot and clasped them under one flipper. I was bounding up the beach towards her now, with the long loping strides of a baby giraffe. She grinned back at me, then scooped up my clothes as well. She secured them beneath her second flipper. Then she took off again across the rocks.

'Hey!' I shouted.

She laughed mischievously as she went.

She was as nimble as a gazelle.

I sped after her. More than once I slipped to my knees and cursed as I scraped them over the surface of the rocks, but I doggedly continued my pursuit. She was a woman. She could keep this going for ever, or until my erection faded. Which it showed no sign of doing. If anyone had been watching it would have looked very strange indeed. And if anyone had been video-taping, it could have been worth a fortune. At least on the Internet. Horned-up naked man pursues nude armless woman, pausing only to gash knees.

She was really enjoying herself; she was laughing aloud – so was I, in between curses.

'Come on, Michelle! You've had your fun! Come on! We can talk about this! We can lie down and talk about this! Come on! You know you want me!'

She threw her head back and cackled. Nice cackle. Women have to get cackles just right, otherwise they can sound like a fishwife. But she did it perfectly.

'Michelle!' I reached for her, but I was flapping at air. I grabbed out again, but missed by a fraction.

She jumped to another rock, I followed.

'You'll never get me!' she cried.

'Just you wait!'

I leaped after her. My arm extended, the very tips of my fingers touched her shoulder. It was hardly more than a butterfly's touch, but it was enough to knock her off-balance as she jumped to the next rock. She landed on it, but her feet failed to find the proper grip. Her left foot slipped to one side on a strand of seaweed; she stubbed a toe of her right. She let out a yelp.

She fell.

Anyone else could have put their arms out to protect themselves. But she couldn't.

'Michelle!'

She fell behind the rock, and for a moment she was out of my sight. I landed on the same rock.

'Michelle!'

I expected her to look up slightly dazed, slimed by seaweed, but with a cheeky grin. But she lay face down, motionless.

I jumped off the rock and landed beside her. Her forehead was sitting flush against another, smaller rock; blood from her head was rapidly oozing out across it. I groaned and bent to turn her. She was limp – her eyes were closed.

It wasn't straight out of the medical manual, but I shook her and bellowed, 'Michelle!'

There was a deep gash across her head; blood was now cascading down her face, her chest, across me. Her mouth opened and I thought she was going to say something, but there was only a cough of blood. A deep sigh followed it and then her mouth closed and her head sagged to one side. Her chest wasn't moving. I checked her pulse. I know nothing about checking pulses. But I was pretty sure she didn't have one.

'Michelle?' I said weakly.

There was no response. There was the gentle beat of the waves on the shore, the easy hissing of the wild grass back beyond the beach, and the wild, wild thump of my heart, but there was no response.

Michelle was dead.

25

There is an inevitability about certain things. That beautiful people will marry beautiful people, that Africans will starve, that America will invade, that teenagers will rebel and that the three chords of rock'n'roll will be revived every ten years or so. That once you set out on a course of evil it will inevitably lead you towards a sticky end, pausing only to slide a knife between your ribs wherever possible along the way. Michelle was dead and I was scraping out her grave in the windblown sand beyond the beach. Then I was carrying her in my arms. Then I was putting her in her grave and piling sand on top of her. Then I was collecting rocks and laying them out over the sand in a kind of random pattern that I hoped didn't look too much like a grave but which would nevertheless provide enough protection from the wind to prevent her young lifeless body from being exposed.

For any normal, moral, sane human being this was not the obvious course of action. The normal reaction would be to raise the alarm, go for help, carry her to the nearest house. Explain the dreadful accident.

But normal, moral and sane are three strands of human

experience which do not figure heavily in my own, particularly here in Everglades City, with millions of dollars' worth of stolen gold in the bank, and there in St Pete's Beach with The Colonel mouldering on a slab. I was a murderer and a thief. I would not be believed. My only choice was flight.

I dived back into the water, washed the blood and sand from my body, dressed quickly and walked back into town along the beach. There were even fewer people on the sand now. When I reached the main drag I made a determined effort to move slowly and casually. I paused to check out a tourist store. From under the peak of my baseball cap I studied the front of the Mountain View Bar and Grill. It was lunchtime, customers went back and forth unconcerned. I crossed to our hotel. EC for once wasn't reading his paper, but chatting on the phone. He saw me cross the lobby, but didn't acknowledge me. When I was out of sight, I took the stairs three at a time.

Davie wasn't in the room. Lunch. I cursed. I packed my bag; then I packed his. I sat on the bed. I should wait for him to come back. Not make a fuss – just explain calmly that we had to get the fuck out of town. But Davie was half-smitten. He wouldn't be content with just lunch. He'd take Kelly Cortez for a walk or a drive: he might not return for hours. What if, in the meantime, someone was to discover Michelle's body?

Christ.

Michelle.

Dead.

She was a beautiful temptress. And I had killed her. If I'd given in to her advances while in the sea, there would have been no chase, no slip on a rock, no head with a fissure in it.

My fault for showing moral courage.

I should have known better. Or I should not then have

changed my mind and pursued her like a caveman. I had all but clubbed her around the head. Fred Flintstone had whacked out Wilma. Worse, he'd murdered Betty.

Shit. I couldn't just sit on the bed and wait for discovery. I had to get Davie; we had to get moving. I didn't even need to ask where he'd gone. There was only one decent restaurant in town.

With luck it would be busy enough for me to slip in and out without anyone really noticing; a quick word in Davie's ear, an apology to the good doctor and we'd be off. With luck, which is always my strong point.

I walked up to the Mountain View Bar and Grill and slipped inside. The bar was as busy as ever. DJ was looking hassled behind it. Good. The restaurant area was off to the right. Most of the tables were filled. I saw Davie sitting opposite Kelly Cortez. She was laughing. So was he, at least until he saw me coming towards him.

'Hi, Doc,' I said. Before she could respond, I said, 'Davie, I need a word.'

He spread his hands and said, 'Fire away.'

'No really – a word.' I indicated with my head that I wanted him outside.

'Relax,' he said. 'Pull up a chair.'

'Davie, I really need to talk to you.'

'Well, do it. Sit down and enjoy a beer at the same time. She's a doctor, man, she can't pass on your sordid little secrets. It's like being a priest, except she can cure your boils as well.'

Kelly giggled.

'Davie, *please*.'

A voice from behind said, 'Excuse me,' and I turned to find DJ. My heart fluttered. He had a tray in his hand. He was trying to get a meal to the next table.

'Sorry,' I said, and moved out of his way.

He set the tray down and an elderly couple thanked him. DJ turned back and said, 'Typical of this town. Here's a man with bleeding knees and the doctor just sits there and ignores him.'

I looked at my knees. Davie, Kelly and DJ looked at my knees. 'Slipped on some rocks,' I said. 'They're fine.'

'Come on, Doc, help the man!' DJ laughed. He returned to the bar.

'You're like a big kid,' said Davie. 'Always wreckin' your knees.'

'Davie, I need to talk to you.'

'Come by the surgery after lunch, I'll clean those up,' said Kelly.

'*Davie!*'

This time he hissed at me: 'What's so fucking important?' He glanced at Kelly. 'Sorry, Kelly. I'm just,' and he looked back to me, 'trying to have a nice time.'

Kelly blushed again.

I said, 'I'm sorry, but it's an *emergency*.' I raised an eyebrow. I gave him a surreptitious wink. He ignored them both.

'Give me half an hour,' was the best he could manage. 'I'm sure we can—'

'We haven't got . . .' I trailed off. I sighed. I looked back to the bar. DJ was pouring a drink for JJ. *Christ*. The car.

I said, 'Hold on a minute,' and hurried across to where the mechanic was sitting with several of his cronies. I touched him on the shoulder. He took about a year to look round. Then he grunted.

'She ready?' I said.

'Who?' said JJ.

'The car – our car – the Land Cruiser.'

He looked vague for a moment, and then the gas finally caught. 'Oh yeah. He who drives into ditches. Sure, she's ready.' He indicated his glass of Bud with a grin. 'Gimme a chance to finish lunch, I be right with you.'

'Look, I really need her now.'

'Her? She's not a woman. She's a *car*.' He giggled. Beside him, CJ and MJ giggled too. He was showing off for the benefit of his friends. Take the piss out of the tourist. 'A car you can fix, but women – you can't fix them, that's for sure.' He grinned again and his mates nodded in agreement.

I tried to stay calm. It was important. 'I need it now.'

'Can't do it, man. Shop's all locked up. Need to get your credit card, receipt . . .'

I moved a little closer. 'Look, JJ, I'm in a hurry. What if I pay you thirty dollars extra, you go and get the car for me now. You bring it down here.'

'Thirty?'

'Fifty.'

'Fifty?'

'*Fifty.*'

He thought for a moment, looked to his friends, raised an eyebrow, and they nodded. So he nodded at me. He got off his bar stool. I turned back to Davie. I heard JJ say, 'Asshole,' for the benefit of his friends, but I ignored it.

Sticks and stones. I was really worried about sticks and stones.

Davie was just ordering his dessert from a waitress.

'I shouldn't really,' said Kelly.

'Be a devil,' said Davie.

'*Davie . . .*'

'Oh, for Christ's sake!' The waitress jumped a little at Davie's outburst. 'Sorry,' he said. 'I'll have the Key Lime Pie. Kelly – just give me a minute, eh?'

She smiled and nodded. He got up from his chair and hissed, 'Come on then, Big Ears, this better be good.'

I led him outside. The sun whacked me about the head

again. I caught a glimpse of JJ disappearing behind the Mountain View, walking in the opposite direction to his auto-shop.

'What the fuck's got into you?' Davie said irritably.

I took hold of his good arm and led him down off the veranda onto the road so that we wouldn't be overheard. There were a couple of tourists sitting at the coffee-table where I'd chatted with the Sheriff the night before. Down the road, EC had emerged from the hotel and was sitting in the shade reading his newspaper. Outside the bank BJ stood with his arms folded talking to Sheriff Baines, who was sitting on the hood of his police ve-hicle.

'Jesus, Dan,' Davie said, 'your eyes are darting about like you're on fucking speed.'

'There's been an accident,' I said.

'What sort of an accident?'

'The worst fucking kind.' I took a big gulp of air. 'Davie – I didn't mean . . . I mean . . . it just happened. She just fucking slipped!'

He finally saw that it wasn't speed, it was terror. He moved a little closer, and this time he gripped my arm. 'Dan, what have you done?'

'I haven't done anything. She just . . . *fell*.'

'Who?'

'Michelle.'

'Michelle? Who's she?'

'The girl in the bar! For fuck's sake, Davie, the girl in the bar with the no-arms.'

'Okay.' He nodded. 'What were you doing?'

'I wasn't doing anything. We went for a swim, all right? We were just messing around, then she slipped on the rocks. Oh Christ, she cracked her head, Davie.'

He was staring at me. I was trying to continue but for the moment the devil was squeezing my windpipe.

'Is she hurt?' Davie asked. 'Come on, Dan. Kelly's in there, she's a doctor. She can take a look at her.'

'It's too late for that!' I spat, clearing the blockage.

'What do you mean? *Dan?*'

I couldn't meet his eyes.

He stared at me. 'Is she dead?'

'Yes. She is.'

'For fuck sake. You're not serious?'

'No, I'm fuckin' jokin'.'

'Jesus Christ.'

'I know.'

'And she's . . . she's out there?'

'Yes. Up to a point.' I swallowed. 'I . . . buried her.'

'Christ.'

'What was I supposed to do? Call the fucking cops?'

Davie put his hand to his jaw and rubbed it vigorously. 'What're we supposed to do now?'

'Get out of here is what we're supposed to do. I've packed up our stuff. We pick it up, JJ's getting the car, we get the fuck out of here.'

He took a deep breath. 'Fuck. Christ. What the hell are you like?'

'I know. I know. It was an accident. Honest to God.'

'Right. Okay. You're right. We'll get out of here. The gold – we have to get the gold.'

I glanced up the road at the Sheriff still talking outside the bank. My instinct was just to leave it. To get as far away, as quickly as possible. Although I knew Davie wouldn't agree, not in a million years. But there was no way I was going to risk falling into conversation with the Sheriff. I would break down and confess all. Or, more probably, he would read me like a book. 'Okay, okay,' I said. 'You get it. I'll go to the hotel and get the bags and—'

At that moment JJ drove out from the car park behind the

Mountain View. He hadn't had to go back to the workshop at all. He'd worked on the car and then driven it down to save him the exertion of walking a hundred yards for lunch. Easiest fifty bucks he ever made. He paused at the car-park entrance to check for traffic. He'd drive up in full view of us and he wouldn't be the least bit fazed by being caught out. And I'd pay up like the biggest sucker in town because I had to.

Behind us, Kelly Cortez came out onto the veranda. 'Davie,' she began, 'your dessert's on the table. Is everything all right?' She paused on the top step and her brow furrowed as she looked out along the main drag.

I looked to Davie to make her go away, but he too was now staring beyond me.

JJ still hadn't pulled out of the car park, even though there was no traffic. He was looking towards us – but not at us. Behind us. Up at the bank, the Sheriff had pushed himself off the hood of his vehicle and was now stepping down onto the road, with EC at his side. Behind Kelly Cortez the swing doors opened and DJ stepped out onto the veranda looking pale and worried. Behind him came CJ and MJ.

They were all looking in the one direction, back up the main street towards the beach.

It was a slow-motion moment stretched to eternity.

When birds beat their wings twice in a lifetime.

When the air freezes and breath becomes impossible.

When every creature but one on God's earth stops and turns to study an object of overwhelming absurdity and horror.

When finally that one creature turns, slower than the rest because he knows all about the curse of inevitability, but that knowledge does not make it any easier to behold the figure staggering up the main street.

The naked girl with no arms.

With the sand stuck by blood to her body.

With the gash across her forehead and the insects buzzing around it.

With the twitching flippers.

With the mouth open and the tongue hanging and the eyes blinking blinking blinking as she forced herself, mind over matter, towards us.

But she just didn't have the strength to do it. She finally collapsed to her knees with an agonised groan. If she could have reached out to me, she would have. But all she could do was to try and make words. Her mouth wouldn't function. She squirmed in the dust of the road like an insufficiently clubbed seal. Her eyes were wide and horrified by her own predicament, she was staring at me, panting, choking on her own blood. She managed to say something through the bubbles of blood erupting from her throat.

'Whhhhy?'

Terror in her eyes.

Terror in mine.

I couldn't move to help her.

She tumbled forward.

'Nooooo!' DJ bellowed from behind and leaped down the steps towards her.

I stood frozen.

'It was an accident,' I said.

26

It was an old-fashioned cell in an old-fashioned wooden three-storey building. There were metal bars and a couple of bunks, just like you'd see in the movies. John Wayne and a boozed-up Dean Martin could have sauntered through the door and not looked out of place. Apart from the fact that nobody could just wander through the door without first getting past Sheriff Sterling Baines, sitting on the porch outside drinking beer from a coffee cup, with a shotgun just out of sight behind him.

Once in a while he came in to check on us. He provided coffee and doughnuts, paid for by the state, and for free he deconstructed our sorry lives for us. He seemed decent enough for a cop, but like most aging professionals was inclined to sentimentalise the past and philosophise at length about the present, when all we wanted was for him to shut the fuck up so we could wallow in our own misery without it being pointed out to us.

'I knew you boys were trouble the moment I saw you,' he said. 'You been in this business long as I have, you know trouble.'

Considering the state we were in when he first saw us, Stevie Wonder could have guessed we were trouble.

'I told you to keep yourselves to yourselves, told you this was my last fortnight an' I wanted it to pass peaceful, but you just couldn't do it. Just couldn't.'

I sat with my head in my hands. Partly through abject misery, and partly because I'd a huge bump coming up on my forehead. When it grew to full size it would match the bump on my arm and be colour co-ordinated with the bruises now emerging on my chest. Davie was similarly well-endowed with external evidence of internal bleeding.

They weren't exactly a lynch mob – they weren't that well-organised. But they showed potential.

It was more of a sudden hysteria, and it would have ended more tragically, especially for me, if they hadn't been torn between venting their fury on me and showing their concern for Michelle, having a fit in the middle of the road. If Dr Cortez hadn't yelled for calm, the numbers taking part in the assault on me and Davie would have doubled; and if Sheriff Baines hadn't discharged a couple of shots into the air then we wouldn't have ended up in a cell at all, but on or in Everglades City's equivalent of Boot Hill.

So we were quite lucky, really.

But, as Oscar Wilde often proclaimed, we were also royally fucked.

The Sheriff knew it too. We didn't even have the nerve to ask for a lawyer. Everything was going to come tumbling out of its own free will: he just had to push the right buttons. But for now he'd make us sweat while he sat on the veranda outside, Methuselah with a shotgun, exuding a calm, confident presence, hoping it would wash out over his city in general and the Mountain View Bar and Grill in particular.

Sheriff Baines had a Deputy called Jesse Stone, an ungainly

big fella who would have been considered handsome if he'd had any kind of a chin; it just seemed to slip away under his bottom lip as if it had been hacked off and then reconstructed without the benefit of a jawbone. The Sheriff was inside getting a re-fill when Stone returned from the Mountain View looking hot and bothered. Kind of the way I'd looked since we'd arrived in Florida.

They tried to talk quietly, but it was a tiny station. Baines gave Stone his drink and poured himself another.

Stone said, 'They're not happy.'

Baines grunted.

'They're talking about coming over here, talking to you.'

'Talking to me?'

'Talking to you with guns.'

Baines nodded. He offered Stone a doughnut. Stone turned it down.

'I'll have it,' Davie said.

'You shut your mouth,' Baines snapped.

I don't know what he was so upset about. At least Davie was talking to him. He hadn't uttered a word to me for hours. Like I'd done something wrong.

'How's the girl?' Baines asked.

'DJ's with her at the hospital. A few of the others. Doesn't look good.'

'So who's leading the war party?'

'No one really. Everyone.'

Baines nodded sagely. 'They're waiting for DJ to come back. They won't do anything without him. His wife, his call.' He glanced back at me. 'I warned you, don't go near her.'

'I didn't,' I said.

Baines shook his head.

'I don't like it,' said Stone. 'We should get them out of here. It's not safe.'

Sheriff Baines lifted his beer-coffee in one hand and his shotgun in the other. 'Deputy, in about two weeks when you get to be Sheriff, I'll give a damn what you think, but right now I'm the Sheriff, and they stay where they are until I get to the bottom of this. Understand?'

'Yes, Sheriff.'

Baines nodded and moved to the door. Stone looked up and saw Davie watching. 'What the fuck are you looking at, asshole?'

'You,' said Davie.

'You want I come in there and whack you with this?' He put a hand on his nightstick.

'Yes, please,' said Davie, 'just so as I can take it off you and ram it up your hole.'

'Would you ever shut up?' I hissed.

'*You* shut up,' Davie snapped back, jabbing a finger at me. 'And I'm not talking to you.'

'Aw, grow up.'

Stone shook his head and went to join Baines outside.

Davie glared at me. 'Yeah, sure, that's fucking rich.'

'It was an accident, I'm sick of telling you.'

'We were *this* close to getting away with it and you couldn't keep your hands to yourself.'

'It was *her*.'

'She hasn't got any fucking hands.'

'You know what I mean. She was all over me.'

'Yeah. Sure. Right. That's just about your fucking level.'

'What's that supposed to mean?'

'Nothing. You and a fucking cripple. Christ.'

'She's beautiful.'

'Not any more she's not. Thanks to you.'

'I didn't do anything.'

'Yeah – right. Your Honour, I was chasing her naked

across the beach and she had a sudden urge to commit suicide.'

'It wasn't the beach. It was the rocks. And it wasn't like that.'

'I don't know what the fuck it was like, Dan, but I know how a fucking prosecutor's going to make it sound. Look at your knees, man. There was a struggle, she was naked, you were chasing her across rocks, she had no arms and couldn't defend herself.'

'She didn't *have* to defend herself!'

'Tell it to the judge, Dan.'

'Brilliant. Great. Don't believe me. Fab friend you are.'

'Fab friend *you* are. If you thought with your head instead of your dick we wouldn't be fucking banged up in here.'

'I didn't . . . ah, what's the fucking point? Here we are. Here we fucking are.'

'*We* being the operative word. What the fuck did *I* do?' He gripped the bars. He called out: 'It was him, Sheriff! Let me go!'

I sat and shook my head at him. Next time he asked me to go on holiday with him I'd definitely dither over it for a while. All I ever wanted out of it was a suntan and a couple of beers.

There was movement at the door and we turned to see Sheriff Baines leading Dr Cortez into the station. She looked grim.

'Howse she doing?' I said.

'Never mind him,' said Baines. 'How's she doing?'

'They're operating on her now. There's a clot.'

'Here's another one,' said Davie, pointing at me.

'Would you ever fuck up?' I snapped.

'*You* fuck up.'

'You make me—'

'Will you both just *be quiet*.' It was Baines. He was an

old guy, but authoritative. We stopped arguing. I came to the bars of the cell and asked if Michelle was going to be all right.

Kelly Cortez shook her head. 'They're going to be a couple of hours at least. Won't really know what the damage is until they get in there. What *were* you thinking of?'

I shrugged helplessly. 'I wasn't thinking of anything. We were having fun. Why doesn't anyone believe me?'

Sheriff Baines came to stand beside her. 'Didn't say I didn't believe you, son. Michelle fucked half this town – if you'll excuse my French, Doctor – no reason to believe she didn't try to fuck you as well. But like I say, I warned you, you play with fire you're going to get burned.'

I put my hands on the bars. 'What about DJ?'

Kelly raised her eyebrows. 'I gave him a ride back from the hospital. Nothing he can do until it's over. He's gonna collect some of her things, take them to her later on.'

'Did he strike you as being in a forgiving mood?'

Before she could respond, a stone came through a side window of the police station. It rolled across the floor and sat there, worrying us.

From outside Deputy Stone hollered, 'Sheriff! You better get out here!'

Sheriff Baines calmly lifted his shotgun again and checked that it was loaded. He nodded at me. 'DJ's back. They've had a few minutes to discuss the situation. Now I expect they've all gone and had a vote. I guess we got ourselves a lynch mob.'

He turned for the door. Davie came to stand beside me at the bars. As Dr Cortez turned to follow the Sheriff he reached through the bars and grabbed her arm. Gently. 'You still owe me a dessert,' he said.

She shrugged his hand off. 'And you still owe me an explanation.'

'That's easy,' said Davie. 'I'm travelling with a cretin.'

I would have responded, but I was too busy cowering down as I caught the briefest glimpse of the angry mob that had gathered outside the station. Sheriff Baines closed the door firmly behind him before Dr Cortez could reach it. Instead she moved to a window and looked out.

'Ten or twenty of them?' Davie asked.

'More like fifty.'

'They have clubs and stuff to beat us?'

'They have guns and stuff to shoot you.'

'Why doesn't he call for help?' I asked.

'Doesn't reckon he needs any,' said Dr Cortez.

'You should go out there and say you're sorry,' said Davie.

'They'd hang me,' I said.

Davie shrugged. There was actually a hint of a smile on his face. I hated him deeply. There was clearly a part of him that was enjoying this situation. I'd seen the same look on his face in the penthouse bedroom of the Don CeSar after I'd shot Michael O'Ryan in the head. It was the exposure to danger. The not knowing whether you'd escape from a given situation. Whereas I knew perfectly well. We were totally safe in our cell. Outside, a United States Sheriff on the point of retirement and his chinless wonder Deputy were having a nice chat with the locals, who were kind-hearted but inclined to let off steam once in a while.

Another stone came through another window. Voices were raised. I recognised two of them.

DJ: 'He attacked my wife, he battered her head off a rock, for all I know he raped her as well, and you're telling me we gotta stand here and wait for some prosecutor to drive up from Naples?'

Sheriff Baines: 'No, DJ, you don't got to stand there, you can go home and wait for the prosecutor to drive up from

Naples. This isn't just a simple case, DJ. It may be these men are wanted for other crimes, or that the FBI need to get involved. In the meantime I haven't even been able to examine the crime scene because I can't risk leaving them in there in case you guys go haywire.'

DJ: 'FBI? We don't need the FBI, Sheriff! If they're guilty of other stuff, then they'll take them out of the county and we won't never see them again. That's not how we do things round here.'

'DJ, we do things right.'

'I don't disagree with you, Sheriff, and the right thing to do is string 'em up.'

There came a roar of support from the rest of the mob.

'Can't do that, DJ.'

'Can, too. You send them out, Sheriff, or we come in and get them!'

There was another roar. Louder.

It was like listening to a bad radio play, but with the added bonus that at any moment one of the characters could step out of the speakers and kill you.

'You don't try and come in here, DJ.'

'What you gonna do, Sheriff, shoot us – shoot us all?'

'Many as I can pick off.'

There was a buzz of excitement through the crowd. A showdown. Like a hoedown, with guns. Other familiar voices:

JJ: 'You tell 'im, DJ!'

CJ: 'Send those sons of bitches out, Sheriff!'

Stone: 'You put those guns down now, folks, and go on home!'

Sheriff Baines: 'I'm telling you, DJ, you don't put one foot on that step.'

'They killed my wife.'

'She's not dead, DJ.'

'It's looking that way. Could have been any of our wives.'

'From what I remember, she was.'

It was a brave but foolhardy point to make.

'You ain't got no call to talk like that, Sheriff.'

'And you ain't got no call to come here with a lynch mob. They done something wrong, they'll pay for it. My way, not your way.'

'Your way they'll get some fancy lawyer and they'll walk.'

'Well, that's America, son.'

'No,' said DJ. '*This* is America.'

There was a sudden explosive blast, and a split second later Sheriff Sterling Baines, thirteen days short of retirement, came flying through the station door with a hole the shape of a medium-sized pizza blown from his chest and out through his back.

Dr Cortez screamed.

And so did I.

27

I was busy thinking my last thoughts on this mortal coil, and they were pretty much the same as ever: they should have been about love and remorse and Patricia, but instead, inevitably, they were of sex and food and rock'n'roll. At least 5 per cent of them were. The rest were about death and how sore it would be. I am not built for pain. I am built for pleasure. Paper cuts and nettle stings can push me over the edge.

I stood frozen at the bars. There was a kind of vacuum by the door; it was open and inviting everyone in, but the death of Sheriff Baines – and he was undeniably dead, you could pitch a tent in the hole in his chest – had momentarily stilled the mob. Dr Cortez was already bending down to the Sheriff, but she didn't even feel for a pulse. If I'd been on the other side of the bars I could have done it for her. I'm good on pulses.

Davie hissed: 'Kelly – please, the keys – get the keys.'

She looked up at him blankly and nodded, but she made no move to clip them off the Sheriff's belt.

'Kelly!'

This second request seemed to shake her from her trance,

but it was too late. Deputy Stone came through the door, his face thick with sweat, his eyes jumping with fear. He rammed it shut behind him and bolted it. But it was a wooden door with a tiny lock. Mosquitoes would give it a hard time. He backed away from it with his gun out. A moment later it was thumped hard. A rock smashed through another window.

'Deputy,' Davie said calmly, 'you have to let us out of here.'

'You just shut the fuck up!' Stone glanced down at Sheriff Baines. 'Christ All Mighty,' he said. 'Christ All Mighty.'

'Deputy, you're in charge now.' Davie sounded for once like the police officer he had been. 'That door isn't going to hold them. No matter what you think about us, you have to get us out of here.'

'I don't have to do nothing!' Stone yelled. Another rock came crashing through. 'Christ, oh Christ,' said Stone. He looked to Dr Cortez for reassurance. 'He's not dead, tell me he's not dead.'

When it was bleeding obvious.

Cortez could only shake her head.

'You have to call for *help*,' I said.

'*Help?*' Stone snapped. 'Where the hell's help going to come from?'

He jumped as Cortez put a hand on his arm. 'They'll come from Naples.'

'Not for hours,' said Stone, 'not for hours.'

There was a sudden thump against the door which rattled violently on its hinges.

'You still have to call them.'

Stone steadied himself against a chair for a moment, took a deep breath, nodded at Cortez, then crossed to the phone. But before he could lift it to his ear, DJ shouted from outside.

'Jesse! Can you hear me, Jesse?'

Jesse hesitated, then put the receiver down and moved cautiously across to one of the smashed windows. I couldn't see what he could see, but it was pretty easy to guess: ranks of angry townsfolk carrying flaming torches yelling, 'Kill the beast! Kill!' The only difference between us and Frankenstein's Monster was that we didn't have bolts through our necks. Yet.

'I hear you, DJ!'

'We've got nothing against you, Jesse, and we're sorry about the Sheriff. Gun just went off – was an accident, y'hear?'

'I hear, DJ. Kind of a convenient accident!'

'I'm telling you, Jesse, and I got a hundred witnesses out here!'

'Well, line them up and I'll take their statements.'

It was an unexpected piece of wit from the man with no chin.

Naturally, DJ ignored it. 'We don't want there to be no more accidents, Jesse, you think about that. All we want is for you to send those two boys out.'

'I can't do that, DJ, you know that.'

'You want us to come in and get them?'

'You can try.' The right words, but the intonation was all wrong; then he made matters worse by yelling: 'And help's on its way! I just called it in! Now you folks all disperse peacefully!' with a voice which broke halfway through, like puberty had just arrived.

'Jesse, first thing we did was cut the telephone line.'

'Don't need no telephone, DJ, we got the Internet.'

'Don't you need a telephone line for that?'

This seemed to flummox Stone for a moment. He was distracted by Cortez holding up her cell phone. Stone smiled gratefully.

'How dumb you think I am, DJ? We all got cell phones. Help's coming, and you had all best go home.'

'We're not going anywhere without those boys, Jesse. Your decision.'

Stone glanced back at us. Then he looked at the remains of Sheriff Baines on the floor. He'd sweated through his uniform and was now dripping on the floor. Cortez was looking at her phone. She bit at her lip. She whispered: 'Low battery.' Stone took another deep breath, and I suffered a stroke.

Another window exploded inwards. Stone ducked down clutching his head as glass sprayed all around him. Ducked down, stayed down. He sat on the floor and let go of his gun. His eyes were tight shut to stop the tears from coming out; his mouth was elongated, showing two rows of perfect teeth clenched hard together in an unintentionally skeletal grin. He was half scared to death. He hadn't joined the Everglades City PD for this. He'd joined for the uniform and the gun and to give out speeding tickets and flirt with the tourists. Not to get shot at or make life or death decisions.

Deputy Stone cowered down as the mob grew louder; the hysteria was growing.

'Deputy,' I said, 'please just let us out. Just get the keys and let us out.'

'I can't.' He wouldn't open his eyes.

Davie rattled the bars of our cell. His knuckles were white against the cool metal, his eyes electric. 'Hey, DJ!' he bellowed.

'Davie?'

'DJ! DJ!'

If he had a plan, he wasn't telling me. Probably because it involved giving me up to save his own sorry arse. He'd blame me for everything and slabber his way out of a premature death.

'Can you hear me, DJ?!'

'I hear you!'

'Well, why don't you come and get us then, you retard fuck!' Davie rattled the bars again. His cheeks were red, his brow furrowed and the grooves on it ran with sweat, as if he had a paddyfield on his forehead.

'Davie, for fuck sake!' I hissed. Naturally, he ignored me. So I tried to pull him off the bars, but he was a trained fighting machine, and I could do shorthand. He threw me across the cell and returned to rattle some more.

'Come on, you inbred fuck! Come and get us!'

'What are you *doing*?' Kelly Cortez hissed.

Davie ignored her as well.

'I'll tell you why you're not coming in, you fucking dough-bag!' he screamed. 'You're fucking scared shitless because Jesse Stone is standing here ready to take you all on! He's one man against a fucking mob! But he's not moving because he's a police officer and he swore to uphold the law and he'll do that and he'll stand here and he'll shoot you one by one as you come through that door, and when he runs out of bullets he'll club you down, and when he can't hit you any more he'll go down fighting and scratching because he knows the difference between right and wrong even if you don't! He's a man, DJ, and you are a bunch of fucking old women!'

It was Davie Kincaid as General Patton, or Sylvester Stallone. It was James Stewart barracking low-down dirty politics in *Mr Smith Goes to Washington*. And it seemed to work, for about thirty seconds. Then there came five separate shotgun blasts which tore holes out of the door and the front wall of the station.

As we ducked down again I yelled, 'That was fucking smart!' at Davie.

'Oh yeah?' he said, and I followed his gaze to where Stone

was slowly rising through the gunsmoke. His gun was back in his hand; he was checking it was loaded. Then he turned and nodded at Dr Cortez.

'Kelly,' he said, 'take those keys off the Sheriff, get the suspects out of that cell and see if you can get them out the back way.'

Cortez hesitated for just a moment, then smiled at the Deputy. She bent to the Sheriff's corpse and felt along his belt for the keys. She had to move him slightly to get at them; she paused to wipe the blood from them, then hurried across to our cell. She unlocked the gate and let us out. She touched Davie on the arm and said, 'This way.'

'I'll come too,' I said.

Kelly led the way. I made a point of not looking too closely at the Sheriff's body as we passed. Davie stopped for a moment. 'Good man,' he said to Deputy Stone. Stone nodded, but didn't take his eyes off the front door.

We moved down a narrow corridor, through a small kitchen towards a solid wooden back door. As Cortez reached up to unbolt it, Davie grabbed her arm. He put a finger to his lips. 'Listen,' he whispered.

We listened.

They were waiting.

They weren't trying to break in, just hoping we'd run into their ambush.

'They must think we're really stupid,' I said.

Davie now took charge. He led us back up the corridor. He only had to shake his head at Stone to bring him up to date. Davie then bent to the Sheriff's corpse and began to remove his gun.

'Stop right there!' Stone pointed his own gun at Davie.

'We can make a fight of this,' Davie said, his fingers tantalisingly close to Baines's weapon.

'You leave it. Maybe I have to save your lives, doesn't

mean we're on the same side.' Davie's fingers nevertheless inched forward. 'I'm telling you, boy, I'll shoot you if I have to. Be doing everyone a favour.'

'C'mon, Davie,' I said.

Davie gave a slight shake of his head, then rose from the Sheriff's body and followed Cortez and me to the stairs.

'This where the teleporter is?' I asked.

'Shut the fuck up,' Stone snapped.

As we hit the bottom step two things happened at once: the front door exploded off its hinges, and a flaming garbage bag came through one of the side windows. It immediately set about burning the station down. Stone raised his gun and fired once through the window, and again through the open door. There was a stampede of footsteps away from both spaces; but moments later shots were returned.

'Move it!' Stone shouted.

We moved it.

I had certain fears about the wisdom of this. I shouted, 'We're going upstairs in a burning wooden building!'

They ignored me, of course. Even I ignored me. I was just pointing out the patently bloody obvious.

The first floor was where Sheriff Baines kept his files and lost property. Davie spotted a fire extinguisher and an axe in a glass case on the far wall. He smashed the glass and removed the axe then followed us on up to the second floor. There was more gunfire from below. The rising smoke seemed to be keeping pace with us.

While Kelly and Davie ran ahead, I paused for a moment at a window on the landing between the floors. It gave me my first real view of the mob. There seemed to be about a hundred of them, but they weren't all involved in the assault on the police station. As far as I could see, there were maybe a dozen taking part; the rest were watching, cheering them on. They were spread out like spectators at an Eleventh Night bonfire; loyal to the cause, but not always willing to participate. Even at this height I could see JJ moving amongst them handing out bottles of beer. Great. There was a free bar at the Mountain View and I was missing it.

As I reached the second floor I found Davie and Kelly examining the far wall. In front of me was a single bed and a desk covered in papers. There was also a suitcase half-filled with neatly folded clothes. Sheriff Baines evidently lived above the shop, but was getting packed up for his retirement. Davie ran his fingers along the paintwork.

'What're you doing?' I asked.

By way of response he raised the axe and struck it hard against the wall; hard paint and splinters erupted. Kelly turned her face away against the shrapnel.

'Ice-cream store next door,' he said. 'If we can get through, maybe we can escape that way.' He raised his eyebrows hopefully, then turned back and started hacking away. I tried to keep look-out on the stairs but the smoke was getting to my eyes; it was thicker, blacker now, harder to catch a breath.

No more gunshots. Maybe DJ had surrendered.

I shouted back to Davie, 'Howse it going?'

'Getting there!' He managed a smile for Kelly. 'Still waiting for that dessert.'

'You get us next door, I'll buy you an ice cream.'

'Let's be devils, and steal one.'

Kelly smiled. I don't know what they were so smiley about. We were going to die, and with the way the fire was raging beneath us, the ice cream would have melted by the time we got to it.

Behind me a window cracked. I turned to it just as there came screams from below; as I peered down at the crowd I saw it suddenly split to make space for Deputy Jesse

Stone as he came charging out of the station. He was on fire.

'Jesus Christ,' I said with enough horror for Kelly and Davie to hurry to my side. Together we watched as Stone fell to the ground screaming and writhing in agony.

The mob watched him helplessly for several eternal moments. Even in their frenzy they knew he was beyond help.

Or the sort of help that would save him.

DJ saved him in a different way. He stepped up, raised his shotgun, and blasted his head off.

28

Safe as houses. That's what my old da used to say.

If you could see me now, Da.

Safe as burning houses.

Kelly Cortez sobbed by the window while Davie hacked away at the wall, pausing only to cough. I would have offered to help, but I was worried about splinters. Besides, I had to keep look-out.

'They're not coming,' I said weakly, peering into the thick smoke.

'They're still not coming.'

'No sign of them at all.'

I was trying to keep our spirits up, but it was a thankless task. I knew they weren't coming, because it was bloody obvious that they didn't need to. The fire would soon do their work for them. It would also cover up a multitude of sins. I could already see the headlines in the local paper. EC reading it at the front desk of the hotel: *Tragic Fire Claims Five* in huge letters, and smaller, beneath, *Sheriff Was on Eve of Retirement* and then: *Tourists Perish*. A sub-editor to the end.

There was a new sound then: the groan of timber as it

cracked and split in the heat. We were on top of a bonfire which would soon collapse in on itself.

'Davie – for fuck sake hurry up!'

'Hold your horses,' he hissed back.

Kelly was now coughing badly. So was I. I was burning from the inside out, and vice versa. It was only a matter of time.

Another half-dozen blows.

Davie dropped the axe to his side and kicked hard against the wall. It collapsed inwards. This wasn't altogether good news. The hole sucked the smoke into it and the flames towards it, and for several moments we flapped about lost in the darkness, but then it cleared enough for Davie to guide us through into the adjoining building.

We knelt on the floor for a minute trying to catch our breath; it was quickly filling with smoke, but it wasn't anything like as bad as next door. This floor was used mostly for storage. There were cartons of ingredients for the ice cream, tins of flavouring, cardboard boxes stuffed full of wafers. We could have had a grand party, but someone had sent Death an invitation.

Davie got to his feet first and urged us to the top of the stairs, but instead of leading us down he stopped and shook his head.

'What is it?' said Kelly.

'We're too close.' He was looking at the far wall, which divided the ice-cream parlour from the vacant building next door. If we could get through that wall as well, we'd be further removed from the mob and stand a better chance of slipping away unseen.

'Go for it,' I said. But instead he tossed me the axe.

'Here,' he snapped. 'I'm supposed to be resting my fucking arm, not chopping down a house.'

Perhaps he had a point.

The Axeman Cometh.

I attacked the wall as if my life depended on it, and it did.

I heaved, I thrust, I whacked, I destroyed. After a couple of minutes Davie took the axe back off me and said, 'You're doing more harm than good. Go and keep watch.'

I was good at keeping watch. It suited me down to the ground.

Kelly came and stood beside me. Her face was black, her eyes were red and her hair was caked to her head.

'Bet you didn't expect this when you had your Frosties this morning,' I said.

She blinked and rubbed at her eye, even though as a doctor she should have known better. 'You mean Frosted Flakes.'

'Why would you do this?' I said, changing the subject.

She glanced back at Davie. 'He has a nice ass.'

'What's wrong with mine?'

'Bony,' she said.

I shrugged. 'I'm married, I would have said no anyway.'

'Yeah,' she said. 'I'm not your type.'

'How come you're not with your mates outside?'

'How do you know I'm not?'

'Ah right – you're a double agent.'

'Yup. And loyal to the end, because I'm going to burn to death.'

'That's often the fate of double agents,' I said.

Davie yelled across from the wall. 'Will you two stop fucking blethering and give me a hand?'

His chopping had exposed a hollow space between our wall and the building next door. He'd already cut through half a dozen of its wooden slats. Together we were able to peel several more of them back until they cracked and split, allowing us to squeeze through the gap and into the vacant building. Here the air was cool and musty and far enough away from the inferno that was now the police station to not immediately suck in all of its fumes. The floor was covered in odd bits of discarded machinery and boxes full of yellowing files.

Kelly went to the top of the stairs, then stopped us again and listened. We could hear the distant yells of the mob, but nothing close at hand. We moved cautiously down the darkened stairs, listened again at the landing on the next floor, then continued our descent to the ground. The three buildings had the same basic design, so even though it was almost pitch black – the only light a very vague orange glow from the fire squeezing through shuttered windows – Kelly was able to lead us across the floor and down the corridor to the back door without any great difficulty. There were a lot of empty beer cans littering the corridor; local kids probably used it as an illicit drinking den – which was good news for us as Davie was able to open the back door effortlessly rather than having to battle with the large padlock which someone had previously cracked apart but left hanging in place so that anyone taking a cursory glance at it would suppose it was still doing its job.

We crossed a small backyard to a white painted wooden fence with a gate which was bolted shut. Davie eased the bolt across and peered out into an alley which ran for several hundred yards along the back of the main street. To the right, but shielded from us by another wooden fence, was the back door of the police station where some of the mob had lain in wait for us. We couldn't tell if they were still there. To the left of us were the backs of the other stores which lined the main street; on the other side of the alley there were the back gardens of several wooden bungalows. There were no lights visible within. Probably everyone had gone out to enjoy the lynching. It was good, that. It showed a strong sense of community.

I said, 'What about the car?'

'You want to go down to the Mountain View and ask JJ for the keys?' Davie turned to Kelly. 'What about yours?'

'I live about five miles out of town. I cycled in.'

'Any chance of a doubler?' I asked.

Davie scowled at me and Kelly looked mystified. 'We have to find somewhere to lie low,' he explained. 'They'll be sobered by the morning.'

I'm not sure if he actually believed that, but it was something to cling to, like a life raft with a hole in it.

We began to jog along the alley.

'How's your arm?' I whispered.

'Sore,' said Davie.

'I could write you a prescription,' said Kelly.

From behind us there came a roar, and we turned to see one of the walls of the police station slowly collapse in on itself. The others quickly followed, causing the first and second floors to concertina down on top of them. There was a cheer from the crowd as flames shot up into the night sky.

One house down, two to go.

We continued along the alley for several hundred yards. I couldn't smell the smoke any more. We were getting close to the water: there was a slight fleck of sand on the smooth breeze and we could hear crisp waves breaking on the beach. It had frightened me before, but now I was ready to make friends with the sea and all of its creatures. They weren't half as terrifying as people were. Ordinary people who sold souvenirs and served hamburgers and cleaned your room by day became wild and unpredictable by night, shooting policemen and burning hapless tourists alive. There were more sharks on the land than there were in the ocean.

At the end of the alley was a long stretch of open ground leading to the beach. It was unlit, but there was a moon high in the sky which might as well have been plugged into the mains.

'If we get caught out there, we're finished,' said Davie. 'C'mon – this way.'

We hadn't elected him leader, he had just assumed the role. I was better with adverbs, and Kelly Cortez could probably have bested him when it came to creating a mean poultice, but Davie was built for this: he was Rambo, to my Dumbo.

He led us into the back garden of one of the bungalows and up to the back door. He sent us left and right along the outside of the dwelling to check for lights and other signs of life.

Nothing.

When Davie tried the back door, it was unlocked. Parts of America are still like that. You can pop out to lynch someone, secure in the knowledge that nobody is going to steal your furniture while you are away.

The house smelled of cigarettes and pizza, mostly because there were overflowing ashtrays in every room and crust-filled boxes piled up in the kitchen. Davie went from room to room, and we followed, because he seemed to know what he was doing.

'You know who lives here?' Davie asked.

I shook my head.

'Not you, you Clampett.'

'Think they're on welfare,' Kelly said.

She was probably right. If the bungalow had had wheels its inhabitants would have been classed as trailer trash. But one country's trailer trash is another's privileged elite. They were poor, but they had cable. They were unemployed, but they had a computer. They didn't appear to have a phone, but they were on the Internet. Davie immediately switched the computer on in one of the bedrooms and called up AOL. Then he said, 'Fuck,' as it demanded a password.

We gathered around him, trying to smother the glow from the screen and guess the password from the odd billion words in existence, a password which was all that stood between us and emailing the cops, the Feds and the Cavalry.

'Fuck,' Davie said again.

'They're fucking trailer trash,' I said. 'They can't know that many words.'

He typed in the two first names he found on an overdue credit-card bill on the floor. John, then Clara. No use. He tried their surnames. He tried Miami Dolphins, Garth Brooks, Elvis, grits, crackers and gravy. I suggested Big Mac, moron, inbred and hillbilly.

From behind us a small voice said: 'We ain't no hillbillies.'

'*Fuck!*' we exclaimed as one, apart from the doctor, who had better breeding.

Davie recovered his faculties first and spun, ready to chop whoever it was with his good arm, but for a moment he couldn't see anyone at all. Then a boy of not more than thirteen began to emerge from beneath the bed. His hair was tousled and he was wearing a grubby T-shirt, boxer shorts and a troubled expression.

'Hi,' I said, always ready to rescue a dire situation. 'We're from the local education board, want to know why you been missing so much school, son.'

'Don't talk garbage,' the boy snapped back. 'I know who you are.'

'Okay,' I said.

The boy raised a cell phone to his ear. 'I just gotta press this button, tell them where you are, you're dead fucking meat . . .'

I have been intimidated by a lot of people in many and varied situations, but I wasn't going to take this kind of crap from a spotty teenager. So I turned menacing. 'And what if we just take the phone off you before you can do that, and break your wrist at the same time?'

'Then I shoot you with this.' He brought his other hand forward. In the glow of the computer screen we saw the outline of a gun.

'Ah,' I said. 'A gun. Every home should have one.'

It could have been a toy.

I felt Davie tense beside me. He was working out the odds. Knowing American gun culture, the chances were about fifty-fifty. Add to that the fact that although it was a small room, the boy was far enough away to make suddenly rushing him a decidedly risky option. Too risky. Davie stood down. Kelly tried the friendly doctor approach.

'So,' she said, 'where are your parents?'

'Fuck them, they went to the wrestlin', wouldn't take me 'cause I got drunk.'

'When are they due back?'

'Tomorrow, some time. It's in fucking Tallahassee.'

'They like the wrestlin', yeah?'

'Who the fuck doesn't?'

'Fair point. So . . . what's your name?'

'Jamie.'

'So, Jamie, what're we going to do about this?'

Jamie shrugged. 'I heard about you.' He nodded at me. 'You're the one boned the spastic.'

He was wrong on both counts, but I nodded anyway.

'Fucking asking for it, that bitch.' Jamie was thirteen and seemed to have an IQ to match. I was getting worried about Michelle's reputation. She needed someone to stand up for her. Oh yeah, he was just down the road.

'Too right,' I said, 'fucking bitch.'

284

Jamie nodded enthusiastically. We were bonding.

'We're not looking for trouble, Jamie. So I hit the bitch, nothing wrong with that, you're going to help us get away, right?'

'Hell no,' said Jamie.

'What then?' I said. 'You going to shoot us all and be the big hero?'

Jamie hesitated for a moment. 'Hadn't thought of that.'

Davie rolled his eyes.

Jamie smiled. 'I gotta better idea.' He nodded at me again. 'You gotta credit card, spastic man?'

'Sure.'

'Well, get it out.'

I handed him a garish First Trust card. He examined it like it was an alien artefact, but then recognising the Visa symbol he nodded and pointed at the computer. 'Here's the deal. We get on the net, I call up some porn sites, I use your credit card to watch whatever the fuck I want to watch for as long as I want.'

'And we get?'

'You get to sleep in the next room until morning.'

'We need to use your email,' said Davie, 'or your cell phone.'

'You get one call – when I'm finished.'

'We need it now.'

'When I'm finished or no deal.'

Davie looked at me, then Kelly. I shrugged. Kelly nodded. She was more decisive than I was. Kelly and the rest of the civilised world.

'Okay,' said Davie.

Jamie smiled. 'Fucking A,' he said.

29

Jamie, already ensconced behind the computer, shouted directions to the bedroom he had assigned to us. Clearly there were other brothers who had been allowed to go to the wrestling in Tallahassee. There were two sets of bunk beds, all with the bedclothes carelessly thrown back. Heavily muscled wrestlers glared out from posters on the wall. Jamie was probably the eldest because he'd graduated to his own bedroom. He was a self-confident little shit, and he had us over a barrel.

I pointed this out to Davie. 'You're supposed to be the killer elite, why don't you just take him down?'

'What's the point? He thinks he has the upper hand, but in fact we have. We get to rest up, he gets to stand guard over us. Someone comes to the door he'll chase them. He's having way too much fun.'

And he was.

The walls could have been described as paper-thin, but that would have been doing paper-thin a disservice. Every beat, every grunt, every groan – and he wasn't even next door; he was along the hall, and turn left.

Davie lay down on one of the lower bunks, and after a

bit of hesitation and a few furtive looks in my direction, Kelly Cortez joined him. He put an arm around her and she put her head on his chest. I had no idea what she saw in him, apart from his good looks and muscles, his commanding ways and roguish charm. But she'd learn. That was all surface stuff. Once she got to really know him she'd soon be begging for a bit of freckle and a bony arse. And I only had her word for the bony arse. Patricia had never complained. At least to me.

So I stood by the window and kept guard. Or, I stood by the window and looked out, but I wasn't really seeing. I was exhausted, but I couldn't sleep, my mind was wandering; it was the kind of hazy twilight world you find yourself in when watching a coal fire late at night, or indeed, a burning police station. There wasn't much of it left. Jamie's brothers' bedroom window gave me a half-view of the back of the main street. The ice-cream parlour had more or less collapsed as well. The third, vacant building was still holding up, but would soon go the way of the others.

Down the hall, and left, Jamie moaned in ecstasy again.

'Christ,' I said, 'how many times can he do it in one night?'

Davie laughed. 'What is he, thirteen? How many times could you do it at that age?'

'Fair point,' I said. 'We could be here for days.'

Kelly *hhhmmmed* contentedly at the prospect.

I'd known Patricia for twenty years and hadn't known her to *hhhmmm* contentedly at anything, unless you count the time she successfully snaffled my Marks & Spencer chocolate éclair while pretending to rummage for an Alpen bar in the fridge. I smiled at the thought of it. It was now after midnight. Back home she'd be tossing and turning in that unsettled hour before the alarm went off. In another life she would already have been up with Little Stevie.

Unaccountably, I felt tears welling up. Stevie in heaven. Usually I detest mawkish things, and always I detest anything Eric Clapton produces, but he had written a song about the accidental death of his son and I had lately found the tune stuck in my head. Even if you didn't know the background to it, it was incredibly moving. Elton John had tried something similar with 'English Rose', his re-working of 'Candle in the Wind' for Princess Diana. It was a pile of shite.

I lay down on the bottom mattress of the second set of bunks and clasped my hands behind my head.

'So what's the plan then, mastermind?' I asked.

There was no response. Their easy, rhythmic breath told me they were sleeping. Dr Cortez had her head on his chest and her left hand on his stomach. She was a good-looking woman, but there was bound to be a skeleton in the closet. Nobody fell for a man that quickly. Or at least, this man. Or at least, without huge amounts of alcohol being involved. I wondered how much Davie had told her about our misadventures. I suspected very little. They'd only had lunch. You couldn't just slip in murder and mayhem between courses. But he might have brought up the gold. Casually. Or thumped the table and said: 'I've got twelve gold bars in the bank!' Perhaps that was it, she was a gold digger.

Down the corridor, and left, Jamie climaxed again.

Davie was wrong, we weren't in control. Jamie held the upper hand. I just hoped he washed it after he was finished.

I had the most perfect dream: dancing with Patricia while Joe and The Clash sang 'Armageddon Time' in the background; Mouse sat in the corner eating a bag of chips; my mum and dad were putting candles into a birthday cake and Little Stevie ran about the dance floor in his bare feet shouting, 'Michael Owen! Michael Owen!'

And like all the best dreams, it ended abruptly: a crash and bang and I sat up suddenly, hitting my head on the wooden slats of the bunk above me. It was daylight; opposite me Davie and Kelly looked as surprised as I was, staring at the door and the three furious kids standing there.

'What the fuck are you doing?' one of them spat.

'Dad!' shouted another.

The third looked wide-eyed at Kelly, who was pulling her shirt down over her bra.

I'd been dreaming about football and chips, and they'd been fumbling in the dark.

'Dad!'

We got to our feet.

Down the hall, and left, a deep, ragged man's voice shouted: 'Jamie! What the fuck! I told you about that stuff!'

'It wasn't me! It was *them*!'

'Dad! There's burglars!'

'It's them, Dad!' Jamie yelled. 'They held me prisoner! They killed DJ's wife! They burned down the police station!'

This was clearly news to the kids in the doorway. They quickly backed away. Davie followed them out into the hall. Kelly went after him. I decided to hold the rear.

'Just hold on a minute,' Davie was saying.

'Jamie, now that's not true. Hi, I'm Dr Cortez, we were just—'

I heard the unmistakable sound of bullets being pumped into a chamber. Davie reappeared in the doorway, with Kelly right behind. He slammed the door shut then hurried to the window and pushed it open. He gave Kelly a hand up and helped her through. I then pushed in front of him and climbed up; he gave me a shove to speed my passage. I tumbled down into an overgrown front garden that fed directly onto the alley at the rear of the main street. Davie jumped down behind me. We'd just reached the top of the garden and were stepping over a low wooden fence, when Jamie's dad started shooting.

He was either a really bad shot, or he only meant to scare us. They were shotgun cartridges, but packed with rice, for maximum effect and minimum damage. It wasn't the sort of rice you could enjoy a good curry with, but if it hit you it could have much the same effect on your arse. If Jamie's dad had appreciated the full extent of our crimes, or the madness that had gone on in the town while he was out at the wrestling, he probably would have used live ammo. As it was the rice shots blasted well above us, but they were incentive enough for us to race away along the alley, keeping our heads down as far as we could without scraping them on the ground.

Jamie's dad might not have been aware of what he had stumbled upon, but the gunfire served as a warning call to the rest of the town. Davie had advanced the theory that daylight would bring sobriety and therefore calm to the mob. Whereas it appeared now that the opposite was true, that instead of subsiding, their anger had mounted with the realisation that they'd dug such a hole for themselves that the only solution was to fill that hole with our dead bodies.

It started with shouting and pointing. With heads appearing at windows and figures at doors.

Then came the abuse and stone-throwing.

We kept moving, ducking down and dancing this way and that to avoid injury. It was like running down the Falls Road in a Union Jack suit. A lump of asphalt whacked into my back and I stumbled. Davie kept me up. 'Come on, Dan!' he shouted and urged me forward.

This was bad enough, and we hadn't even encountered the real players. These were just scared residents who believed everything they'd heard about us.

Davie led us into another back garden and then around a house which fronted the main street. We took cover behind a bush and sneaked a look back up the several hundred metres to the Mountain View Bar and Grill. Several vehicles, including our own, were revving up, and as we watched, DJ came down the steps, shotgun in one hand, bottle of wine in the other. Behind him came all his regulars, plus a few I hadn't seen before. One tripped on the top step and pitched forward onto the road, smashing the bottle he was carrying. The others laughed and swore at him.

They'd been drinking all night. Not good.

It was also bad because Davie chose that moment to lead us across to the other side of the road. He had no choice, really, because behind us the stones were starting to land again as the residents ventured closer. But if we'd turned and said *Boo* they might have scattered. Instead we hurried across the road as fast as we could into the shelter of a yellow awning over a hamburger joint, but not fast enough to avoid being spotted by the driver of the lead vehicle.

He let out a shout, the rest of DJ's lynch mob jumped on board, and in a moment their little convoy was speeding up the street after us; they were hanging out of the doors and clinging onto the roof, screaming and yelling and blasting their horns as they came.

Davie pushed us forward again, skirting the restaurant and leading us down amongst the trash cans behind it. Kelly stopped abruptly.

'Kelly!' Davie yelled.

She shook her head. 'Go on,' she said. 'I'll talk to them.'

'Don't be fucking daft, they'll tear you to pieces!'

'No, they won't. I haven't done anything.'

'Kelly! Please! That's not how mobs work!'

'Davie, go!' She was doing her Captain Oates. Her 'leave me here to die'. If it bought me some extra time, then I was quite happy for her to do it, but Davie looked devastated.

'You don't have to do this,' he said.

'I know. Just go. I'll be fine.'

There came a roar of overly souped-up engines from the forecourt.

'Go!'

Davie hesitated for just a moment longer, then turned away. Possibly he was influenced by me pulling his shirt as well. Kelly stepped back towards the front of the restaurant. We started running again, this time through the back gardens of the houses on this side of the street. Most of the fences were low enough to hurdle, and we took several with matching strides as if we were runners competing in an Olympic event, albeit one in which spectators were free to throw stones and aim garden implements at you.

We came to a taller fence which Davie climbed effort-lessly, but despite several efforts I just couldn't pull myself over it.

'Come on, you fat fucker!' he yelled.

'I'm doing my fucking best,' I screamed back, and I was: it just wasn't good enough.

Perched on the fence, he must have been aware of them coming. He must have known that whatever Kelly had mounted in way of our defence had been brushed utterly aside, because the evidence was there before him. DJ, JJ, CJ, all of them, streaming across the gardens behind us, clambering awkwardly over the fences we had taken in one stride. Drunk but determined, a ragged army, but still an army. We had had a lead, but it was like being in front in the Grand National. You still had to get over Becher's Brook. It was a great leveller. They must have seen him, because a shout went up and then they were all hollering. Davie grabbed my hand and pulled me up onto the top of the fence; it was a rickety wooden effort and could hardly hold both our weights. I jumped down onto the other side before it gave way. I was already bounding away towards the next fence when I realised that Davie wasn't following.

I stopped. 'Davie?'

He looked back and shrugged.

'Davie, don't be so fuckin' stupid!' I shouted.

'Toffo,' he said, then slipped back down the other side of the fence to face the mob.

30

Davie gave them a run for it, that's for sure.

I heard yelps and screams and the crack and split of picket fences being demolished; I heard the dull slap of punches and the curses that followed their connection. There were yells of, 'There he is, get him!' 'Don't let him go!' 'Hit him! Hit him!' There were scuffling sounds and screams of pain, then a rush of feet across sunbaked earth as he made a break for it. 'Hold onto him, you fucking asshole!' 'Fuck, he's broke my nose!' and 'After him!'

I heard all this, cowering down behind my fence.

And then, when they'd caught him, I saw it as well as I stood up and peered through a knot-hole in the aging wood.

They'd caught him about five gardens away, back the way we'd come. The only way he could have gotten there was to burst through their on-coming ranks. He was done with running away. Davie had *attacked*. To save me. To save this yellow son of a bitch crapping himself behind a wooden fence while his best friend, his face bloody, his clothes ragged, was pinned against the wall of a wooden shed and beaten with gun butts and whacked with baseball bats.

And it wasn't even Davie they wanted.

They struck him again. He grunted. He did not scream.

'Where is he?' DJ roared for the third time.

Davie's split lips opened over bloody gums. It was finally time to speak. My leg was beating a frantic rhythm against the fence.

'Go . . . fuck yourselves . . .'

JJ barrelled forward and punched him hard across the jaw; Davie's head snapped to one side and his legs buckled under him. He would have fallen if two of DJ's cronies hadn't held him up.

DJ pushed his face right into Davie's, close enough to taste the blood. 'You tell me, asshole, or I swear to God . . .'

Davie managed the faintest, groggiest nod. When he spoke he spat blood out over DJ. 'I tell . . . you where . . . he is. He's in . . . he's in fucking bed with . . . your mum.'

This time DJ didn't react immediately. He stood back. 'JJ,' he said, and nodded at the shed. 'Go in there, see if you can find a hammer, some nails.'

JJ's brow furrowed for a moment, then he smiled appreciatively. He yanked open the shed door and stepped inside. Davie was spitting blood. JJ held a hammer up through the glass. 'This big enough?' he asked.

It was a rhetorical question.

Unlike the question I was asking myself, which was: Am I going to stand here while my best friend gets nailed to a shed? It was obvious what DJ was planning. He wasn't about to do some DIY while he pondered Davie's fate.

I had been living the quiet life at home with Patricia. She might have thought that we weren't coping with Stevie's death, but I was fine. I didn't ask Davie to drag me halfway around the world to kill The Colonel. He had made me a fugitive. We hadn't been friends for years. In fact, the more I thought about it the more I realised we hadn't ever really been friends at all; we had been geographic acquaintances who happened to share an interest in music for a few months. Friends were for life. No, everything that had happened to me in the past few days was Davie's fault. He was his own worst enemy. I owed him nothing. They could nail him to the shed and I could still walk or skulk away with my head held high.

In hell.

JJ was holding one of Davie's arms out straight against the shed. They were going to crucify him.

I stood frozen behind the fence, drenched in sweat and horror.

Davie knew exactly where I was, I was sure of that. For a moment I even thought our eyes met through the knot-hole. But he would not give me away. It was not in his code. He was all about bravery and courage. He would die protecting me.

DJ raised the hammer. He placed the nail against Davie's palm.

'You tell me, you Irish asshole!'

Davie shook his head.

DJ turned and yelled: 'If you're out there, you shout now or we'll do this!'

I bit at a nail. They were just trying to scare me into revealing myself. They wouldn't do it at all. It was barbaric. Not in this day and age. Or they might only do one hand. I could let them do one hand, see if that satisfied them.

Christ.

DJ moved to one side to give himself room for a proper swing. He stretched his arm back; his teeth showed over his bottom lip. Davie closed his eyes; the nail was already dripping with his sweat and glistening in the morning sun. DJ swung the hammer forward . . .

Davie, I'm sorry. Davie, I'm sorry. Davie, I'm . . .

'Stop!'

It was just enough to put DJ's aim off by a fraction; the hammer crashed into the shed wall, punching a hole through it. DJ spun round, fury etched on his face.

Sometimes you've just got to stand up and be counted. Conquer your fear, face your enemy, spit in his eyes if required. A man's gotta do what a man's gotta do.

And I woulda done it if Dr Kelly Cortez hadn't beaten me to it.

She pushed her way through the mob, as I pressed my eye back to the knot in the fence.

'Stop it now, DJ!' she shouted.

'You don't tell me what to do, you—'

'I'm not!' She was holding something up. I couldn't quite see what. 'It's your wife, DJ. Talk to her!'

She held it out to him: a cell phone.

A puzzled look squirmed its way onto DJ's face. 'Michelle?' he said. 'But she's . . .'

'She's alive and kicking, DJ. And these guys didn't do anything.'

DJ took the phone. He held it hesitantly to one ear. 'Michelle?' he asked tremulously. And then a smile enveloped him. *'Michelle!'*

Behind him JJ let go of Davie's hand, and he slumped down to his knees. Kelly immediately ran to him.

'Davie . . . Davie?' she cried.

He managed a bloody smile. 'You took your time.'

She kissed and hugged him.

He was a quick mover, our Davie. He had won her over in the time it would take me to work up to buying her a drink. He deserved a hug from me as well, for saving my life and being brave and heroic and standing up under torture, but I stayed behind the fence for another ten minutes in case DJ changed his mind. I'm a journalist,

I don't take part in stories. Instead, I observe. There has to be someone left at the end to report them, otherwise who would ever know? DJ was crying down the phone to his wife, and presumably I was now being absolved of any crime. But it was still too early to venture out: events had gone way beyond the simple fact of my guilt or innocence. There were two dead cops, three buildings burned to the ground – little details that couldn't and wouldn't be forgotten. Everglades City wasn't a city, it was a tiny rural community, and communities stick together. We weren't out of the woods yet.

But we were a couple of minutes later. I heard a police siren and peeked over the fence in time to see a patrol car roll up. Two uniforms got out, with EC from the hotel and BJ from the bank behind them. Several of the lynch mob dropped their weapons and started to back away. With what was left of my strength, I hauled myself up onto the top of the fence, paused for several deep breaths, and then launched myself off. I landed untidily on the sunbaked ground, then stepped over two flattened picket fences and approached the scene. What had started as a gradual withdrawal became a wholesale running-away. DJ had done all the shooting, so he could carry the can for it. There was community, and then there was looking after yourself. DJ stood with the shotgun under his arm, apparently not caring one way or the other; JJ was beside him. Everyone else had fled. The cops didn't make any attempt to stop them. If they wanted them, they knew where to find them. Most were heading home. Others were forming an orderly queue at the hospital for Michelle's hand in marriage; she would certainly be available now that DJ was going to jail.

Nobody paid much attention as I sauntered up. I smiled down at Davie and said, 'Howse it goin', big lad.'

'Been better,' he said.

He didn't look quite as excited as I was to be alive. Perhaps because he'd had a severe beating. Perhaps because one of the police officers was Cody Banks of the St Pete Beach Police Department. And his partner was his partner, last seen looking really annoyed from the boot of a $500 car.

'Hey,' said Cody, 'fancy seeing you guys again.'

I looked at Davie. He raised one helpless eyebrow.

'You, ah, just passing through?' I asked.

'Sure, looking for you. And found a whole lot more besides. Sat up in our hotel room last night, watched you squirm like the dogs you are.'

'It wasn't us.' I pointed at DJ. 'It was *him*.'

'We really don't give a fuck,' Cody's partner said.

Somehow, I wasn't surprised. But it was a bit of a shock for Dr Cortez. 'What are you talking about?' She waved her hand in DJ's direction. 'You have to arrest him. He killed—'

'Ma'm, if you don't mind, just shut your aperture.'

Kelly's mouth dropped open a little. She had thought it was all over, that everyone would live happily ever after. But how often does that happen? Davie put his good arm around her and she helped him back to his feet. 'So,' he said, 'what's your plan?'

EC spoke for the first time. He had his newspaper tucked under his arm in case things got boring. 'Well, son, there's two schools of thought on that.'

'One,' said Cody, 'we feed your ass to the 'gators, which would be my favoured option.'

'Or two,' said BJ, 'you get back to where you came from, no more said about it, and we clear up the mess here with the help of these two very fine gentlemen.'

BJ and EC both smiled glowingly at the police officers, as if they were two Boy Scouts who done good.

'Your choice,' said BJ.

'Mind, you're so scrawny,' Cody said, nodding at me, '"gators probably turn up their noses. Somebody find the body then we're all in the shit again.'

He was the second person in the past few hours to comment on my physique. I would have punched his lights out if he hadn't been bigger and stronger, and possessed of a big gun and a surly demeanour.

'Do I take it,' Davie said, 'that our choice also includes going home without our valuables?'

BJ wasn't embarrassed about this at all. 'Take a whole heap of money to rebuild the station. Then a lot of people have to turn a blind eye to what went on here. That's not cheap.'

Davie nodded at Curtis and co. 'And I don't suppose you guys are working for charity.'

'Split fifty-fifty. Reckon that's about fair.'

BJ smiled benevolently. 'But I'll tell you what I can do for you. I can give you a couple hundred dollars just to see you through, until you go home.'

'Well,' I said, 'thanks a bunch.'

'No trouble at all.'

Americans. Sarcasm. Will never change.

But inside my heart was bouncing. We were going to get out of this, we were going to get out of this, we were going . . .

On the outside I remained cool and calm.

'You just expect us to walk away?' Davie said.

'Not walk,' said Cody's partner. 'You can take the Land Cruiser. I guess we can afford another.'

JJ handed me the keys. 'It works okay,' he said, 'but it still smells of ditch shit.'

I looked at Davie. 'Well?'

He was battered and bloody, but there was more than

a hint of defiance in his eyes. Better nip that in the bud. 'Come on, big lad,' I said. 'We're going home. We've had a good run.'

His eyes flitted from Cody to BJ and DJ without blinking. They finally settled on Kelly. He sighed. He pulled her to him and gave her a squeeze. 'You still owe me a dessert,' he said.

There were tears in her eyes. She gave him a hug. He grimaced. She said sorry and kissed his lips. He grimaced again. It was a painful business getting smoochy after being in battle. Or so I'd heard.

31

I knew it was going to happen, it was just a question of where and when. But the fact that it happened so soon took me by surprise. We were hardly outside the city limits. I thought he'd at least wait until we were close to Naples, so that it would look like he'd really given it some thought. But no. He just couldn't wait.

We'd gone back to our rooms in the Bank, had a shower, got cleaned up as best we could and then driven out of town past the smouldering ruins of the police station. There were a couple of news crews filming reports, and I saw BJ being interviewed. He was probably paying tribute to the two police officers who'd perished in the fire. Dr Kelly Cortez was there as well, no doubt telling a reporter that the bodies were burned beyond recognition, but that there was no doubt about the cause of death. She wouldn't mention that there was a huge hole in Sheriff Baines's chest, nor that Deputy Jesse Stone was minus one head. Elsewhere palms were being greased and reports were being doctored. I was from Belfast. I knew how it worked.

We weren't far past the ditch I'd reversed into a million years ago when Davie told me to pull over.

I switched off the engine and we sat there for a couple of minutes without talking. Farmer Giles chugged past on his tractor and I gave him a wave. He waved back. It was a friendly kind of a place.

'So,' I said.

'So,' said Davie.

'So I suppose you've got something to say.'

'Something to do.'

'Davie, we're home free.'

'They have our gold.'

'No, Davie, they have *the* gold. It was never ours. Leave it be. Let's just go home.'

'I can't do that.'

'Yes, you can. You go back there, they won't let you walk away. Not a second time.'

'I don't intend giving them that option. Dan, I've a gun in my bag. Last thing they'll expect is for us to go right back.'

'That's what Butch and Sundance thought.'

'We're not Butch and Sundance.'

'You can say that again.'

He drummed his fingers on the dash. Farmer Giles had the right attitude. Stay on your tractor and mind your own business. Do a good deed if you have to, but don't hang around afterwards.

'I have to do it, Dan.'

'No, you don't.'

'I do. It's the right thing. It's your money too. Reparations. You deserve it, you and Patricia.'

'No, we don't. And we don't want it. It's bad news, mate. Walk away.'

'Can't do that.'

'Davie, you got me out here to kill The Colonel. I've done that. It's enough. Let's go home. If you still want to get your kicks shooting people, do it with your mates, the whaddyacall them . . . the revengers.' He gave half a shrug. 'Except,' I said, with sudden clarity, 'there are no revengers. You're the only one. The Colonel was the only one.'

'End justifies the means, Dan.'

'Not always.'

A pair of love bugs were mating on our windscreen. A few days ago I would have put the wipers on and squished them. Now I let them be. I just wanted to be doing the same thing with Patricia, although in a less public place.

'I'm sorry I never kept in touch,' I said.

'You went on to bigger things.'

'Not really,' I said.

'Your face was in the paper. You wrote good stuff.'

'You were out there risking your life, I was writing gossip.'

'Dan. I was a traffic cop. I never even saw a terrorist. I chatted to someone from the Animal Liberation Front once. I always wanted to do something important, but I never had the chance. Then I lost my licence and they bucked me out. You see—'

'You don't have to explain, Davie. We're mates.'

'I know I don't, but I want to – because we are mates. The punk stuff was brilliant. Could have lived those couple of years together for ever. I went to see The Damned last year. Place was bunged with old punks. I stood at the back and watched this showband on stage, and in front of me there were hundreds of bald, fat heads. Punk's not dead, Dan, it's in late middle age.'

I sighed. He sighed.

'I could have been a good cop, but I never got the breaks.'

'And you probably pissed them off.'

He smiled. 'There's that. And then peace broke out any-way. I always felt like I hadn't done my bit, do you know what I mean?'

'No,' I said.

'And what happened to you always annoyed me, was always in there eating away at me. When I heard he was out there, I had to do something. And I had to bring you with me, because it was about you.'

'No, you didn't. And I'd like to say I appreciate the thought, but it would sound like I'm thanking you for a crap Christmas present. I never wanted any of this. But it's done, Davie, it's over; we can both go home and try to forget about it.'

Davie shook his head. 'I'm going back. Come with me.'

'No, Davie. I'm going home.'

He looked at me for a moment, then nodded abruptly. He climbed out of the car and walked round to open the boot. He opened up his bag, reached inside and took out his gun and a box of ammunition. He loaded the gun, then threw the rest of the bullets into the ditch.

'Can't do it with nine,' he said, 'then I can't do it at all.'

We stood awkwardly for several moments, then we moved forward together and hugged.

I kissed him on the cheek and said, 'You're a stupid fucker.'

He kissed me back and said, 'Takes one to know one.'

Then he turned and started to walk back towards town.

I was just getting back into the car when he shouted: 'Hey, Dan. Remember Karen Malloy?'

The fifteen-year-old girl from Groomsport. As if I could ever forget.

'What about her?'

'One night you went home early, I screwed her in the bushes.'

'I know,' I shouted back, 'I was watching.'
He was lying. So was I.

That was the last time I ever saw Davie Kincaid. A big lanky traffic cop with a gun in his shirt and gold on his mind.

I watched him in the mirror as he disappeared around the bend into Everglades City. I suppose he was a punk rocker right to the end. Anarchy. No respect for authority. And vaguely silly with it. I sat there by the side of the road, knowing I should get well away, but quite unable to move. I pushed buttons on the radio until I found Van Morrison again. He was still singing about the bright side of the road when the first gunshots rang out.

I waited another ten minutes, then started the engine and drove away. I made sure to stick to the speed limit, and indicated when I wanted to overtake. I wasn't taking any chances. I didn't think I had any left.

I didn't tell Patricia that Davie was dead. I said he'd decided to stay in America, that he'd met a girl, a doctor, and was going to settle down out there and raise goats. She said she was happy for him, but didn't ask for too many details; I think she knew I was lying.

She didn't even ask about The Colonel. She knew he was dead because it had eventually made the local papers, once his identity had been established. Michael O'Ryan had been murdered, nobody was arrested, it was dismissed as a drugs deal gone wrong. A reporter called her and asked if she wanted to comment on The Colonel's demise. She said no.

A week after I got home we went out for dinner. Patricia told me she'd met a woman in the library and they'd got talking and gone for coffee, and the upshot of it was that we had someone who was willing to act as a surrogate. She wouldn't do it for free, but she wasn't charging the earth either. We were going to have another baby.

I smiled and held her hand.

'It's good to have you back,' she said.

'It's good to be back.'

Only I wasn't sure if I was back at all. I returned to my job selling Ulster as the ideal place to live. At night I drank and listened to my punk records. To Joe and Joey and Johnny. I checked out the Everglades City newspaper on the Internet and read a detailed account of the fire that had destroyed the local police station and obituaries for the two police officers who had perished in it. There was no mention of a bank robbery or a lynch mob. In one edition under a headline *Home from Hospital* there was a photo of Michelle with a bandage around her head, blowing candles out on a cake. She'd been injured in a swimming accident, but was now making a full recovery with the help of her loving husband, DJ Turner. She would have had her arms around DJ, but she didn't have any. The rest of the initials, full of stomach and beer, were crowded into the back of the picture, their thumbs up, displaying massed ranks of crooked, stained teeth.

One night we went out for dinner with the surrogate lady. She was very nice. She worked as a publisher – had her own small company. She knew about me and had enjoyed some of the books I'd written. Perhaps I could write something for her? What about a travel book? I promised to give it some thought.

Four weeks after my return from Florida I drove down to Groomsport. I had been putting it off and putting it off, but it had to be done.

Davie's mum was pleased to see me. She ushered me in and made me tea and brought me biscuits and chatted away about the work she was getting done to the house and how she was taking a computer course at the tech and that she was thinking about learning to ride a horse, even at her advanced age.

She was putting a brave face on it. Neither of us had mentioned Davie, or the holiday. I had no idea how much he'd told her; she had certainly been very convincing in her distress over Davie being dropped just before his wedding.

Eventually I said, 'Mrs Kincaid . . . about Davie.'

She set her tea cup down and clasped her hands in her lap. 'I know this is very awkward for you, Dan. There's always one gets left behind.'

'It's just . . . I feel terrible about it.'

She nodded sadly. 'These things happen.'

'But . . .'

'It was his choice, Dan.'

I sighed. I could feel the tears starting to come.

'Dan. He sent me some photos from your holiday. Would you like to see them?'

I cleared my throat. I nodded. She crossed to a small bureau, opened a drawer and pulled out a padded envelope. I had a vague memory of Davie taking some snaps with a crappy disposable camera during the first few days of our vacation.

Mrs Kincaid opened up the envelope and handed the photos across. There were only four of them. 'You really look like youse were enjoying yourselves.'

'We were.'

The first showed me lying by the pool in the Del Mar with a baseball cap pulled down over my eyes. My chest and shoulders were bright, bright red, but I was laughing.

I must have taken the second; it was Davie posing by our $500 car, arms folded, chest puffed out, Hawaiian shirt, and giving me the fingers.

The third was Davie with his arm around my shoulders,

both of us grinning drunkenly. I had a vague memory of asking somebody to take it in a bar in St Pete. Back when we were just on vacation, before I had any notion of the death and destruction to follow. Whoever it was had left half of their thumb over the lens, but it was still a good picture. Sure, we were boozed up, but our eyes were bright. We had been friends, once, in Groomsport, two decades before, and we had become friends again in Florida. But it was an Ulster kind of a friendship, an unacknowledged one, one built on verbal abuse, sarcasm and huffing. Friendship wasn't about how often you saw someone, it was about how relaxed you felt in their company, about being yourself. We had, undoubtedly, been ourselves. Davie had been mad, unpredictable, frustrating and violent; he had also saved my life. I had been drunken, sunburned and when called upon to save his life, I had chickened out. He was a better man than me. No two ways about it.

I blew air out of my cheeks and moved to the final photo.

Davie, sitting in a bar with his arm around Dr Kelly Cortez.

This time I did wipe a tear from my eye. True love, snatched away. Mrs Kincaid came up, slipped a supportive arm around my waist and looked at the photo with me.

'They look so happy,' she said.

I nodded miserably.

'I always wanted to go to Mexico,' she said. 'Don't suppose I'll get the chance now.'

I didn't know whether to correct her or reassure her that she was young yet.

And then I didn't do either, because I realised that the photo hadn't been taken in the Mountain View Bar and Grill. That the bar in the background was festooned with small Mexican flags. That Davie had had a hair cut. That there was a great whalloper of an engagement ring on Kelly's finger. In the bottom left-hand corner of the photo there were small digital figures showing the date on which it had been taken.

Less than two weeks before.

The son of a bitch had walked into the sunset, but instead of burning up, he'd walked out the other side with a girl on his arm, and judging by his choice of relocation and the sparkler on Kelly's finger, a huge amount of gold in his suitcase.

The fucking fucker.

'I'm so happy for him,' Mrs Kincaid said. 'He says he's going to go travelling for a few months. She seems like a lovely girl. She's a doctor, you know. I always knew he'd meet the right girl eventually.'

I shook my head in disbelief, then smiled, and handed back the photos.

'So did I,' I said.

He was alive, and in love, and rich.

I drove back up to Belfast blasting The Clash out of the CD player.

Davie was alive, Joe was dead.

His music would live for ever, but he had moved to a different label. Davie had also moved on. Maybe it was time for me to shake up my life. Or at least my music. You couldn't always live in the past, because you only ended up trying to recreate it. There was bound to be fresh young rock'n'roll out there, it was just a question of finding it.

We were young yet. Patricia and I could still set the world on fire.

I burst into the house full of the joys of spring, able at last to tell my wife the truth about Davie's fate.

She met me at the bottom of the stairs. She was clutching

our Visa bill in her hands. Her face was red and her eyes were bulging. This was not a good sign.

'Two thousand dollars,' she screamed, 'to Big Fuck Porn Websites plc?'

I swallowed. 'It wasn't me,' I protested. 'It was a thirteen-year-old boy.'

This did not help matters.

Author's Note

Joe Strummer died in December 2002, but to stop this being a Christmas story, with trees and presents and ho-ho-ho's, I moved his death forward to the summer. I trust he would have appreciated the extra six months.

The Don CeSar is a real hotel, and Al Capone did indeed stay there, but don't try knocking the walls down as it will be added to your bill. Everything else about the hotel in this novel is completely fictitious.